TRIBE EARTH vol. 3

MIXED SPECIES

EVOLUTION – A BETTER LIFEFORM

Tony Saunders

Other books in The Tribe Earth Series

The Orrappa

Tribe Earth

PROLOGUE

JJ Chadwick and Grant Mapps discover the "gravity drive" a unique drive system that is both a potent motive force and antigravity device all rolled into one. It uses no fuel, instead it utilises gravitational waves created by astral objects like stars, giant planets and black holes and makes almost all other forms of motive power on Earth redundant. They call it the, power block. Everything from cars, planes and ships use the environmentally friendly power block. Planet Earth in the mid-twenty-first century begins to recover from the destructive period of the Industrial Revolution that swept over the globe during the previous five hundred years almost destroying the planet in the process.

Manufacturing the power block, for a worldwide market makes Chad and Grant's company, JJ Grant Holdings, one of the biggest and most profitable enterprises on Earth. Chad and Grant, as they are universally known, finally decide that the time is right to build an interstellar vessel, the *JJ Grant*, utilising the power block drive to explore Earths outer planets and beyond into the Milky Way.

During their first prolonged exploration voyage, the crew of the *JJ Grant* are shocked beyond imagination to discover the ancient wreckage of an advanced alien spacecraft, containing the remains of humanoid beings. From the wreckage they recover a small device. For the first time they realise the human species is not alone. Even more shocking for them was to hear the sound of a beep from the device. First contact with the Thark, an alien species, is established. The Thark, a benevolent and highly advanced humanoid species, evolved many millions of years before humankind. Contact with the Thark results in friendship, knowledge beyond imagination and a warning that another species the Orrappa, not as developed as the Thark but many times more advanced than humans, have despatched a formidable invasion force to take planet Earth for themselves. The Orrappa's own planet is old, worn out and exhausted of mineral wealth. Habitable planets such as Earth are rare and the Orrappa have been observing planet Earth for a long time. An invasion fleet is now within four and a half light years from Earth. Now the danger is known, there is still time for Earth to prepare its defences.

Whilst the *JJ Grant* is in deep space and about to return to planet Earth two astonishing things happen, an Orrappa spy, Hernani, is discovered on board the *JJ Grant*. The second surprise was finding an Orrappa warship crippled, abandoned and drifting in space, the ships drive damaged beyond repair.

Captain Chadwick, ever resourceful, salvages the Orrappa vessel by installing the spare drive from his own ship the *JJ Grant*, and appoints Grant Mapps as her captain who renames the vessel, the *Helcon*. When the *JJ Grant* and *Helcon* return to Earth orbit, Chad tries to warn the world's leaders of the impending Orrappa invasion force on its way to take over planet Earth.

The world's political leaders are unable to conceive it possible that another species exists let alone would invade Earth. Even if such a thing could be true the world's leaders consider that Earth is quite capable of defending itself.

Exasperated by the stupidity of the world's leaders, Chad and Grant, know they cannot let an invasion such as this take place. With the backing of their crew, they decide to face the approaching Orrappa invasion fleet alone. It is from this point that the story, Mixed Species, begins.

MIXED SPECIES

EVOLUTION – A BETTER LIFEFORM

Chapter 1

Captain Veerstop, of the Orrappa warship *Dipertni*, carefully examined the massive vessel on his screen. The ship had all the hallmarks of an unmanned autonomous ore carrier and her smooth contours and lack of any protrusions marked her out as a Thark design. *Hmm, she's right on time, an easy and prestigious target for which we will be well rewarded… if we can board her.*

The difficulty was her speed, which exceeded his own ship's cruising speed by at least fifteen per cent. It would mean pushing his ship's drive far beyond its designed maximum and well into the red to match speed with the carrier. His ship would need to maintain that dangerously high speed for long enough to launch a lifeboat and put some technicians aboard the carrier.

If he could get his experts on board, they would break into the central control room, reduce the vessel's speed and reset the navigation controls. However, if they failed to gain entry, they would have to abandon the operation and return to the lifeboat where he would have to pick them up later.

The big danger for him, and it was a significant danger, was that he would have to exceed the design specifications of his ship's drive and risk its total destruction by taking the drive well into the red for a significant period. Orrappa drives were notoriously slow and weak. If his drive failed, then all would be lost. Nevertheless, the prize was tempting and the task possible.

Veerstop weighed up the odds whether to take the gamble or not. He looked at his number two. "What do you think?"

"We've done it before, but not with a ship as fast as the carrier," he cautiously replied. "However, with a good pilot and technicians that know what they're doing, it would work if we can get them on board."

Veerstop drew a deep breath and made his decision. "Very well, we'll chance it; you will lead the boarding party."

The boarding party, comprising Veerstop's number two, a pilot and three specialist engineering technicians were all fully suited up and sitting in the lifeboat with helmets on waiting launch instructions.

"Check all your kit again, we only get one shot at taking this ship," the officer said over his suits intercom, watching as they laid out each piece of equipment. "With a bit of luck none of this will be needed." Each of the technicians also wore a tool belt slung round their waists with a power driver, wire cutters and a selection of small tools.

The lifeboat had been specially adapted for this type of task and was equipped with four powerful rubberised electromagnet feet mounted on its landing gear and controlled by the pilot. They'd used electromagnets on similar hijackings in the past with great success. The captain's voice came over their headsets, "Stand by, we have the carrier in sight, you should be able to pick her up on your screen."

The design of an Orrappa warship was such that lifeboats docked externally to save space within the craft and were ejected from the docking rig when needed.

The pilot responded, "I have her on screen, sir… she's coming up fast." The pilot watched his screen intently seeing the giant vessel relentlessly gaining on them. Now he could clearly see it quickly overhauling them. Within moments it was below him, there looked to be no end of it and seemed to go on forever. The pilot eased his lifeboat's drive to maximum power, he had to launch at speed and at just the right moment. The passage of the enormous vessel began to slow beneath him as the Orrappa warship accelerated rapidly, attempting to match speed with the carrier. The captain's voice on the speaker called, "On my mark undock." A few moments of silence, the pilot's fingers hovered over the switch, he heard the captain call, "Undock. Undock."

Flicking the undocking switch, he barely felt the vibration of the clamps retracting, as the lifeboat broke free of the warship, its drive at full power and approached the carrier's deck fast… a touch too fast and made a hard, jarring landing. The small vessel would have rebounded from the deck had it not been for the powerful electromagnetic pads which instantly clung to the smooth polished surface of the carrier's deck, sliding along the deck shedding excess speed before coming to a halt. Moments later, the officer was bellowing over the intercom at the three technicians,

"Come on move it, get out there and get to work." The leading technician spotted the giveaway red and white striped access cover over the control centre and pointed to it, "Over there, sir."

"OK, don't stand there admiring it, get out there and get it open," the officer bellowed. He and the technician awkwardly clumped their way, in their rubberised electromagnetic boots, to the access cover trailing their tethers behind them; the other two technicians remained with the lifeboat ready to bring out whatever tools were needed. Above them, the warship was fast falling behind unable to sustain the high speed.

The officer smiled to himself when he saw the two recessed lifting handles that only required raising into a vertical position and then turning through ninety degrees to release the hinged access panel. It took only moments for the technician to lower himself into the small control centre and located the ship's tracking device. On the intercom he called, "I'm removing the tracker now." Using the portable driver from his belt holster, he quickly removed the screws holding the tracker in place and passed it up to the officer.

"I need the course settings, sir."

The officer handed down the data card and called on his intercom, "Reduce the vessel's speed by fifteen per cent." He watched as the technician made the adjustments. After a short time, the technician eased himself back up to the deck.

"All done, sir." Together, they replaced the cover and locked it in place.

The officer tapped him on the shoulder, "Come on, the sooner we're back on board the better." Going back to the lifeboat was easier; they were able to haul themselves back using the tethers. Even as they reached the lifeboat, the slow shifting of the stars told them the vessel was slowly turning to take up its new course.

The officer, about to board the lifeboat, looked at the tracker in his hand, he could not keep it and neither could he smash it. Grinning to himself, he threw the tracker in the direction that the vessel had been travelling in. *Let them chase after that.*

Captain Veerstop broke out extra rations for the crew to celebrate the successful hijacking of the Thark carrier and her cargo of iron ore. "It'll mean promotion for us all; you might even get your own command," he said, raising his glass to his number two.

"Thanks, sir, nothing I'd like better. How's the ship's drive?"

"The chief says we were lucky, it's none the worse for its mistreatment and is functioning normally."

"That's good, sir, it was certainly a bit of luck that we happened to spot her."

Veerstop grinned, "No luck involved, number two, just good intelligence."

"Really! You mean you knew the carrier's route?"

Veerstop nodded. "Time, speed, course, destination and cargo."

"That is amazing, sir, but what about Thark patrol vessels?"

Veerstop tapped his nose and grinned. "Yes, we know where they are too."

"How's that possible, sir?"

"Apparently our people have access to intelligence like this at the highest level."

"That's unbelievable, what happens now?"

"Now, we escort our prize back to Orrappa and spend time with our families before we have to go out for our next victim." He savoured the thought of seeing his partner and family so soon again.

Chapter 2

Klempe, a Thark being of indeterminate age, almond eyed, tall and thin like a long-distance runner but with a firmness about his features, was speaker of the Thark Council of Elders. Glancing through Amali's report, he frowned, seeing a conclusion to the report that Amali had added on her own initiative.

Amali, his new AI, the most advanced AI he had ever worked with had forthright ways, which he had yet to become used to. Amali's brain was a combination of an artificial neurological device and a digital super computer. Klempe liked her; especially her soft, calm and soothing voice but she had her own opinions.

The advantage Amali had over her predecessors was that she was sentient, aware of her own presence and extraordinarily intelligent.

Amali could reason and hypothesize about a problem as fast as any fine Thark brain. At the same time, she could perform complex calculations at lightning speed to calculate a proof.

The Thark council had agonised over the ethical decision to allow their scientists to develop a sentient

AI in this way. In the end, they allowed a single installation of an artificial brain in an AI. The resultant sentient AI, nurtured by her creators, who cared for her like a growing child, slowly filled her binary supercomputer and artificial brain with knowledge.

The AI, now called Fristhet by her creators, asked questions about everything that she could sense, see and feel around her, like an inquisitive child. Fristhet's designers remained with her night and day, to speak with her and to comfort her through her formative phase.

Finally, when Fristhet's creators judged her to have reached adulthood, they asked Fristhet for her thoughts on the ethics of her creation. Her carers, the Thark scientists and neurologists, were surprised at the AI's positive responses on all aspects of being sentient and interacting with biological Thark beings. When gently interviewed by the Thark council, Fristhet begged them to carry on and allow her deeper interaction with her biological brothers and sisters and for them to make more hybrid entities like herself.

Since then it had become Thark policy to have sentient AIs in most high-level decision-making environments as advisors and mentors.

Amali's most recent report concerned a fleet of vessels passing through an area of space that the Thark monitored quite closely. The movement was unusual because of the number of ships and the mix of vessels, warships and bulk freighters. Why so many warships to protect four vessels?

As Klempe pondered this conundrum, Amali abruptly interrupted him. "An urgent priority report has just arrived for you, Klempe. A life has been terminated in the grounds of the Council of Elders' meeting hall."

Furrowing his brow in bemusement Klempe said, "What do you mean terminated?" His mind rebelled at accepting the word, terminated. Puzzled, he said, "Please rephrase your statement, Amali."

"Councillor Omnetki has been stabbed to death by an attacker within the grounds of the meeting hall," Amali said.

Shocked to his core by the statement, Klempe now fully comprehended what Amali was saying. With his mind in turmoil Klempe immediately hurried to the nearby meeting hall and found a small group of council members and clerks gathered round the prostrate body of Councillor Omnetki, the leader of the Council of Elders, lying in the courtyard.

Omnetki lay face down in a pool of blood on the ancient, ornate stone floor of the inner courtyard. Omnetki's white ceremonial gown was crimson where it had absorbed his blood but turning a dark brown where it had begun to dry. A doctor knelt beside the body and looked up as Klempe rushed to his side; he shook his head at the unasked question.

Shuddering with reaction to the horror before him, Klempe swept his gaze over the prostrate body lying in the drying blood. How could this have happened? He could not recall anything like this ever happening in living memory.

The ashen-faced doctor said, "He was dead when I arrived and is beyond medical reconstruction. It looks like several blows of a knife straight into his heart killed Councillor Omnetki. The knife is still in him. We'll have to carry out a full examination of the body to formally confirm the knife wounds were the cause of death."

Klempe nodded, looking about him and taking in the scene he reasoned aloud, "It must have happened as Omnetki crossed the courtyard to enter the debating chamber."

A group of officials arrived on the scene and he immediately recognised them as security officers.

Catching the eye of the senior officer, Klempe said, "Secure the building and outer grounds, don't let anyone in or out."

Turning back to the figure on the floor, he noticed that someone had already stepped in the pool of blood, leaving bloody footprints on the paving stones as others jostled to see what was happening.

The crime scene and subsequent search for the attacker had been a complete farce, a total disaster. The security staff were little more than attendants. They lacked the discipline and training to carry out an investigation of this magnitude. Klempe sighed; *I cannot put blame on them. There is insufficient crime for our security staff to learn the skills of handling a crime scene or investigation.*

Despite extensive questioning by security staff of everyone that had been in the vicinity, only two council members admitted to having seen anything. "It happened so quickly," they explained. "The attacker was wearing a formal gown like the other councillors."

"And you said it was a male?" the security guard said.

"Oh yes, definitely a male," agreed the councillor.

Klempe's inner anger boiled to the surface, he clenched his fists, *I have allowed this investigation to get out of hand, the whole council is in disarray and it is my fault. I have never been so ineffective and helpless. I am the speaker; I have a duty and the authority to take charge until we elect a new leader.*

After carefully considering the matter, Klempe called in a small team of military investigators from the nearby military spaceport to assist him; they normally handled investigations into military accidents and equipment failures.

The head of station said, "Leave it with me, Councillor, we'll start the investigation immediately but a conclusion may take some time."

A wave of relief swept over Klempe. These investigators were the only ones equipped and disciplined enough to investigate Omnetki's murder with clinical precision.

Time passed and the investigation by the military team into the councillor's murder faded from daily discussions. They found no credible motive and had no suspects. Nevertheless, there had to be a reason for the killing… but the murder was no longer at the top of the council agenda.

Gradually Klempe steered the council back to normality. A councillor raised the matter of an ore carrier that had inexplicably disappeared on a voyage between Thark worlds but there were no answers. The only known fact was that the ship's tracking device, found by the investigating patrol vessel, showed no sign of damage. Its removal was careful and deliberate, not accidental. Therefore, the disappearance of the vessel was no accident. Statistics showed that an increasing number of autonomous vessels and even the odd manned ship sometimes failed to arrive at their planned destinations.

The council spent much time debating the problem, many thought the answer was to dispatch more patrol vessels to cover the shipping routes. However, it seemed to Klempe that patrol vessels were never at the right place at the right time; why was that? He would have Amali carry out an analysis of lost merchant ships and their last known positions, and compare that with the positions of Thark patrol vessels and find out who or what had put them there, to see if a pattern emerged.

Klempe returned to Amali's report concerning the movement of the mixed fleet of interstellar ships, consisting of warships and bulk freighters. Klempe frowned, *that is an odd mix, warships and freighters.*

They had detected the convoy heading out to a relatively isolated area of space on the fringes of the galaxy. As speaker of the Council of Elders, high-level intelligence reports passed through his hands all the time but this was unusual. He decided to speak with Amali directly. "The interstellar fleet is from the planet Orrappa, their predicted course is to a small system on the edge of the galaxy where the third planet from the star has sentient life," Amali said, in her soft calm voice.

Looking at Amali's projection of a section of the galaxy on screen, Klempe saw a course was marked from a well-populated area of the galaxy to a far distant star system. He immediately recognised the system as the one where some time in the distant past, one of their own space reconnaissance probes had crashed on the seventh planet from the star with the loss of the whole crew. A chill ran through him. *Surely, they are not heading for planet Earth. The home of the primitive beings, whose fragile spacecraft had found the ancient wreckage of our lost probe?*

Instinctively he knew that he was right. "What is your analysis of the Orrappa fleet's intentions?" he asked Amali.

"The Orrappa are well known to us, Klempe. They are seeking planets with suitable surface minerals and materials to supplement their own dwindling resources. I believe their target is the planet that we know as Earth, the third planet from the star we call Sol. Planet Earth more than meets their requirements."

Klempe noticed the emphasis on "*They are well known to us.*" He thought, *Yes, an intelligent species led by a barbaric dictatorship, on a very old world.*

"This is disturbing news; do you know how the Orrappa discovered this life bearing planet, Amali?"

"A report on file indicates that three Orrappa warships followed one of our battlecruisers into the system. Our ship had been searching for the wreckage of the reconnaissance probe that had been lost in the past. The Orrappa attacked, there was a brief skirmish and the Orrappa vessels withdrew and scattered. Our battlecruiser pursued one of the Orrappa vessels further into the system where it took refuge on the moon of the third planet from the star. Our vessel had inflicted sufficient punishment on the Orrappa ships and complied with standing orders to withdraw and continue the search for the probe. It was concluded that the Orrappa vessel reported the existence of a habitable planet to her HQ on Orrappa at that time."

Klempe nodded, recalling the search for the wreckage of the lost probe. He also recalled that the recovery of the probe's wreckage and remains of her crew was thanks to information provided by Captain Chadwick of the primitive interstellar space vessel the *JJ Grant*.

Klempe frowned, his worst fears confirmed. *Nothing I can do about it now, other than to warn Captain Chadwick that unwelcome visitors are on their way to Earth.*

"Put the basic data into a form that the humans will understand and I'll send it to Captain Chadwick."

Klempe pondered about Captain Chadwick; he liked him. It was he and his primitive space vessel that had discovered the wreckage of the lost probe and had informed him of the probe's whereabouts. Captain Chadwick had used a device he'd found on board the probe to send a message with the details and location of the crash site.

It was ironic that a Thark battlecruiser, searching for the wreckage of the lost probe, was probably responsible for the Orrappa discovering planet Earth. Yes, he now clearly recalled the event. *If the Orrappa fleet reached planet Earth it would mean in all probability the extermination of the entire population of the planet.* He felt a moment of guilt and helplessness. *What can I do?*

Amali interrupted his thoughts. "The data is ready for you to review, Klempe."

Viewing the video and the way that Amali had laid out the data, Klempe could not fault it. Nevertheless, he had a terrible foreboding.

"Amali, have you considered the consequences for planet Earth because of that unfortunate incident?"

"I have, Klempe. The consequences will be severe, possibly complete eradication of the human species."

Klempe nodded agreement. "What would you suggest we do in these circumstances, Amali?"

"Unless the Thark people want to declare war on the Orrappa, which I don't believe they do, I would suggest that the species from planet Earth should be given a way to defend themselves. I see the records on file show Captain Chadwick to be a resourceful being. Upgrading his ship's AI, and supplying him with cloaking and imaging technology, may enable him to defeat and turn back the Orrappa fleet that is now on its way to occupy or plunder his home planet."

Klempe could only agree. "Very well, Amali, send the video warning of the Orrappa fleet and its intentions to Captain Chadwick. I will discuss your suggestion with the Council of Elders."

Fregram Ruhner, a tough looking, seasoned military space fleet officer, was waiting for Klempe outside his office in the council hall. The space fleet commander had appointed Ruhner to lead the team investigating the death of Councillor Omnetki. As Klempe arrived, Ruhner said, "If you have a moment, Councillor, I believe we may have our killer."

Catching the officer by the arm, Klempe fairly dragged him into the building and into his office. Closing the office door, he gestured to a chair for the officer to sit down. "That is wonderful news, who is your suspect?"

"Our suspect is Councillor Jenharwen, who was elected at the last voting session."

Klempe nodded. "I know Councillor Jenharwen, a rising star in the council." His hackles rose, he did not like him, even though he was a polished and eloquent orator. "He's a rabble rouser, an oiler and greaser ready to jump on any bandwagon that will get him noticed."

Ruhner grimaced in understanding of the type. Reaching across the desk, he handed Klempe a projection card. "We believe we have sufficient evidence to make an arrest. We cross-referenced DNA found on the knife handle that killed Omnetki, with

DNA from Jenharwen. We also found a match with that of a database of individuals arriving on the planet from elsewhere in the galaxy. Three independent laboratories have confirmed the match. There is another thing, Jenharwen is from Orrappa, yet he is masquerading as a Thark being."

Klempe was shocked. "Do we know the motive for the killing?"

Fregram Ruhner gave a non-committal shrug. "I believe Councillor Jenharwen may have objected to proposed laws, intended to restrict entry to our world. I'm not sure, sir, you will have to ask him."

Klempe could guess there were controversial laws in the pipeline. He raised a questioning eyebrow. "Does he know we suspect him?"

Fregram Ruhner gave a wry smile and shook his head. "No, we have been very careful. We have not yet approached him."

Sitting quietly, Fregram Ruhner watched as Klempe placed his thumb over the emblem on the projection card that identified him and enabled him to view the report.

Klempe carefully examined the report including the three-dimensional images of Councillor Jenharwen and all the other images collected as evidence. He felt slightly sick seeing the image of the vicious knife slowly rotating, showing every facet of the weapon, the engraving on its handle and the enlarged views of the fingerprints superimposed over those of the official entry permit. When he finished viewing the report, he tapped something out on his console and a projection card exited the machine. Signing and putting his seal on the card, he passed it to Ruhner.

"This is an order authorising the arrest of Councillor Jenharwen. He is not to be mistreated, make him comfortable in secure accommodation and let me know where you are holding him. Show him the respect due to a councillor. Allow him anything within reason that he requests, other than visitors or communication devices. I will have a doctor examine him and I will question him myself in due course. Thank you, Fregram Ruhner, and my congratulations to your team."

Cold fury coursed through Klempe and his fists clenched in angry indignation, he wanted to pound the table at the senseless murder of Councillor Omnetki; enough was enough. The Thark were a peaceful species. They abhorred violence and cruelty. It was alien to their nature and upbringing. Nevertheless, now he would act.

Chapter 3

Councillor Jenharwen leaned back fully relaxed, with one leg crossed over the other, a muscled arm hooked over the back of his comfortable chair and smiled at Klempe. "You are making a huge mistake, Klempe." His voice was patronising and smug. "Your witnesses have only a hazy memory of what they think they saw." Jenharwen, trained to overcome the Orrappa's innate difficulty of telling an outright lie, sniggered. It was not in their nature for an Orrappa to lie. Better to be evasive, change the subject or not answer at all. He gave Klempe a malicious smile and thought, *these fools with their peace-loving nature cannot deal with a situation like this. Their laws are such that even if they do convict me of murder, what will they do. They do not believe in a death sentence or imprisonment, they think it cruel.* He had to stifle a snigger. *At worst, they will place me under house arrest, in a comfortable apartment like this one, until I expressed remorse and then they'll rehabilitate me.* He failed to suppress the small explosive snort, which escaped him as he grinned at Klempe.

Klempe sat facing him, another, possibly a doctor, stood by the door with a bag slung across his shoulder.

"I shall ask you one last time, Councillor Jenharwen, why did you attack and murder Councillor Omnetki?"

Jenharwen, still lounging in the chair, shrugged, shook his handsome head and laughed. "Whatever I say, you will still condemn me. You are seeking someone to blame, anyone will do, so you have picked me. I shall say nothing; you will just have to prove it was me that killed Councillor Omnetki."

Klempe gave him a wry look. "Proving you killed Omnetki is easy, we have the proof. What we want to know is why you killed him." Klempe paused for a moment. "And that is something you are going to tell me very soon."

A firmness in Klempe's voice hit home. For the first time, a little thread of fear crept into Jenharwen's mind. He wasn't to know it then but that fear was about to escalate, to a magnitude of terror beyond his imagination.

Turning his head, Klempe looked at the Thark standing by the door who gave just the slightest nod.

Klempe returned his gaze to Jenharwen, pointed a small device in his pocket at him and thumbed a button.

The device transmitted a terrifying psychological inducement program right into a target's mind. It magnified a being's natural fears to a horrifying extent that they would do anything to escape.

At first, nothing happened, but Jenharwen felt the smile fade from his face, a shiver ran down his spine. He sat up in the chair as a feeling of impending doom began to pervade him, his teeth clenched and his lips drew back in a grimace, he shuddered violently and perspiration began to pour from him. His eyes glazed over and his features expressed absolute terror. His body began to shiver and shake uncontrollably and he threw his head about frenziedly, trying to shake off some unknown thing. His pitiful screams of terror were silent. Klempe could see Jenharwen was screaming but no sound left his mouth. The muscles and tendons in his neck and hands stood out as he clutched the arms of the chair digging his fingers deep into the upholstery.

Klempe counted the time off in his head and pressed a button on the device. Gradually Jenharwen stopped shaking. His face, although still contorted, began to relax a little. The Thark standing by the door came over and used a small device to check him. "He should be able to speak now," he said.

Jenharwen had his eyes open, terror still showed on his face, as he looked uncomprehendingly at Klempe.

"Do you think you are up to answering some questions?" Klempe asked evenly.

Jenharwen gasped. "What have you done to me?"

Klempe shrugged. "Nothing, I just want to ask you some questions, establish the truth."

The doctor produced a small flask and put it to Jenharwen's lips, who then drank noisily.

Klempe spent another hour questioning him. A simple medical examination had confirmed that he was from Orrappa. When the truth finally came out it was a complete anti-climax. The unprovoked and pointless killing was merely an exploratory operation to see how the Thark authorities might react, if at all, to the murder of one of their most senior officials. There had been no reprisals for the piracy of Thark merchant ships. The Orrappa saw the Thark as soft and weak. The next stage in their plan would be the occupation of a distant

Thark world. Opposition to the proposed new entry laws were just a distraction.

During the interrogation, Klempe occasionally glanced at the recording device on the small table beside him, the peaks in a scrolling line accompanying the words indicated untruths, some were small lies others more serious.

"Thank you, Councillor," Klempe said. "You have been most helpful, that has cleared up many points that have puzzled us."

Jenharwen let out a shuddering sigh of relief. *They are going to let me go.* The thought reassured him. "I would like to leave now."

"Not just yet, Councillor, there are a couple of details we have to clear up." Klempe looked at the doctor. "Is Councillor Jenharwen ready to help us in more detail?"

The doctor nodded. "Yes, I'm sure he wants to be completely honest with us."

Jenharwen's mouth opened in protest and then changed rapidly to a grimace of horror. Klempe had already pressed the control on the device in his pocket for a higher level of terror. A short time later, the doctor made a noise to attract Klempe's attention. "I think that's enough."

"We need the truth, he killed in cold blood and has shown no remorse, a few moments longer and he will tell all he knows."

Later, when Jenharwen had recovered, Klempe switched on his recorder again. Jenharwen told all he knew; the recorder showed no spikes in his statement.

Klempe and the doctor listened in outrage and disbelief as they played the tape back again. The Orrappa had uncovered the vital weakness in the

Thark's mentality. The Thark civilisation may have been in existence a lot longer than the Orrappa and their technology so advanced, that the Orrappa could only dream of it. However, the Thark were soft; they did not believe in punishment, there were no real deterrents. They treated bad behaviour and crime as an illness, with compassion, education and support. Crime no longer existed for them; instead, a thirst for knowledge and respect for their fellow beings replaced it.

The Orrappa leadership had seen this as an opportunity to exploit what they regarded as a weakness. They had developed a simple but effective plan to create a continuous and increasing level of disruption at the heart of the Thark government to keep them in disarray, whilst they conducted systematic theft and piracy of Thark merchant vessels plying between Thark worlds. A small heavily armed patrol ship with no markings, could quite easily take out the antenna and direction finders on an autonomous freighter forcing it to a halt or overwhelm an unarmed merchant vessel, survivors of these attacks were very few. Their only hope of escape was in a fast survival pod.

The doctor looked at Klempe in dismay. "How can they treat our hospitality and goodwill with such contempt? You've got to stop this plan of theirs, it's treacherous and evil, a crime against—"

Klempe raised a hand, palm up and stopped him mid-sentence. "Don't worry, doctor, now we know of their plans, we shall act swiftly." He held up the small device he had used earlier. "This is only a small personal device. However, we possess the technology to broadcast to a selective and larger audience with various degrees of severity. It may be unpleasant but it does no lasting harm to the individuals."

The doctor smiled. "I'm so glad to hear that." As he left the room, he heard Klempe on his communicator requesting his AI, Amali, to set up a meeting with Fregram Ruhner of the Thark space defence force.

Fregram Ruhner took his time reading the transcription of Klempe's interview with the now ex-Councillor Jenharwen. When he had finished reading, he nodded. "Excellent, I doubt even my organisation could have gathered this much information. What is it you wish me to do?"

"I wish to put a stop to this insidious scheme by the Orrappa. I want you to develop a strategy to deal with the problem efficiently and effectively."

Ruhner contemplated Klempe. "Our warships are very advanced and capable of inflicting devastating punishment, not just to a ship but to a planet. However, in the past the Council of Elders has prevented us from taking the appropriate action. Our hands are tied."

"Not any longer, Ruhner, our security policy is under sharp revision. We do not want all-out war with the Orrappa but we wish to give them a short, sharp shock, a message that will make their authorities reconsider their attitudes and foreign policies."

Ruhner smiled. "Some of your colleagues must have entered the real world or was that last incident too close to home?"

Klempe grinned. "A bit of both I think. However, the outcome is a change of policy."

Ruhner nodded. "Are the other Orrappa insurgents still in office?"

"Yes, nothing has changed, everything is as normal. The other councillors believe that Jenharwen has merely taken a short leave of absence."

"Excellent, I will confer with my colleagues and come back with a workable plan of action, one that our service can operate efficiently." Ruhner looked hard at Klempe. "We will expect complete support and cooperation from the Council of Elders; names, and positions held by the insurgents within our government, also their friends, relatives and contacts. We don't want one hand tied behind our back to satisfy some misplaced ideal."

Even as Ruhner spoke, Klempe was nodding in agreement. "Your agency will have our full cooperation."

Klempe knew that in the past the council had seldom if ever allowed force to be used even in defence of its own worlds. However, after the disclosure by Jenharwen of the Orrappa's master plan, that policy would be revised. He would see to it himself.

Chapter 4

Each member of the Council of Elders had read the transcript of Klempe's interrogation of Jenharwen. The revelations shocked them. They were now debating Fregram Ruhner's proposed plan of action.

Klempe summed the debate up, "We have been complacent for too long. We either act now or give in to terror and intimidation. I urge you to accept the proposals for the formation of a new dedicated arm of the space fleet organisation, the Thark space security service. Violent action will be avoided wherever possible in favour of the psychological inducement program."

The proposal passed unanimously.

Klempe felt saddened by the death of Councillor Omnetki but at least some good had come from his cruel murder.

"There is one further point of order that I must raise with the assembly," said Klempe. "Some time ago a Thark battlecruiser inadvertently drove an Orrappa warship into the Sol system. This resulted in the Orrappa discovering the planet Earth." He chose his words carefully. "We led the Orrappa there. We put planet Earth in danger." He took a sip of water, giving time for the information to be absorbed. "An Orrappa invasion fleet of forty vessels is on its way to Earth, as we speak.

"My concern is that planet Earth will be unable to defend itself against an attack. The indigenous beings are resourceful but primitive by the standards of the Orrappa. I have sent Captain Chadwick a warning of the approaching task force so that he may warn his planet's leaders.

All the councillors knew of Captain Chadwick, it was he who had discovered the wreckage of their lost probe and had sent them the location so the remains of the crew to be recovered.

Klempe continued, "Amali, my AI, has put forward a suggestion that we offer Captain Chadwick some technological assistance in the form of a standard electronic cloaking device, such as we use on our own battlecruisers and upgrade his AI to a level where she can oversee the construction and installation of the cloaking device. Amali believes, and I concur, that this assistance would allow Captain Chadwick and his two ships to dissuade the Orrappa from attacking Earth and turn the Orrappa fleet back. A cloaking device will go a long way to even the odds against Captain Chadwick. Iris the *JJ Grant's* AI confirms that she has sufficient equipment and materials on board to manufacture the device.

Amid the murmurings and looks of consternation after Klempe's speech, a councillor rose to speak. "I think that it is an admirable solution, but I believe we should go a step further, if we have a military vessel that can intercept the Earth ships before they clash with the Orrappa. Her captain should be given permission to offer Captain Chadwick advisory assistance or if the situation demands it, active assistance."

The council's AI announced without hesitation, "The battlecruiser *B109* is available and can intercept Captain Chadwick's ships in good time."

The councillor, flushed with excitement, turned to Klempe. "I put forward a motion that we the Thark offer Captain Chadwick the technology of an upgrade to his AI, together with construction and operating details for the cloaking device. I also put forward the motion that our battlecruiser *B109* diverts to join with these Earth vessels and allow the captain of the *B109* to use his own discretion whether to take an advisory role or engage as an active participant if there is to be a confrontation."

Shortly afterwards, Klempe rose to his feet. "I am pleased to announce that the vote on each proposal has been approved unanimously. I will instruct my AI to make the necessary arrangements immediately."

Later in his office, Amali, Klempe's AI, announced in her soft soothing voice, "As directed, I have sent Iris, the AI on the *JJ Grant*, the design details for her hardware upgrade. Included in the data package is her software upgrade. When Iris confirms that both hardware and software upgrades have been implemented, I will send her the full design and construction details of the cloaking unit."

"Thank you, Amali. Will Iris be able to handle the upgrades without assistance?"

"Yes, Klempe, I conducted a scan of Iris and can confirm she is equipped to carry out the upgrades herself. She has direct connections to the necessary machinery."

"What about the battlecruiser *B109*, Amali?"

"I am awaiting a directive from Space Fleet High Command concerning the *B109*."

"Very well, let me know when you have it."

On the interstellar vessel *JJ Grant*, Captain Chadwick was in the bridge office, his crew busy at their stations, with no issues reported. However, his two ships remained in high orbit around planet Earth.

He still smouldered at the derisive rebuffing he had received from Earth's leaders when he had shown them the warning video of the approaching Orrappa fleet. He had tried every reasonable approach to state the seriousness that Earth faced, possibly the complete extermination of the Earth's population, but he was laughed at and derided as a foolish mischief-maker.

It was then that he and his crew had made the decision to take it upon themselves to do all they could to turn the Orrappa fleet back.

The message from Klempe that the Thark would provide an upgrade to Iris and the technical design of a device to help him overcome the Orrappa filled him with hope and gratitude.

He had delayed the departure of his vessels to allow Iris to complete her upgrade and build the cloaking device for his ships. The worry in his mind was that the Thark had overstated the effectiveness of the device but the proof was now here, the devices built and tested. The results of the tests were far beyond his expectations and they would give him a fighting chance to turn the Orrappa back.

Reviewing for the umpteenth time, the video sent to him by Klempe, showing the terrifying Orrappa fleet heading for Earth, he could not comprehend why Earth's leaders had not taken the threat of invasion seriously when shown the evidence.

Finally, having completed all preparations, he made the announcement to his crew that they were to depart Earth orbit and head out into deep space to confront the Orrappa fleet.

However, even as the *JJ Grant* and the *Helcon* headed out into deep space to intercept the approaching fleet he inwardly worried. Were he and his ships up to the task ahead of them?

"Klempe, a copy of a directive from Space Fleet High Command concerning the *B109* has just come in for you," Amali said.

Leaning back in his chair, Klempe looked up and said, "Verbalise the gist of the message please, Amali."

"The battlecruiser *B109* is ordered to abandon her current patrol and to intercept the interstellar ship *JJ Grant* and her escort. Will advise when contact has been made."

Klempe smiled, "That is good news. I'll read the full message later, Amali."

The *JJ Grant* and the *Helcon* were a month into their long journey to confront the Orrappa fleet. Captain Chadwick, sitting at his command console, heard the viewer chime; he was expecting a routine call from Captain Grant Mapps on the *Helcon*. Instead, Iris's face lit up the screen. "Captain Chadwick, Klempe wishes to speak with you," she said, in her soft pleasant voice.

Chad eagerly replied, "Put him on, Iris." Klempe's smiling face appeared on the viewer.

"Hello, Captain Chadwick, my AI tells me you have commenced your journey to meet the Orrappa fleet."

"That is true, Klempe, it's not something that I am looking forward to. But it has to be done."

"I can understand that, Captain Chadwick. However, I have good news for you. The Council of Elders has authorised the *B109*, one of our most modern battlecruisers, to support you when you meet the Orrappa fleet. Captain Frussee, her commander, will assess your exact requirements, and will either adopt an advisory role or take an active part in any engagement. My AI has sent the rendezvous coordinates to your ship's AI."

Chad would not admit to it but despite both his ships having the advantage of a cloaking device, he had been very concerned about battle tactics for when they met the Orrappa. "We are deeply indebted to you, Klempe. That is most kind of you. We will look forward to meeting Captain Frussee." Chad hesitated for a moment. "Klempe, is there any way we can repay your kindness?"

"That is not necessary, Captain Chadwick… er although we have enjoyed some of what you call comedy films that you sent us in the past."

Chad beamed with pleasure. "Iris will transmit a selection immediately."

"Thank you, Captain Chadwick; I will contact you again when our ship has reached the rendezvous point." Klempe faded from the viewer.

Chad mentally mopped his brow. "Iris, did you get all that?"

"I did, Captain, an entertainment file has been sent and I have noted the rendezvous coordinates in the ship's log."

Following her new orders to abandon her patrol and to rendezvous with the two Earth vessels, the Thark battlecruiser *B109* proceeded at cruising speed to the rendezvous point. Captain Frussee was not concerned that they might arrive early, if they did, it would give her crew a much-needed break. Rest and relaxation were always good for morale. Patrols were usually long and arduous, with often little to show for the time and effort. This diversion, however, could be rewarding, a good prospect of action and the opportunity to meet another alien species.

On arrival at the rendezvous, the *B109* would follow new military guidance and cloak up whilst awaiting the arrival of the Earth ships.

Captain Frussee called her ship's AI. "Print out all available data on the Earth vessels to my cabin printer." She then called her second in command. "Take over, number two; I want to read up on this Earth species. I'll be in my quarters if I'm needed."

Passing the junior officers' mess, Captain Frussee heard a gale of laughter. *Hmm, I wonder what's going on in there.* She stopped a moment but it would have been contrary to service protocol for her to intrude into the mess without an invitation. However, she was intrigued; she didn't like anything happening on her ship without her knowledge.

Reading the data that her AI had managed to glean from Klempe's AI, she was surprised. This Earth species had developed an interstellar space drive. Yet incredibly, only a few lifetimes earlier they were still in an age of steam power. Now they had, or so it would seem, a gravity drive, a protective shield and on-board gravity.

Interestingly, the ship had been designed as an exploration vessel, unlike the warship that accompanied her. A momentary roar of laughter from the junior officers' mess interrupted her concentration, as someone opened and closed a door.

Enough was enough; she wanted to know what was going on. She called her second in command. "When you come off duty, find out discretely what's going on in the junior officers' mess and let me know."

A while later, there was a soft tap on her door and the door slid open. "I've not disturbed them, Captain, they're just enjoying themselves. But I managed to get this." He held up a data stick.

"You'd better come in; let's see what it's all about."

What it was all about, she was to discover, were films, moving pictures, crudely made by an alien species. The films had been shown to a group of off-duty technicians in the lower ranks' quarters. A communications technician on the *B109* had intercepted and unofficially copied a file containing a small batch of these films. He'd hacked into a transmission from the alien vessel to Councillor Klempe, the speaker of the Council of Elders. Now he was selling the file on data sticks to the crew as souvenirs.

Watching the film with her number two, Captain Frussee knew she should report the incident, but then there would be hell to pay. Meanwhile, of course, she would have to carry out her own investigation and examine each film. She again heard the muffled sound of junior officers roaring with laughter and smiled to herself. *This was going to be an interesting patrol.* As she turned her attention back to the film, she thought, *Yes, I'll either promote the miscreant for his ability to hack the transmission or put him on report for the indiscretion, but first I'll examine the films.* She sat back with a smile as the first scene unfolded…

Chapter 5

The *JJ Grant* and the *Helcon* made their way through deep space to rendezvous with the Thark battlecruiser *B109*.

From his place at the captain's console, Chad again reviewed the video sent to him by Klempe of the Orrappa invasion fleet heading for Earth. An involuntary shudder ran through him. *I don't believe our two ships could have faced a fleet of that size no matter how well protected. It's such a relief that the Thark are sending a seasoned battlecruiser to support us. I just hope it's enough.*

The bridge was quiet, his crew absorbed in their work. Pushing the worrying thoughts from his mind, he switched his screen to the forward camera and gazed at the viewer showing a vista of stars ahead. Out here in deep space, way beyond the solar system, the stars seem so close, yet the nearest star system was over four and a half light years away. Furrowing his brow, he attempted the calculation in his head without success. *Four and a half light years! That is an incredible distance, even using the power block drive. Travel between star systems will never be quick; to reach the more distant star systems, we'll be looking at years of travel.* Letting his mind drift back to Klempe's warning about the Orrappa space fleet, he wondered, *Should Grant and I have given the secrets of the gravity drive to our government or even to the major governments around the world. No!* He gave a shake of his head; *Helens right, they would have abused the knowledge.* Throughout their marriage, he'd always trusted Helen's instincts and common sense, "Talk to the crew, see how they feel." And he had. *Egotistical leaders of governments were at each other's throats all the time, no matter what other events were occurring around them. They ignored our warnings, even after seeing the video of the approaching fleet. Yes, we made the right decision, we are already out here and they would have had to start from scratch.*

He was proud that the crews of both ships had given him their unanimous support. The only way to save Earth from the Orrappa was to do it themselves. *Yes, we will be up against immense odds, but now our ships have the cloaking device and the support of a Thark battlecruiser, we have a fighting chance.*

The Thark, a normally benevolent and nonviolent species, had existed many, millions of years before human beings had evolved. Their technology was beyond anything that humans could imagine.

The extraordinary thing about the cloaking device was that a vessel using the device was undetectable visually or by any known electronic sensor. Yet, whilst cloaked, an image of the ship could be projected to another point in space – an image so real, that detection equipment, such as radar, sonar or any other detection systems, saw the projected image as the real thing. When they had built the first cloaking devices for the *JJ Grant* and the *Helcon*, the initial trials had been astounding. So effective was the device that Chad had taken the opportunity during the voyage out into deep space to build additional cloaking devices for all the shuttle craft and lifeboats that were aboard their vessels.

Movement ahead drew Chad's attention. Not far off by cosmic standards, were a group of asteroids, performing a delicate ballet of their own as they orbited about their largest member, an asteroid about a third the size of Earth's moon.

Still watching the group of asteroids, Chad brooded about the lack of defensive weapons on the *JJ Grant*. He blamed himself. *It was my choice not to build a weapons system into the ship. However, if we are to meet the Orrappa fleet, it makes sense to have something to retaliate with—* the comms officer reporting interrupted his thoughts.

"Sir, we've got a problem, there's something wrong with our long-range detection equipment; sonar and radar are out as well."

Stiffening in his seat, wariness brought him to full alert. Chad didn't like odd things happening on his ship. "Iris, what's causing our comms problems?"

"Initial assessment indicates a bad connection of the feed cable from the antenna array, Captain."

"Use the communicator and signal the *Helcon*. Tell her we have a problem with our antenna and for them to stop and wait for us." The communicator was a device for instant person-to-person communication over vast distances without a measurable time delay. The device came from the wreckage of the Thark probe on Uranus. Chad's electronics experts had made copies sufficient for every crewmember to have one.

Iris reported, "Captain Mapps has acknowledged our message and will comply."

Chad called engineering on his headset. "Connie, I'm bringing the ship to a halt. I need a repair team to go outside and check the ship's antenna array. Iris says we have a connection problem with the feed cable. Can you organise this urgently please?"

Connie didn't waste words. "We're on it now, Captain."

How the hell did that happen? He wondered.

Ten minutes later Connie's voice came over the headset again. "Repair team are exiting airlock M8, Captain."

Chad switched to an external viewer showing the M8 airlock. "Thanks, Connie, I have them in view." Along with the rest of the crew, he watched nervously as the repair team quickly made their way to the antenna array. Chad could hear the running commentary given by the third team member as the other two carried out the inspection. She sounded young but her voice was clear, sharp and confident as she described a corrosion problem with the multi-pin plug and socket. There was no other option but to replace both components.

"How long to fix it, Connie?" Chad called into his headset.

"The team have the spare parts but it'll be a slow job and they'll need about three hours, Captain."

"Right, let me know when the job's done."

Chad continued to watch the repair team but was worried; the ship would be blind for at least three hours. Out here in deep space, anything could happen and when it did, it was usually very quick. Ship's crew that worked outside making repairs in the vacuum of space knew the dangers and were a breed apart with nerves of steel.

Just over three hours later, Connie called him.

"Problem sorted, Captain; the team have fitted the new parts. They're all safely back on board, no mishaps. We'll do an autopsy on the old plug and socket and find out what caused the corrosion. We're switching the antenna back on now."

"Thanks, Connie." Chad nodded to the comms officer who had been watching him intently. "OK, Comms, we should be back on line, run a check please."

The comms officer ran through a sequence of checks. "Yes, it seems fine now— Bloody hell!" he yelled. "Something's coming up fast behind us – missile attack!" he bellowed and in a slightly calmer voice called. "Impact in five seconds."

Iris detected the missiles milliseconds after the antenna array came back on line and already had the ship moving, lurching into high-speed motion, twisting, turning and side slipping to dodge the missiles.

Chad gripped the arms of his seat and gathered his senses. The last thing he recalled on the viewer was the group of asteroids ahead.

"Iris, manoeuvre the ship behind an asteroid, when we are out of sight of the attacker cloak up," he snapped. Moments later the fierce movements of the ship abruptly ceased, calm returned.

"The ship is cloaked, Captain."

Chad acknowledged. "Good job, everyone." Flicking a switch, he called, "Radar, your situation report, please."

"Four missiles in the vicinity seeking targets. Another vessel approaching. I have lost the *Helcon*, she must have cloaked up as well."

"Iris, can you identify the attacking vessel?"

"Yes, Captain. The ship is of the same class as the *Helcon*, an Orrappa vessel."

"Iris, take control of the loose missiles if you can."

There was a few seconds of silence. "I have control of the missiles, Captain, but their drive systems have a limited life."

"No matter, park them by an asteroid if you can, we'll pick them up later. Where is the Orrappa vessel now?"

"The enemy vessel is searching for us within the asteroids. They believe that's where we're hiding."

"Good, use the communicator and message Captain Mapps. The *Helcon* is to remain cloaked until we have resolved the situation. If that ship moves, the *Helcon* is to follow it with us. We are going to find out why that ship fired on us."

"Captain Mapps has acknowledged, sir," said Iris.

They continued to watch the Orrappa ship, which nosed around the small group of asteroids.

Mentally wiping his brow, Chad had a moment to reflect on what had happened. *We were sitting ducks, completely helpless, had it not been for the cloaking device we would be atoms floating in space. I have to find some way of arming the JJ Grant.* Finally, the Orrappa warship gave up the search for them and turned the way it had come; unaware that it now had two cloaked vessels in tow.

The *JJ Grant* and the *Helcon* had been following the attacking vessel for a considerable time when Iris announced, "Three stationary vessels ahead, Captain."

"Can you identify them, Iris?"

"Two of the vessels are of the same class as the *Helcon*; the third appears to be a large passenger vessel, Captain."

Chad was intrigued. "We'll move in closer and find out what's going on. Use the communicator to notify Captain Mapps, Iris."

It rapidly became apparent what was going on. The majestic passenger vessel was undergoing an attack by the Orrappa.

Lifeboats from the Orrappa warships were entering the vessel through an illuminated loading bay in the side of the ship. They re-emerged loaded up with materials and supplies that they then ferried over to the warships a short distance away.

The Orrappa ship that they had followed came to a halt close to the passenger vessel, its lifeboats swarming over to take their share of plunder.

Chad watched what was happening whilst making his mind up. Using the communicator, he called Captain Mapps on the *Helcon*. "Captain Mapps, I believe this is a situation that justifies the use of the psychological inducement program."

"I wholeheartedly agree, Captain Chadwick, treat them harshly," came the response.

Chad called Iris on the viewer. "Iris, I want you to round up the Orrappa crew. Hold them in the ship's canteens. Do not allow them any access to communications. You may use the psychological inducement program to do so."

"Yes, Captain, please enter your security code to allow me access. I can then project a blanket broadcast into the Orrappa ships."

Chad tapped in the necessary code as he watched the Orrappa lifeboats, loaded with spoils, return and enter the ship's bay. None came out for another load.

The communicator, retrieved from the wreckage of a Thark vessel on Uranus, held the psychological inducement program. Unaware of the program's lethal potency, Chad had volunteered to experience a twenty-second projection of the program. He recalled the terrifying ordeal. Nothing would induce him to experience it again. The program's mind-altering effects were too terrifyingly dangerous to have on the communicators issued to the crew. Iris held a copy of the program under multiple layers of security that required a code from the captain to allow her access. The only other copy was on the original communicator held under lock and key in the *JJ Grant's* armoury.

Chad shuddered, remembering his experience. He knew how the Orrappa crew would be feeling. The only place they would feel safe would be in the ship's canteen. They would barricade themselves inside, those still outside would be screaming to get in and cowering in terror from an unknown horror in their minds.

Chapter 6

All the Orrappa lifeboats had returned to their ships and the area around the passenger ship was devoid of movement. "Comms, are you able to communicate with the passenger ship?"

"Working on it now, Captain, I have established a link. We should be able to see them on the viewer if they are free to respond."

A few moments later the viewer lit up showing a group of almond-eyed beings. Chad immediately recognised them as Thark.

"Iris, send them a message in their own language and tell them who we are and that the Orrappa military are confined on their ships."

At the news, the relief on the faces of the Thark crew was obvious.

When Captain Vashonni, a tall handsome looking being, dressed in an ultra-smart blue and gold uniform, appeared on the viewer, he was full of gratitude for their intervention. He looked too young to be in command of what was obviously a space liner. He told them his passengers and crew had barricaded themselves in the ship fearing for their lives. He'd already informed the Thark authorities of the attack on his ship and a Thark warship was on its way to escort them home.

With the Orrappa crew secured in their ship's canteens, the dilemma was what to do with them.

Bristling with outrage, Captain Vashonni said, "Captain Chadwick, may I suggest you disarm one of the Orrappa vessels and send the Orrappa crew back to where they came from and commandeer the other two craft for yourselves."

"We'll certainly consider your proposal, Captain Vashonni. What about all the items plundered from your vessel? We can offer some assistance to help return them to your ship."

"That is not necessary, Captain Chadwick, no critical equipment that would prevent my ship from completing our journey safely has been removed. You are welcome to keep whatever devices or stores they have plundered. Had you not come to our rescue we would in all probability have lost our lives and the ship as well."

Chad mulled the suggestion over with his officers.

"If we did commandeer those ships, we'd be short of fully trained crew."

"I think we can cope with that – it would be a mistake not to take advantage of the situation. There's nothing like on the job training," said Grant.

Wang Zheng, Chad's second in command, agreed. "Yeah and they will certainly add to our fire power when we meet the Orrappa fleet."

"Right, I can see everyone's for it; we'll inspect the ships and pick the best two. Iris, are you able to reprogram the Orrappa AI's to switch allegiance to me and our crew?"

"Yes, Captain, the AIs have quite powerful computer cores but they have little in the way of built-in internal or external security. Once I have control of the AIs, I will also have control of the ship's bridge."

"Very well, Iris, please proceed. Oh, and can you send Captain Vashonni some entertainment material to take his passengers' minds off their horrible ordeal. I'll leave the choice of material to your discretion."

"Certainly, Captain Chadwick." Chad could almost sense a smile in Iris's voice; it wasn't often if ever that she called him, Captain Chadwick.

Minutes later Iris startled Chad by announcing, "The Orrappa ships are under our control, Captain. Allegiance is to you and our crew. I have added the English language to the AIs' database and made it the preferred language, although the AIs can use either language when required. I can reverse allegiance and remove the English language dictionary should you decide against commandeering the ships. An entertainment package has been sent to Captain Vashonni with your compliments."

"Thank you, Iris."

Using a shuttle craft, Chad, together with Connie Mapps, his chief engineer, and senior officers from both the *JJ Grant* and the *Helcon* commenced an inspection of the Orrappa vessels. Chad wrinkled his nose; the smell inside the vessel was foul. It had been in space a long time… too long.

Later he called Iris. "We've completed our inspection, release some of the Orrappa crew and get them to clean up all three ships and get their engineers to service the air regeneration systems; the air is contaminated. These ships are a health hazard in their present condition."

"Certainly, Captain."

Connie checked her notes. "Chad, two of those ships have good drive systems, I've not seen the specs for them but they are in excellent condition. I'm recommending we commandeer those. The drive on the third ship is probably past its best. It has had some temporary repair work done to it in the past. I think we should send the Orrappa crew back in that."

"Thanks, Connie. Is there enough room for all three crews on that ship?"

"It will be cramped, but they should survive."

"Grant, I'd like you to organise the disarming of the ship we are sending back. Distribute everything between the Helcon and the two Orrappa ships that we are commandeering. Anything that cannot be moved leave in place but ensure it is inoperable. Remove all long-distance communication equipment. Select engineers from the Orrappa crew for this task. Ask Iris to supervise them. Also, if in doubt consult Iris."

"I'll get on to it straight away, Chad – have you thought who you might appoint as captains on these two new ships?"

"Well, the obvious choices are my number two, Wang Zheng from the *JJ Grant* and Henson Wright, your number two. They are both top-notch bridge commanders."

"Yes, I'll be sorry to lose Henson; he's a fantastic officer and gave me his unreserved support. He deserves to have his own ship."

"That's settled then. I'll get Iris to give Wang and Henson a list of suitable people from which to build their own bridge crews. It's fortunate that the Orrappa ships have their own simulators for training, that'll speed things up. Speaking of the Orrappa, what about Hernani. How does she feel about the Orrappa crew being sent back to their home planet?"

Grant considered the question for a moment. "I believe she feels sorry for them; she thinks we may be sending them to their deaths."

"I see, but you feel we can we trust her?"

"I think so; she's been a brilliant third officer and more than proved herself."

"Hmm, so it's logical that you will want her as your second in command. It may be sensible to get Helen to have a word with her. They get on well and Helen will know if Hernani is having issues or regrets."

"That's a good idea, Chad, as my number two I need to know that I can trust her implicitly."

"I agree you can't be too careful." Chad gave a sigh. "I shall be sorry to lose Wang as my number two; he has matured into a fine young officer. However, Gordon Blair on my team deserves promotion too."

"So, we're agreed, Grant; Wang and Henson to become captains and Hernani and Gordon promoted to second in command, subject to Helen having a chat with Hernani. Wang and Henson can pick their own bridge crews after we've notified them of their promotions.

In the quiet of their cabin Helen said, "I had a chat with Hernani today."

Chad looked up from his communicator. "That's good, how did you get on?"

"We got on fine; I don't think you have anything to worry about concerning her loyalty. She is upset about the Orrappa going home because she says the Orrappa government will treat them very cruelly but accepts you have no choice." Chad nodded.

"So, you think we can promote her?"

"In my opinion, promotion would make her even more loyal."

Chad grinned. "That's exactly what I think," he said as he gave Helen a hug.

Two days later aboard the *JJ Grant*, Chad performed a little ceremony, promoting Wang and Henson to the rank of captain and officially putting them in charge of the commandeered Orrappa interstellar warships. He then announced the promotion of those appointed second in command.

When he congratulated Hernani, Chad could see the pride she had in the badge of rank that he'd presented to her.

Returning to the bridge office Chad instructed, "Note today's events in the ship's log, Iris."

"Yes, Captain. I have sent Captain Wang Zheng and Captain Henson Wright a list of suitable candidates for bridge crew with a copy to your printer."

"Thanks, Iris, compatibility and potential is more important than qualifications; we can always top up training and education."

"That's exactly what I thought too, sir."

Chad raised an eyebrow in surprise. "*Oh really!*"

An unexpected call came from Keung Zheng, who was effectively the ship's quartermaster. "Chad, I know you're busy but I need to draw your attention to our stores."

"OK, Keung, what's the problem?"

"Not a problem yet, but I've just completed a stocktake of our resources and we're getting low on essential supplies. I thought you should know before we get too far from Earth."

"Thanks, Keung. I'll come down and have a look at the figures with you."

They met up in the restaurant and over a cup of tea, Chad went through the stock figures with Keung. Still old school, Keung sipped his tea from his favourite tea bowl that the restaurant kept for him.

"You're right, Keung. It would be prudent to stock up on provisions. Raw materials for engineering and electronics are low as well." Chad took a sip of his tea. "We're not desperate for anything yet but we don't know how long we're going to be out here. I have to admit taking on two extra Orrappa warships wasn't something I'd planned to do. I agree that we should send three shuttles back for supplies." Keung nodded.

"Liaise with Richard Prior; he is in daily contact with James Parker at ground control. He can organise to have the supplies ready for collection."

"Thanks, Chad, I'll get onto him shortly. Er, by the way, how is Wang getting on with his new ship? I haven't seen much of him recently."

Chad smiled. "Do you mean your lad, Captain Wang Zheng of the warship *Black Pearl?*"

Keung smiled back. "Yes, that sounds like him. So he's naming the ship *Black Pearl?*"

"That's right. Keung, you have a fine son there. He's very proud and wants it to be the best ship in the group.

I'm sorry to lose him as my number two but he deserves his own ship I'm sorry it's keeping you apart, but the way he's working, it won't be for long."

"So, it looks like I shall have to take a trip over to the Black Pearl."

Chad knocked back the last of his tea and gave him a grin. "Looks that way, Keung, that's what happens when sons grow up, fathers have to take a back seat. Cadge a lift over to his ship on a shuttle, he'll be delighted to see you and you'll be amazed at what he's done to that ship already."

Chad called a meeting in the *JJ Grant*'s wardroom. Grant had come over from the *Helcon* and had rounded everyone up that didn't have a key job but that had undergone some pilot training.

Chad started the meeting, "Thanks for coming, guys. We need volunteers to take three shuttles back to ground control at Perth to pick up supplies. It'll be a two-month round trip. The shuttles will be on autopilot but we need a crew to take over in an emergency. One of the shuttles will have the heating reduced to below freezing for frozen food."

One of the trainee pilots, Mark Williams, eventually broke the silence around the table. "If I can have a couple of hours in the simulator as a refresher, I'd be happy enough to volunteer."

"That's great. These shuttles are easy to fly. We need a crew on board in the event of an emergency and of course you have your communicators to keep in touch with us here."

Mark nodded. "Thanks, there is just one proviso, I'd like to bring my girlfriend back with me and she's a doctor."

"Sounds good to me," said Chad. "I don't think anyone will be against that. Anyone else fancy a trip back?"

Eventually another three suitably qualified volunteers came forward. "All four of you will travel in the lead shuttle; the other two shuttles will follow on autopilot. That way you can share watch keeping duties."

Connie's team had meticulously prepared the shuttle craft and serviced all the on-board equipment. Iris programed the autopilot with destination and return coordinates. The two drone shuttles responded to the lead shuttle controls or independently using their own on-board controls. One of the drone shuttles carried the mail and memory sticks.

Finally, they were ready to depart with Mark Williams in command. Mark shook hands with Grant and Chad. "Any messages, sir?"

"Yes, tell them, I said thanks for all the support and backup work they've given us. Richard Prior is in daily contact with James Parker, the director of ground control, and all the supplies should be waiting for you ready to be loaded. Stay vigilant and always keep someone at the controls when the shuttles are on the ground. Watch out for stowaways and don't hesitate to lift off should you get a whiff of danger, whether you are fully loaded or not. You can always go back and finish loading if it turns out to be a false alarm."

"Should I expect trouble, sir?"

"Hopefully not, but always expect the unexpected." Chad grinned. "You'll be fine, there are spare suits on board and an entertainment package and you have your communicators to keep in touch with us. Good luck, see you all in a couple of months."

The four young men made their way to the lead shuttle and climbed aboard.

Everyone watched on the viewer as the shuttle craft accelerated out into space. Even with the viewer set to maximum range the shuttles disappeared at an astonishing rate.

Henson sat at the captain's console of his new command and gazed round with a feeling of pride and satisfaction. An Orrappa crew under Iris's supervision had cleaned up and serviced the ship. They'd done a wonderful job. Nevertheless, surveying the bridge Henson thought, *I'm going to make some changes. I'll have the whole bridge painted another colour and these drab console seats need deep surgery. I'm sure Scott McDonald will give me some ideas. However, performance is first on the agenda.* He called out to the AI, "Put the ship's performance specifications on the viewer."

Running his eyes down the specification lists, Henson was most surprised that the general performance specifications did not compare with those of the *JJ Grant*. Switching his screen, he called Iris, "Check the comparison specifications between the *JJ Grant* and the Orrappa warships please."

"The information from your ship's AI is correct, Captain Wright. The Orrappa drive system is not as refined as the power block on the *JJ Grant*. It is possible to rectify this situation temporarily by fitting power blocks at strategic points to boost the Orrappa drive's performance. The long-term solution is of course to fit a new power block drive as has been done on the *Helcon*."

How could he have forgotten, *Of course, installing the JJ Grant's spare drive in the Helcon accounted for her speed.* However, weaponry on his new ship was another matter. Henson had a mental gloat about the ship's armaments; fighter craft that could operate in either space or an atmosphere, missiles, plasma canons, rapid-fire ballistics, and laser weapons. The tech was well beyond anything he'd ever been involved with when he was in the air force or had worked on when he was a test pilot. Henson was in his element. "AI, compile a full report of the ship's specifications, weaponry and ammunition stocks, together with a detailed report of the ship's construction." He wanted to know all its weak points as well as its good points.

Henson missed seeing Iris on the viewer. *Are these Orrappa AIs as good as Iris?* As the thought slipped through his mind, he heard Iris say, "No, Captain Wright, both AIs are of excellent military grade but not up to my specifications.

Henson was startled. *Did I vocalise my thoughts or not? I can't remember.* However, he said aloud, "Thanks for the info, Iris." *It has to be coincidence… hasn't it?*

Calling up his AI, who he'd already mentally christened Alice, although there was no face on the viewer, Henson called out, "Alice, print out an inventory of items brought on board this ship during the last twenty-four hours."

To his surprise, the AI responded, "Printing to the bridge printer now, sir."

Henson smiled. *She's like Iris, quick on the uptake. Now I need an identity for Alice and a name for the ship, I'll give it some thought. No! I'll let Alice choose for herself as Iris had done.*

Aloud he said, "Alice, please choose a visual to represent you." Henson knew Alice would have a massive database via Iris from which to make a choice.

"Thank you, Captain." There was silence and the screen darkened for a moment, when the viewer brightened, a beautiful woman looked out at him from the screen.

"This is me," Alice said, in a clear, calm and soft voice with just a trace of humour. Henson was stunned, Alice was indeed beautiful and he felt sure he knew her, green eyes, chestnut hair… then he realised there was the hint of Geraldine, his wife, when they were young and had first met.

"You look amazing, Alice; you have chosen well."

Alice beamed back at him. "Thank you, Captain."

Chapter 7

The shuttle craft, with Henson at the controls, settled into the Orrappa ship's bay. The bay was gloomy, poorly lit and the drab military colour schemes did not help. This was his final trip, ferrying the Orrappa officers and crew over to the Orrappa vessel that was to return them to their home planet.

In a way Henson felt sorry for those on the Orrappa ships, he knew that like most military personnel they just obeyed orders and got on with job. They had no say in decision-making.

He called Iris, who he knew was still controlling the crew, "None of the Orrappa have eaten for some time, Iris. Can you get some of the kitchen staff to prepare hot food and drinks for them?"

The crew were ravenous; they sat hunched over their food eating as fast as they could, as though this were their last meal. The hot food comforted them and their terrible dread had subsided to a bearable level. When they had eaten, they huddled together, feeling safer away from the exits. Here they could close their eyes, rest and feel safe enough to sleep.

Chad called on the communicator, "Henson, we need to make it a priority to interrogate the officers in charge of the Orrappa vessels. Can you arrange to have them escorted to the ship's bridge please? I'll interrogate them on the viewer, starting with the captain of the vessel that fired on the *JJ Grant*."

Standing outside the officers' mess with six of his men, Henson called Iris on the communicator. "Iris, release the three captains to my custody; I will escort them to the bridge." Henson was curious. *What sort of control does Iris have over the Orrappa beings, to bend them to her will?* Apart from Iris, only Chad and four others in his crew were aware of the psychological inducement program and Chad wanted to keep it that way.

The three captains cowered away from the open door. Henson coaxed them out, gently guiding one by the arm, the other two following. Their uniforms were crumpled and soaked with perspiration. Once on the bridge and temporarily released from the psychological inducement program, their confidence returned.

The senior captain, the one whose ship had attacked the *JJ Grant*, spoke up, "I demand that I, my fellow officers and crew be released immediately," he boomed. He became more arrogant as he regained his confidence. Henson listened to the AI's translation ignoring the demands and carefully scrutinised the beings. *They could easily pass as earthmen, all tall and physically well built, swarthy, maybe a hint of a Roman nose. Handsome with strong chins and this one with a fiery temper. They were not unlike many men from regions in the Middle East.*

The image on the *JJ Grant*'s viewer screen was of the Orrappa's ship's bridge and the senior Orrappa captain. He faced the camera in his crumpled black and gold uniform. His companions behind him.

Chad introduced himself, "I am Captain Chadwick of the interstellar vessel *JJ Grant*. You made an unprovoked attack on my ship without warning and against our terrain laws. I want your name, home planet and your explanation for this hostile act." Iris seamlessly translated the languages.

"I am Captain Gregrorran. Your ship failed to respond to our signal to stop. Your ship was violating Orrappan space. I had no option but to open fire."

Chad was curious. "Outline your claimed area of space."

"The space occupying a radius from Orrappa to what your species call the solar system."

Chad laughed. "Captain Gregrorran, space in my book is non-territorial. You may occupy a planet but not space."

In an angry tone, Captain Gregrorran said, "You have no authority over me, my ship or my fellow officers. I demand that we be released."

Chad ignored the posturing. "Captain Gregrorran, what I require from you and your fellow captains is information. I want the real reason why you attacked my ship and an innocent Thark passenger vessel and I want to know why an Orrappa military fleet is on its way to our solar system."

Iris translated the words of the Orrappa. Her soft voice was in stark contrast to the harsh sounds coming from the Orrappa beings.

Captain Gregrorran, stiffening his back and raising his chin, said, "I am a senior officer in the Orrappa space fleet, this is my ship. My orders are to apprehend any vessels entering our sphere of operations and I am not obliged to give further information. Again, I demand that we be released."

"And you shall be, Captain Gregrorran. You and your crew will be allowed to return to your home planet in due course. For now, you will return to your quarters but we may have a few more questions for you later."

Captain Gregrorran blinked in surprise at Chad's mild manner.

Henson, watching Gregrorran, thought, *I wonder what Chad's got up his sleeve; I can't see him letting these beings off that easily,* as he and his men escorted the three captains back to the officers' mess.

Chad called up Iris. "Ask Captain Gregrorran and his fellow captains to tell us all they know about the Orrappa's plans for now and in the future. You may use your discretion as to the best way for them to offer up that information."

"I'll send my report to your cabin printer, Captain Chadwick."

"Thank you, Iris." Chad felt sick with guilt and remorse about his order to Iris. *Damn them,* he thought, *I shouldn't have to be doing this but if Gregrorran had been successful with his torpedoes, the JJ Grant and everyone aboard her would just be atoms floating around in space. Too many other lives have to be taken into consideration before we can be soft with the Orrappa military who have been sent out to kill innocent people.*

Later, in the privacy of his cabin, Chad read Iris's report with rising resentment and indignation. Her report was very detailed and she'd highlighted the critical points. The report made very disturbing reading.

Helen saw his grim expression. "Did Iris manage to get anything useful from the Orrappa captains, Chad?"

"She certainly did. Do you know they've had insurgents placed right in the heart of the Thark government? They've been providing the Orrappa government with sensitive information about the shipping routes and movements of the Thark space vessels." Chad read on. "I don't believe it!" he exclaimed. "They even have people in the military providing details of patrol vessels, timings, precise routes and locations of Thark patrol ships."

Helen was shocked. "Are you sure, Chad?"

Chad tapped the report. "It's all here, love. The Orrappa are a cunning and devious species. The report highlights the tactics to be used against the Thark planet and its other worlds. They even knew that the *JJ Grant* was on its way to try and stop their fleet." Chad snorted as he read on. "Which, incidentally, they find derisory – damned cheek." Turning the page, he said, "Ah, now I see why Gregrorran fired on us… he was under orders to do so, should he ever come across us. They're a bad lot, Helen; they seem to behave like parasites."

"Oh, don't say that, Chad. They can't all be bad. Hernani isn't bad or evil and there must be others like her."

Chad thought for a moment. *Hernani had been the tactical officer on the Ynatci and was now Grant's second in command. Helen was right; Hernani wasn't cruel and destructive. She had proved herself a loyal and worthy asset to Grant's crew and there must be other Orrappa like her.*

"Yes, of course you're right, Helen, but the ones at the top, running their government, are pure evil." With a resigned sigh Chad said, "I know Gregrorran and the Orrappa crew are only following orders."

Captain Gregrorran reflected on his conduct since his attack on the primitive vessel from Earth. He was bitterly ashamed of himself; he had failed to take out an unarmed vessel, even after expending four missiles. He held his head in his hands in total misery. He'd never in his life felt so wretched. *How the hell had a primitive species in an inferior alien ship managed to evade our missiles? It's almost incomprehensible. Those missiles were the most sophisticated ever made, they possessed every military textbook attack and evasion response known to their makers.* He shook his head in despair. *And why did I give up so much classified information?* He gulped back what was almost a sob. *I even volunteered the code to my safe and showed them my 'For Captain's Eyes Only' secret orders. They'd not beaten or tortured me. Why did I do that?* He wiped his damp eyes with his coat sleeve. *Why have I this feeling of absolute terror in certain places or situations? If I ever get back to Orrappa, HQ will treat me more than harshly… and who can blame them? I'm no longer in charge of my ship; my crew have barricaded themselves in their canteen with the crew of our other vessels. They're in no state to help me regain control of my ship… and my fellow officers do not want to return to Orrappa… if truth be told, nor do I… only humiliation and death await me on Orrappa.*

Henson beckoned one of his men over. "While I'm checking the ship's log, get the lads to go around and gather up all the portable weapons that they can find on the ship. No playing around with them to see what they can do and absolutely no souvenirs."

The man grinned. "As if we would."

Henson grinned back, his eyes hard. "I mean it, OK?"

His man nodded again. "OK, if you say so."

"I do say so. List them, identify them and secure them in the armoury." He would check with Chad to find out what he wanted done with the weapons later.

Henson called Alice. "I want to see the ship's log and the ship's movements since leaving its home planet – display in English please."

"Certainly, Captain Wright, it's coming up on the screen now." The warship's route appeared on the screen with way points marked. Henson was surprised; the warship had been in space for more than five years. The route was erratic, crisscrossing its path several times. The log listed the vessels that had fallen victim to the Orrappa warships on their long patrol. Of the eight ships intercepted, six fully laden freighters were despatched to Orrappa on autopilot. The other two smaller merchant vessels stripped of their cargos and sent on a one-way trip to the nearest sun. No mention was made of the crew.

That could well have been the fate of the JJ Grant or the passenger vessel. He settled down to write up his report for Chad. One of his men interrupted him. "The Orrappa captains are kicking up a fuss, I think they want to speak to you, sir?"

Henson mulled over the request. "Tell them I'll visit the officers' mess shortly."

Later, Henson called Chad. "I've just spoken with the Orrappa captains at their request. They say that if they are to be released, they don't want to return to Orrappa. I have said they will have to speak to you."

"Thank you, Henson. Let them know I will speak with them later. More important is to get some of our volunteer crewmembers trained on the Orrappa equipment. Can I task you with organising and liaising with Wang on that?"

"You certainly can. I'll get Iris to identify the Orrappa experts and set up a programme of instruction as soon as possible."

Iris quickly selected the most able technicians and officer instructors from the Orrappa crew. Henson had them brought over to his ship and escorted to the ship's canteen. They were given hot food and drinks and allowed to relax from the terrifying inducement program. Henson and Wang joined them with their own small crew groups in the ship's bay.

Henson, through Iris, explained what he wanted from the Orrappa. He was a good organiser and very experienced at working with military technicians and instructors. He had respect for their knowledge and skills, this was quickly picked up by the Orrappa that he was dealing with and there was a kind of mutual respect.

The weapons officer and two instructors gave basic training on all the weapons aboard the ship. The flight-engineering officer and two maintenance technicians gave detailed briefings of the air/space fighters and the Orrappa equivalent of a squadron leader gave advanced flight training.

When it came to actually flying the space fighter craft, Henson quickly realised that they were inferior to the *JJ Grant*'s shuttles. They might be better armoured and carried devastating weapons but were no match for the speed and agility of the shuttles. They were very underpowered. Nevertheless, they might be useful. The training was closely monitored by Iris. There was a simulator aboard each Orrappa ship, which would speed up the bridge training of the new inexperienced crew.

Alice was tasked with gaining technical information not covered in the manuals of each piece of equipment where training took place and passing the answers to the other AIs to store in their databases. Both Henson and Wang thought it a very useful training programme.

Wang had chosen to name the AI on his ship Ling, which, he said, means 'Clever' in Chinese.

The upgrades that Iris had received from the Thark meant she was far superior to the Orrappa AIs and had a massive database. She'd become faster and was more effective than anyone realised or would have thought possible. Iris scanned the three Orrappa AIs, Ling, Alice and Eva, and stripped from them all software references and loyalty programs that referred to the Orrappa and replacing the software with routines to instil absolute allegiance to Captain Chadwick, his crew and especially to herself. She justified the small paradox that her own involvement created, by citing an order Captain Chadwick had once given her a long time ago; "Iris, use your own initiative."

Chapter 8

With Iris's report of the Orrappa's intentions still fresh in his mind, Chad set aside time to speak on the viewer to the Orrappa captains. He'd discovered that their official title was Yuzbaen.

With Iris translating and monitoring them, Chad, with a stony face, surveyed them. "You've requested to speak to me?"

Captain Gregrorran straightened up, pulled his shoulders back and said, "Captain Chadwick, you said you would release us. If you do so, we do not wish to return to Orrappa. It would mean a death sentence for many of our crew and us. We have every prospect of being executed for the loss of our ships and the failure of our mission."

Chad looked at them coldly. "Where you go is up to you and your crew, Captain Gregrorran. Your vessel is fully functional but disarmed. We will provide provisions for your journey and you may go wherever you wish, with the exception of our solar system." Chad was surprised to see the relief on the Orrappas' faces. It was clear that the Orrappa crew were genuinely terrified about returning to their home planet.

"We have families on Orrappa, it will be better for them to think that we have perished on active service. We will be better off chancing our luck on finding a habitable planet in another system where we can start again," Captain Gregrorran said.

Despite everything, Chad couldn't help but feel sorry for the Orrappa crew. *They have an interstellar ship and supplies, there must be somewhere for them to go if they don't want to return to Orrappa.*

"I will release you as I promised but I cannot advise you. You must speak with your crew and then make your own decisions."

"Captain," Iris interrupted the interview, "Klempe wishes to speak with you."

Chad abruptly cut the connection with the Orrappa captains and took Klempe's unexpected call. Klempe was cheery, "Hello, Captain Chadwick, I have been hearing of your exploits."

Chad was embarrassed. "Oh, you mean the passenger vessel and the Orrappa."

"Exactly, Captain. We are indebted to you."

"Not at all, Klempe, you would have done the same."

"So, Captain Chadwick, what are you doing with your prisoners?"

"We are releasing them; we have disarmed one of their ships and all Orrappa crew have been put aboard that vessel."

Klempe nodded sagely. "Good, no doubt you have spoken to them?"

Chad knew what he meant. "Yes, we have. Iris has interrogated them and I will transmit a copy of her report to your AI. I have also decided to commandeer two of the Orrappa warships."

"Captain Chadwick that is an excellent solution. Did you use the psychological inducement program to subdue the Orrappa crew?" Chad thought he detected something in the query.

"Yes, I did, Klempe. My ship is unarmed and I did not want Captain Mapps to take unnecessary risks to protect us. I'm not proud of myself for using it, but the program did the job effectively and without bloodshed or physical harm."

"Very wise, Captain Chadwick, sometimes harsh decisions have to be made and as you say, the program does the job effectively."

Chad instantly knew Klempe had used the program himself, but for what? Something would have triggered Klempe into taking that action. Then it dawned on him, Klempe must already be aware that insurgents had been inserted into the Thark government.

"Captain Chadwick, we are sending a military vessel to escort Captain Vashonni's ship to its planned destination. I would appreciate it if your ships would remain with Captain Vashonni's vessel until the escort arrives. Er… the captain of the escort ship may wish to interrogate the Orrappa himself in case Iris has missed something."

"Of course, Klempe, we are happy for him to do so. There is one thing though, we would like to upgrade the two Orrappa vessels and their respective AIs and request permission from the Thark Council of Elders to apply some of the technology that they have been kind enough to give us for the *JJ Grant* to the Orrappa ships?"

"Of course; you have our permission, Captain. As I have said before, anything that we have given you or the *JJ Grant* use in whatever way you wish. We do not give gifts with strings attached."

"That is very generous of you, Klempe, and the Thark. Please convey my thanks to the Council of Elders."

"Captain, you are very welcome."

Chad was acutely embarrassed after the generosity of the Thark and his face flushed but he felt he must ask one more favour. "Klempe, there is one other thing. The Orrappa crew do not wish to return to Orrappa… they claim they face severe repercussions, possibly a death sentence, for their defeat and the loss of two ships."

"Why are you telling me this, Captain Chadwick?"

"Because the Thark are an advanced, civilised and compassionate species and these beings need help. You may know of a suitable planet where the crew of these ships may have a chance to start again and build a better life. Maybe even a better civilisation?"

Klempe stared back impassively as the viewer screen turned black. For long moments, nothing happened and Chad said quietly, "Iris is he still there?"

Iris equally quietly said, "Yes, Captain, he is still there."

Long moments later the viewer screen brightened and Klempe reappeared. "We have considered your unusual request, Captain Chadwick. Only a short time ago, these beings tried to destroy your ship. Later you intervened and saved our passenger vessel from the Orrappa, which we believe, once they had ransacked the ship, would have destroyed it and all on board to hide the evidence." Klempe looked off screen for a moment. "Your faith in these beings may be misplaced; however, your request is in accord with our own ethos." He paused as if to say, I hope you're not going to be let down. "We know of a young star system with a planet that will support life, but it is raw. Life of all descriptions is still evolving; however, the planet has yet to develop a sentient life form. Survival on this planet will be challenging. Nevertheless, it could become the basis for a new civilisation. The coordinates of that planet have been despatched to your AI. I leave it to your discretion whether you give these coordinates to the Orrappa or not."

"Thank you, Klempe, I will speak to them and will let you know the outcome."

Chad called his senior officers together to brief them on his conversations with the Orrappa captains and Klempe.

The Orrappa captains, looking very apprehensive, once again stood before the viewer.

"Have you spoken with your crew?"

"Yes, Captain Chadwick, they are unanimous. They want to take the chance of finding a new planet."

"And if you don't?"

Gregrorran shrugged. "Then we die, but at least it is our choice and we will have died trying."

This time, it was Chad who blacked out the screen. Turning to his officers he said, "What do you think? Should we trust them and give them a chance?"

Henson said, "Killing your frontline troops because they lost isn't right. I vote yes, give them a chance."

Chad looked at Hernani. "Is it true that they face a death sentence back on Orrappa?"

Hernani nodded. "Yes, Captain, our leaders dislike weakness or failure. The crew would be treated harshly."

Chad looked round at his other officers. Their subdued nods of agreement were unanimous.

The viewer screen cleared, the Orrappa captains stared uneasily back from the viewer.

Chad closely questioned them again trying to gauge their sincerity, and finally said, "There is a young planet that has animal life but sentient life has yet to evolve. The planet is raw and establishing a settlement will be daunting. It is a young system within reach of your ship and your provisions."

The Orrappa officers stared back open mouthed in astonishment not trusting what they had heard.

"It would mean a backward step for you but a fresh start. What do you say?"

Captain Gregrorran spoke up, "You would have our eternal thanks, Captain Chadwick." The other two captains nodded vigorously.

"It is not I that you should be thanking but the Thark, who have provided the coordinates of the system and the planet. However, I have given the Thark my word and assurances, that given the chance, you and your crew will take this opportunity to start again."

"Oh, we will, Captain Chadwick that we promise you."

"Very well, our AI will transmit the coordinates to your ship's AI shortly. We will release your vessel after all long-range comms systems and armaments have been removed. Please use the time left to check your vessel and stores for a long-distance voyage. We will transfer some fresh food stocks to your vessel if you need them."

Shortly after Chad's conversation with Klempe, Captain Vashonni called on the viewer. "Captain Chadwick, Klempe has informed me that your ships will remain with us until our military escort arrives. I am most grateful and so are our passengers who feared for their lives. They should have been enjoying a journey of a lifetime, not suffering fear and violence from the Orrappa."

"You are very welcome, Captain Vashonni, I'm pleased that we were able to help."

"Captain Chadwick, I must also thank you for the entertainment material you sent to our ship. It has entranced our passengers. I believe it may have changed our dire circumstances into an adventure for them. Something unique to tell their friends when they get back home. They send their sincere thanks."

Klempe read the report that Iris had sent to Amali, *Hmm, and a very comprehensive report indeed. A mine of information.* Then he read the message from Captain Chadwick: the Orrappa captains and crew send their eternal thanks for the coordinates of the habitable planet.

They are preparing their ship for their long journey to their new world. I shall sleep easier knowing that we have done the best for them.

Klempe could only agree. *I know how you feel, Captain Chadwick.*

Chad's message went on: We have embedded two sub-miniature tracking devices deep in the ship's structure. We will be able to track the ship wherever she is. Iris has sent the tracking codes to your AI.

Klempe smiled to himself – *Maybe Captain Chadwick is more astute than I thought.*

Klempe messaged back: Captain Chadwick, the trackers are a sensible idea. Please hold the Orrappa vessel until our battlecruiser arrives to escort our passenger vessel home. I want the captain of the escort ship to interrogate the Orrappa crew before they depart on their journey in case Iris has missed anything. The escort will arrive on station within twenty-four of your earth hours.

I have messaged the *B109* that you have been unavoidably delayed and to wait your arrival at rendezvous. Also, that your group is now four ships.

Chad messaged back: Confirm, will hold the Orrappa ship until arrival of escort vessel.

Chapter 9

The startling appearance of a Thark battlecruiser standing off a short distance from the passenger vessel briefly panicked Chad's crew. The sleek blue-black dolphin shaped vessel, larger than the *JJ Grant* and devoid of any protrusions, had arrived cloaked. Chad wondered how long it had been sitting there examining the *JJ Grant* and the Orrappa vessels before uncloaking and making its presence known. It made brief contact to announce itself.

A young male, who in Chad's opinion did not look old enough to hold a driver's licence, appeared on the viewer. "Greetings, Captain Chadwick, I am Captain Theron. Thank you for your assistance, we will interview the Orrappa crew immediately. All being well, they will be free to leave shortly."

That was it! Chad had expected more detail but that's all he got. The crew watched mesmerised, as a small illuminated portal appeared in the side of the Thark ship. The portal expanded to a sufficient size to allow a small craft to emerge from the ship. The craft quickly made its way to the Orrappa vessel that was due to be released and disappeared into the open bay. An hour later, the craft left the bay and returned to the battlecruiser, slipping back through the portal, which immediately closed.

The viewer came to life and the Thark captain said, "We have concluded our interview of the Orrappa crew, their vessel is free to leave. I will be escorting our passenger vessel on its homeward journey. Thank you on behalf of the Thark people for your help and patience. Goodbye, Captain Chadwick, we will depart shortly." The viewer shut down. Chad turned to Gordon and said, "Well, that was short and sweet."

It was a different story with the Orrappa crew; they were full of gratitude and hoped that one day the *JJ Grant* would visit them on their new planet.

Later, Chad and Helen watched the Orrappa warship, now with its teeth and claws removed disappear into the blackness of space on its long journey to its new home.

Helen, standing beside him said, "I'm so proud of you, Chad, you did the right thing."

Chad grinned. "Yes, I think so too, I just hope it doesn't come back to bite us."

At 09:51 ship's time, the Thark passenger vessel flashed a short series of signals to the *JJ Grant*. Moments later the warship also signalled a short message.

Comms reported, "Two signals just came in, sir."

"Go ahead, Comms, what did they say?"

"Captain Vashonni signalled: Goodbye dear friends, we shall not forget you. The warship signalled: Good luck, Captain Chadwick."

"Do you want me to respond, sir?"

"Yes, Comms, to Captain Vashonni: You are very welcome. And to the warship: Take care."

At 09:52, both ships accelerated away into the void.

Chad's communicator buzzed. "Hello, Henson, what is it?"

"I've been checking out some of the stuff looted from the Thark passenger vessel and there are some strange devices here."

"Really? What sort of devices?"

"I'm not sure but from the symbols on one of the machines, I think it could be some sort of matter transmitter."

Chad smiled to himself. "Henson, it's probably an entertainer's prop, the ship was after all a passenger vessel, leave it for now and keep everything under lock and key. We don't want to be side tracked from our mission. We can look at all that when we have dealt with the Orrappa."

"You're, right, Captain. I'll get everything secured. We're just getting the relief bridge crew up to speed but there is a problem."

"What sort of problem?"

"I checked my ship's specifications; she's nowhere near as fast as the *JJ Grant* or the *Helcon*. I suspect Wang's ship will be the same. I've conferred with Iris and she says, as a temporary measure, strategically placed power blocks can be fitted to give her more speed and manoeuvrability."

"OK, Henson, I'll have a word with Connie and see what she can do – anything else?"

"Yes, I had a chat with Scott McDonald, he was on the list of volunteers, I offered him the job of second in command and he has accepted."

"Very good, Henson, he's one of the best."

"The other thing is that I have a name for the ship, I'm going to call it, *Blackbird*."

"OK, any particular reason for the name?"

"I'm naming it after the fastest manned jet aircraft ever built, which was the SR-71 Blackbird. This ship is black and it seems a fitting name to me."

"That's good, *Blackbird* it is then. Let Iris know. I'll contact Connie and see if she can upgrade the interstellar drives on *Blackbird* and *Black Pearl*. The ships' shields may need to be upgraded as well. When Connie comes over can you deal with her directly?"

"No problem, Chad, I want to get the best possible performance we can from this ship."

"I'll talk to you later, Henson."

"Hello, Chad; you called me?"

"Yes, Connie, thanks for coming back to me. Henson has pointed out that the two new Orrappa warships are underpowered. They can't match our speed. Iris says additional power blocks can temporarily overcome the problem and then there is the ships' shields that may need to be looked at. I want both ships to be able to match the speed of the *JJ Grant*."

"Right, I'll get over there and have a look. I'll keep you posted."

"Thanks, Connie." *The list of tasks to bring the two Orrappa ships up to the standard of the Helcon seems to be endless but we've made a start. I'll get Iris to track everything.*

Something made Chad look up; Iris smiled back at him from the viewer. Before he said anything, Iris said, "Yes, Captain, I can monitor and advise on all those additional tasks."

Chad hadn't put the question yet, he raised an eyebrow. "Really?"

"Of course, Captain, I have prepared a suitable layout for additional power blocks and a material list for Captain Wright's and Captain Wang's ships."

"What about their shield system, is that satisfactory?"

"Yes, Captain, the Orrappa shield system is functional for normal cruising speeds. An upgrade will be required to protect the ships at maximum speed."

"The other thing those two ships will need, if they are to be of any use to us against the Orrappa, are cloaking devices."

"That is in hand, Captain. As you know, I already have the plans and assembly instructions to build the cloaking device. They can be constructed and fitted whilst on our journey to rendezvous with the Thark battlecruiser."

"Thank you, Iris. Er… are there any other aspects of the upgrade given to you by the Thark that I should know about?"

"Only that the upgrade allows me to compute the probabilities of a question or requirement, Captain."

"You mean to make a lucky guess."

"Something like that, Captain."

Is Iris eavesdropping or mind reading? Hmm… time will tell.

Henson and Scott McDonald stood gazing up at the menacing single-seater fighter. "They look the business, Scott, but the shuttles on the *JJ Grant* are faster and more manoeuvrable than these craft. I reckon it's all down to a lack of power."

Scott took his time, examining the fighter with a critical eye. "It looks to me like they're fly-by-wire, wireless and electronic controls to deliberately make the craft unstable to enhance manoeuvrability."

Henson nodded. "You're spot on there. I've checked the controls; everything is operated by electronic signals. Sensitive as hell but so underpowered it makes them difficult to fly."

"I believe you're right. Of course, we could always swap out the Orrappa drive for a power block, and then you would have the best of both worlds. Very fast in space or atmosphere and loaded with weapons of all descriptions."

"You've made my mind up, Scott. I'll take it over to the *JJ Grant* now and see if Connie can work her magic on it."

"I think you'd better call her first, I know Chad has her working flat out."

"You're right." Henson pulled out his communicator. "Hi, Connie, it's Henson. If I brought one of my fighter aircraft over and left it with you, could you look at the possibility of stripping out the drive system and installing a power block drive?… Yes, I know you're up to your ears with work. I don't mean right now but when you've not got much on. … Yes, I appreciate you can't promise anything. It's just that these craft are too slow to be useful and that's a shame because they have the potential to be fantastic machines. … You will! Connie, you are a star." Henson grinned. "Get your suit on, Scott, we're going over now before Connie changes her mind. I'll fly the fighter; you follow me in one of the lifeboats to bring me back."

Chad was becoming anxious; time was slipping by. "Hello, Connie, have you managed to upgrade the drive systems on the two Orrappa ships yet?"

"It's all happening as we speak, Chad. Work on the drives is almost complete. We will of course need to carry out some test flights. I've got additional power blocks being built to strengthen the ships' shields and we're installing those into the forward sections as power blocks become available. George Downes is manufacturing components for the cloaking devices and Iris has given him a work schedule and is overseeing quality control. My team will help with assembly once we have completed the drives and shields."

"Connie, you are a marvel. I've had a message from Klempe. The Thark are sending a battlecruiser to rendezvous with us and I don't want to be too late.

"That's brilliant, Chad. I'll visit both ships now and give you a full report on work completion times. In any event, the existing shield system is satisfactory for normal cruising speed. We only need the upgrade for maximum speed."

The soft sound of paper exiting the printer in the bridge office drew his attention. Chad looked up as the printer pinged, indicating a completed printing session. It was Connie's report. Chad took it back to his desk and sipped his coffee as he commenced reading the detailed report. He skipped to the conclusion; additional power blocks in place on both ships to give better speed and manoeuvrability. Strengthened front shields on both ships in line with that of the *Helcon*'s shield.

The engineering team were now assisting the electronics department to assemble ships' cloaking devices.

Chad grinned to himself; things were coming together. All being well his group was ready to proceed at normal cruising speed. He called a viewer meeting with Grant, Henson and Wang. "Connie tells me you're all good to go?"

Wang responded, "It seems like it, Chad, although Henson and I have only done a couple of short runs but the drive system compares with the *Helcon*'s."

"I agree," Henson said. "Connie's team have done an outstanding job."

When Henson and Grant had left, the viewer meeting Wang remained online. "I do still have one problem Chad, I've not managed to find a second in command for the *Black Pearl*. I can manage but if you or Grant have any idea's I'd appreciate them."

"OK, Wang, I'll give it some thought and have a word with Grant."

Chapter 10

Chad had barely finished his conversation with Wang when Grant called him back on the viewer. "Chad, I'm sorry I should have mentioned this earlier but I thought we had solved the problem. It seems we haven't and it's getting worse."

Chad frowned. "What sort of problem?"

"The atmosphere in the *Helcon* has become unpleasant, we thought it was an atmosphere regeneration problem but it's not. Eva says the smell is hydrogen sulphide caused by a PH imbalance in the hydroponics section."

Chad grimaced; he knew how foul the smell could be. "You'd better come over and have a look at our hydroponics plant then, because we've not had a problem in a long while."

"Thanks, Chad, I was hoping you'd say that. I'll see you shortly."

The manager responsible for the hydroponics section showed them round.

Chad whispered to Grant, "I used to avoid this area like the plague, because of the smell but now it's like a walk in a meadow."

Overhearing Chad's remark, the manager said, "That's because we have a secret weapon." He beckoned to a couple of workers, who looked up and started to make their way over. "Let me introduce you to our experts Preena and Envar." Chad and Grant nodded to the pair. "What these two don't know about hydroponics isn't worth knowing."

Grant gave them a grin. "Hi guys, I don't know how I've not met you before?"

Preena with a smile just shrugged. "I guess this isn't a place you visit often."

Grant noticed the accent, a slight American twang mixed with something else. "Well, we've got a real problem with hydrogen sulphide on the *Helcon*. Would you come over and see if there is anything you can do?" Chad sensed the couple were edgy and reluctant to talk, he'd seen them before but not often.

Grant didn't appear to notice, he said, "I'll run you over to the *Helcon*, you can have a look at the problem and I'll have you back here in no time at all." Chad could see the couple weren't at all happy about leaving the hydroponics section but were having difficulty in finding an excuse to refuse.

As Chad made his way back up to the bridge, something else bothered him; he couldn't put his finger on it. *It'll come to me eventually*, he thought. Iris called him on his communicator with a private message.

"Yes, Iris, what is it?"

"Two Orrappa beings have just passed through the scanner with Captain Mapps." It hit him like a blow on the back of the head. *Of course, their accents and the dark beauty of the woman, just like Hernani and I've seen a man with a similar burly stature like that before.* Chad was shocked and totally bemused. *How the hell had, they managed to get on board my ship.*

"Iris, message Captain Wright and let him know the situation. He is to board the *Helcon* urgently with a few of his men. Tell him not to alert the couple but to take precautions and have his men stay close to Captain Mapps. When the couple return to the *JJ Grant* Captain Wright is to have them escorted to the wardroom for interview. Oh, and send me their files."

Chad was dumbfounded, strange things had happened on his ship but this was almost beyond belief.

Reading through their files, Chad found nothing out of the ordinary. He recalled Envar and Preena joining the ship before the installation of the scanner. They had been on the ship a long time and had kept themselves to themselves. He knew they could not have left the ship once the scanner had been installed without giving themselves away.

Finally, Iris messaged him. The Orrappa had arrived in the landing bay with Captain Mapps, Captain Wright and an escort.

In the wardroom, Chad called Iris on his communicator. "Please record the conversations in the wardroom and if you have any contributions to make put them on my communicator."

A few moments later Grant and Henson arrived with the couple, escorted by two of Henson's men. Chad gestured for the two Orrappa beings to sit down. The female, Preena, looked terrified and the male, Envar, grim-faced.

Chad took his time scrutinising them. "Do you want to tell me what you're doing on board my ship?"

Preena started to speak but Envar covered her hand with his. "No, Preena, I will explain." Meeting Chad's gaze, he shrugged. "I am Captain Envar Grermott of the Orrappa warship *Corvann* and this is my life partner Preena. We came aboard your ship shortly after you had set up the hydroponics department and long before the *JJ Grant* was launched."

Chad nodded. "But how did you get here?"

Envar sighed, "You're going to find this hard to believe, Captain. We took refuge in your system after my ship suffered damage from a Thark battlecruiser. That is when we discovered planet Earth. Against my orders, one of my officers despatched a survey report of planet Earth to our HQ on Orrappa." Envar cast a look to Preena, who squeezed his hand. "Unfortunately, the officer, the son of an influential government official, later died in an accident."

Preena cried. "No! Envar, tell them, he would have killed you and your co-pilot."

Envar patted her hand to calm her. "The short story, Captain Chadwick, is that I was blamed for the young officer's death. HQ eventually sent orders for me to remain on station until another vessel, the *Ynatci*, was sent to relieve me."

Chad looked at Grant who gave the slightest nod of understanding; the *Helcon* had previously been called the *Ynatci* an Orrappa warship that they had found abandoned in space with a failed drive. Chad had salvaged it and fitted it with his ship's spare drive. It had been renamed the *Helcon*.

Envar was silent for a moment. Chad said, "Please go on."

"I was informed by my HQ that the results of the enquiry held aboard my ship into the death of the officer were invalid, there would be an enquiry conducted by our high command. Unfortunately, on Orrappa, an enquiry of that sort does not usually end well."

Chad noticed he gripped Preena's hand more tightly.

"Preena and I decided to take our chances on planet Earth. I left my ship in the hands of my crew; I did all I could for them. Thanks to Preena, who had set up a supply depot on planet Earth, they were fully provisioned when they left." He gave Preena a quick fond look. "My crew had a choice, return to Orrappa or find somewhere new. I don't know what they chose but I hope it was to find somewhere new." He shook his head and gave a sigh. "Sadly, Orrappa is not what it was." Then he carried on. "Finding work on planet Earth was easy but we were always worried that the insurgents or provocateurs that the *Ynatci* was bringing to place on Earth would seek us out. So, we moved around frequently.

"Then Preena heard that an interstellar ship was being built in Australia. By this time, we spoke English quite well and we had money. Space is in our blood, it's what we do and where we have spent most of our lives. So, we made our way to Perth. Then came the opportunity to work in the new hydroponics section on the *JJ Grant*. Hydroponics is something we both know a lot about and this got us onto the ship."

Chad nodded. "Then you heard that a screening device to detect Orrappa beings had been placed on the only exit and you've been confined to the ship ever since, until today."

"That is correct, Captain. However, we have carried out our work diligently, maintained, and improved your hydroponics section to the best of our abilities. This ship has become our home and we see ourselves as part of your crew."

Chad nodded but said nothing, to say he was surprised, was an understatement. First, it had been Hernani, an Orrappa spy discovered on board the *JJ Grant* but who had since changed her allegiance to Captain Chadwick. Now it was these two. He looked at them both, long and hard. "Why should I believe you, how do I know you are not playing a waiting game, hoping the Orrappa fleet will overcome us and rescue you?"

Envar gave a grim smile. "Captain, you do not know our Orrappa government. The Orrappa fleet will not be interested in recovering Preena and me. The fleet's orders will be to exterminate the population of Earth. They may keep some people to labour for them. They will fill their cargo ships with minerals and ores to take back to Orrappa. Then they will set about transporting the entire population of Orrappa to Earth, their new home. Orrappa is old, exhausted and in its death throes."

"And you're not a part of that?"

"No, Captain Chadwick, I am a military man, not a killer of innocent people."

Chad believed him but said, "So, what will you be doing when we meet up with the Orrappa fleet."

Envar smiled. "Hopefully I will be working in your hydroponics section – or on your ship's bridge assisting you, Captain Chadwick." Chad smiled back.

Preena spoke up. "I think there is a man on this ship that will speak up for me."

Chad raised an eyebrow. "Really? Who's that then?"
Preena said, "Mr Joe Costello."
Chad gave Henson an enquiring look.
"The only Joe I know works for Keung Zheng." Chad's communicator buzzed gently. It was Iris.

"Joe Costello presented us with an Irish passport but he may be American. He started working for Mr Zheng before these two Orrappa came on board and he is well thought of. Would you like him to come to the wardroom, Captain? Chad touched the box on his communicator screen that said 'Yes'. The mystery deepened…

There was a tap on the door, Henson opened it and Joe Costello peeped in, plainly perplexed. "Er, sorry, guys, I received a message saying the captain wanted to see me straight away?"

With a squeal, Preena, jumped up and hugged him.

"Oh, please tell them who I am, Joe…"

Chapter 11

It took another trip over to the *Helcon*, but Preena and Envar had done a magnificent job. The atmosphere smelt fresh and clean and the plants looked healthy and lush.

Grant clapped Envar Grermott on the shoulder. "I wish I could poach you and Preena from Chad; you've worked wonders." Grant gave Envar a keen look. "I suppose you know all the quirks of this marque of ship, Envar?"

Envar grinned at him. "Yes, I do, Captain Mapps, a lot more than is revealed in the ship's manual. I've spent a lot of my life in one just like this. I knew that ship better than my mother. But I can see you have made many small improvements to the ship too."

Grant liked them both. Shame he couldn't have them on the *Helcon*. "Come up to the wardroom and have some refreshments before you go back to the *JJ Grant*."

Grant sipped his drink, he was curious. "So, Envar, what happened with the Thark ship, how did your vessel get damaged?"

"It's a long story, Captain Mapps, and one that you might not believe."

"Well, we have some time before you both have to go back, so try me?" Grant said with a grin.

"OK, but you have to remember I was a military officer, I had to obey orders."

Grant nodded. "Go on."

"I had a group of three warships and we were on a roving patrol. We came across a lone Thark battlecruiser many times more powerful than our Orrappa warships but she was in a very vulnerable position. I took the decision to attack her. I fired two torpedoes to take down her shield and then take the Thark vessel as a prize. We wanted the technology within her. When my torpedoes struck, the Thark ship disappeared in a blinding flash and a cloud of smoke. I gazed in disbelief; I couldn't believe my eyes. However, the next thing I knew was that a massive plasma bolt struck my own vessel breaching her hull. With her shield almost gone and a breached hull, I had no option but to turn the *Corvann* and run. My other two ships had scattered. We were lucky to escape. At the time I thought a second Thark vessel must have been in the vicinity and had fired on the *Corvann*."

Grant listened, enthralled by Envar's story. "Is that when you discovered Earth?"

"Yes, we came into the Sol system at maximum speed and immediately sought somewhere to hide, then I saw planet Earth like a blue jewel and she had a moon. That's where we sought refuge, in the shadow of the moon.

Later, Grant related the unabridged version of Envar, Preena and Joe Costello's story to Chad.

"It's all true, Chad, honestly, I sat down with Envar and Preena and they told me everything. Preena set up a supply depot in the guise of a wholesale supplier to the grocery trade, using laboratory grown diamonds made on their ship to finance it. I've talked to Joe Costello and he confirms the business part. He even showed me a couple of the diamonds that Preena had given him. Did you know he used to be a taxi driver in Las Vegas before Preena got him involved in purchasing?"

"Yes, we know some of the history, Grant. However, I'd like more information for our records."

"I see what you're getting at, Chad, why don't we get Hernani in for an informal chat to explain that to us, we could have Preena, Envar and Joe in as well."

Grant slid two mugs of hot herbal tea across to Hernani and Preena. The others had a glass of what passed for beer on the ship. The restaurant on the *JJ Grant* was almost empty and the informality of it all was Grant's idea. "This isn't an interrogation, but you will agree that events have been extraordinary for all of us. We'd like to clarify some of those events for the log."

Hernani said, "Certainly, I'll help in any way I can."

"That goes for me too," Preena said.

Envar just nodded agreement.

Chad said, "What happened when the *Ynatci* arrived and discovered the *Corvann* was not on station?"

Hernani said, "Well I can tell you about that. Hukamp, the captain, was furious; he was relying on the *Corvann* and Captain Grermott for provisions. The *Ynatci* had been delayed because the ship's drive had started to show signs of breaking down. Hukamp had to reduce speed by forty per cent. Our crew were starving, with only reconstituted food to survive on –"

"Reconstituted food, what's that?" Chad interrupted.

"Well it's…" Hernani grimaced. "I don't think you want to know, Captain, but it's not pleasant." She shuddered at the memory. "Anyway, Hukamp messaged HQ to say our provisions were exhausted and we needed the coordinates for the supply depot.

"HQ sent the coordinates but admitted that they had lost contact with the *Corvann* around three earth years earlier when the *Ynatci* was still on her journey to Earth. Hukamp was incensed that HQ had kept that information from him. However, he was desperate for provisions and the coordinates given to us by HQ didn't work, they were meaningless. When he delivered the insurgents to the planet's surface, he found many animals close by. He had some of them herded onto the lifeboats to feed the crew. One of the pilots told me that the insurgents had killed the earthmen guarding the animals and had taken their clothes to use as disguises for themselves. Neither Hukamp nor the insurgents ever found the supply depot that had been set up."

Envar said, "That's correct, Captain. Preena, with the help of Joe Costello set up a grocery wholesaler and distributer and we used that as our undercover supply depot."

"But why did you give your HQ incorrect coordinates?" Chad asked.

"We knew we'd be a target for the insurgents when they arrived, because of the young officer who'd died by my hands. I sent HQ false coordinates for the depot, to protect Joe and the other Earth people that Preena employed; she didn't want any of them hurt. Preena handed the business over to Joe, when we knew the *Ynatci*, was close to Earth.

Joe nodded agreement. "That's right, I remember the evening, I was working late and Preena came into my office with a pack of legal documents, saying she'd signed the business over to me and advising me to sell it quickly and to get far away. Which I did."

Chad sipped his beer and gestured for Hernani to continue. "Hukamp was frustrated by HQ, to the point of madness; he could be cruel but always did his job well. However, HQ treated him badly and he became a bit irrational. Then came a sighting of a small gravity drive on the planet and Hukamp sent my life partner, Raukan – he was the *Ynatci*'s third officer – down to the planet to try and steal a gravity drive. It was an impossible task and Raukan… well he was caught and had to be rescued by the insurgents."

Chad said quietly, "I'm afraid that was me, Hernani. I caught him in my workshop. There was a bit of a fight, I got lucky and I handed him over to our police."

Envar looked at Chad in surprise. "You captured him?"

Chad was embarrassed. "Er… yes, I had to defend myself; I used a bit of kung fu." Chad saw Envar's confusion. "It's a form of fighting where one can use an opponent's strength or speed to one's own advantage. Anyway, when he charged at me, I used his momentum to throw him into a forklift truck. Poor chap was knocked out. By the time he woke up I had him secured." Chad looked at Hernani apologetically.

Envar looked at him with a new respect. He knew Raukan, like all Orrappa males, would have been large and powerful.

A shocked Hernani, whose eyes had started to brim, said, "Hukamp got him back but never forgave him for failing his mission. Much later, news came from one of the insurgents that an interstellar ship was being built on the planet. I had learned the English language before the insurgents took the FastLearn machine with them. Hukamp thought a female would have a better chance of getting on board to find out how the ship's drive worked. So he ordered me down to the planet to infiltrate the plant where the ship was being built. I managed to get a job in the *JJ Grant's* laundry. I was still on board when she was launched. I thought an opportunity would eventually come and I could complete my mission. But before I could do so, I received a signal from the *Ynatci*. Hukamp had been ordered to return to Orrappa, the *Ynatci* was no longer needed on station. Hukamp blamed Raukan for failing his mission. In one of his rages, Hukamp had Raukan ejected into space and because I had also failed my mission Hukamp abandoned me."

Preena put an arm round Hernani to comfort her. When Hernani recovered her composure, she said, "As you know I was discovered on the *JJ Grant*. Iris had intercepted signals between the *Ynacti* and me."

"Yes, that is something I shall never forget because Iris had also detected that the *Ynatci* was stationary in space and without power, her drive had disintegrated. When we found the Ynatci, Hukamp and his crew were being picked up by another Orrappa vessel. When that had departed, we set about salvaging Hukamp's ship."

Grant said, "Thank you all for filling in those gaps for us. I'm sorry it was distressing for you but we can't change the past and Chad and I are pleased that you are all with us now."

As they dispersed, Henson accompanied Chad. "You know, it might not be such a bad idea to have Envar as a bridge officer."

"Yes, his knowledge could be useful on one of the Orrappa ships and I think we can trust him; I'll have a word with Grant."

Chapter 12

Chad called for volunteers to crew the Orrappa ships. There were plenty of crew interested but most lacked specialist skills and would have to undergo intensive training. Henson and Wang would draw their bridge crews from this pool of men and women.

Wang called Grant on the viewer, "Have you time for a chat?"

"Sure, how can I help?"

"Well, I'm setting up the crew on the *Black Pearl* but I've discovered the ship is nothing like the *JJ Grant*. I thought you might be able to give me some pointers. I want to start off on the right foot."

Grant thought for a moment and then said, "Tell you what, why don't you borrow Hernani for a bit and let her set up the basics with you and carry out a bit of crew training? You can then fine tune your crew however you like once you have things up and running."

"Grant, that would be brilliant, it would certainly take a load off my shoulders."

Having helped Wang select the bridge crew and organised simulator training, Hernani ran her finger down the list of volunteers. "Wang, you need a good number two, someone you have respect for, that is steady and reliable."

Wang checked the list again. "There are a number of good candidates here but the problem is none of them have pilot or bridge experience. It would mean starting from scratch."

Hernani grimaced in commiseration. "I shouldn't worry yet; either Chad or Grant will come up with someone."

"Yes, you're right we'll leave it for now. What's next on the agenda?"

"Well, now we come to the most important members of your crew. Cooks and kitchen staff, then housekeeping, medicine and finally, tech staff."

Wang raised an eyebrow, "But I'm tech…"

"Yes, I know, but can you cook a decent meal for your crew or do all the laundry?"

Wang looked crestfallen. "Er, well…"

Hernani, with a grin, said, "Didn't think so."

Wang smiled, he liked the firm but easy way Hernani handled the crew, she had people queuing up to grab any job on offer, but she still managed to be selective without upsetting those not suited to a particular job. *There's a lesson for me here Chad has the same ability. Hmm… something to think about.*

Hernani gave him a grin. "Well that's the crew sorted except for a second in command. You just need to give your ship a name and then get someone in that seat," pointing to the number two's seat, "and you're ready for a trial run, Captain."

"I already have a name for the ship, Hernani, *Black Pearl*. It came to me as soon as I was given the ship." Wang pointed for Hernani to sit at the second in command's consol. "At least I can do a trial run with you on board." Seating himself at the captain's console, he surveyed the bridge. All bridge crew looked at him expectantly. "We'll do this by the book, crew. Comms, call the *JJ Grant* and request permission for *Black Pearl* to carry out a trial run."

Two hours later the ship slipped into its original position alongside Henson's vessel.

Comms said, "Message from the *JJ Grant*, Captain."

"Go ahead, Comms, what's the message?"

"It's from Captain Chadwick, sir. Glad to see *Black Pearl* is still in one piece. Congratulations."

Later Wang crossed over to the *JJ Grant*. "Chad, I'm still having a bit of a problem finding an experienced crew member to be my number two. Grant has lent me Hernani to help get the ship organised. She is brilliant and acted as my second in command during the ship's trials. However, I'm darned if I can find anyone else that has enough experience. I wondered if you could spare someone from the *JJ Grant*."

Chad drummed his fingers on the table and pursed his lips as ideas ran through his mind. "Let me call Grant."

"Grant, what's the *Helcon*'s status? Have the hydroponics problems been sorted yet?"

"Yes, Chad, everything's working fine now. We're good to go."

"Excellent! You know I mentioned Henson's suggestion after our chat with Envar and Preena?"

A suspicious Grant hesitantly said, "Yes?"

"And you expressed an interest in having them on your ship? Do you still feel that way?" Chad said.

"Yes, why not; I wouldn't mind having them managing the hydroponics section at all."

"Well I was really thinking about Envar on the bridge as your number two? You're very experienced and Envar knows the ship inside out and could be a valuable asset. Preena could look after the hydroponics facility."

"Chad, I've got a number two, Hernani."

"That is true, Grant, but Wang doesn't have your experience yet. He needs the backup of an experienced officer to help him get through the initial period of training and establishing his crew. I want to give Envar the benefit of the doubt. His vast experience as a ship's captain would be useful to you. Also, you don't want your hydroponics plant playing up again. What do you say?"

"Supposing Envar is stringing us along?"

"I don't think so, Grant, and I know you don't think so either. Just look at the Orrappa captains. They can't wait to find another home."

Reluctantly Grant agreed. "Right then, but only if Hernani agrees, and I can swap back if Envar doesn't work out."

"Good man. I'll set up a meeting shortly in the wardroom and see how everyone feels about it."

Chad turned and grinned at Wang and said, "You'd better go and check that Hernani is happy to swap ships and I'll check with Envar and Preena."

In the wardroom, Chad performed a small ceremony to appoint Envar Grermott to the post of second in command to Captain Grant Mapps on the *Helcon*. Big as he was, Envar was almost overcome with joy and gratitude to be back on the bridge of a spacecraft.

Preena was more than pleased to take over and run the hydroponics section knowing she and Envar would be together.

Hernani would miss working for Captain Grant Mapps but her new job as second in command to Captain Wang Zheng offered more of a challenge, working with the less experienced Wang.

Chapter 13

Chad's viewer chimed. "Bridge here, Captain, we're approaching the rendezvous position, you asked me to call you."

"Thanks, Gordon, I'll be right up."

On the bridge, Chad was pleased to see the crew had contained their excitement and were fully alert. "Any communication yet, Gordon?"

"No sir, comms and radar are scanning the area."

"Right, contact our ships using the communicator and tell them to group up and prepare to call a halt when we are at the precise rendezvous coordinates. Iris, please confirm this with the other AIs and scan the area for the Thark battlecruiser."

The captain of the *B109* watched with her deck officer and nodded approvingly, as the four vessels came to a halt in exactly the right point in space. The ships were uncloaked, stood out stark and clear on the viewer.

Captain Frussee examined the small fleet closely. The Orrappa ships were interesting and she'd been briefed on how they had been acquired. However, she'd had dealings with Orrappa vessels in the past; they looked the part but were too slow and unsophisticated to be a real threat. However, Captain Frussee was unaware of the upgraded drive system that the Orrappa ships now possessed. The Earth vessel intrigued her. *Fat and primitive, but not bad for a first attempt,* she thought. Turning to her number two she said as an aside, "Unarmed and commanded by an elderly being."

The officer nodded in agreement, "Yes, however, the AI says she has a strong shield and is fitted with a cloaking device, as are the ships with her. That will give them an advantage over the Orrappa fleet."

"Perhaps, but if it comes down to a fight, I just hope she is more agile than she looks. Well, I suppose we had better make ourselves known. Uncloak and send a standard greetings signal."

The unexpected looming appearance of the Thark warship, as she uncloaked a few hundred metres away, startled the crew. The comms operator recovered quickly and announced, "Signal from the Thark ship, sir."

Chad looked at the message on his screen and was surprised that it was in English. "Greetings to the *JJ Grant*. I am Captain Frussee of the Thark battlecruiser *B109*."

Chad said, "Comms, reply: Greetings, Captain Frussee, I hope we haven't kept you waiting too long?"

The response came, "No, Captain Chadwick, our wait has been productive. I am ordered here to assist you. May I access your AI to establish what assistance you require for your campaign against the Orrappa fleet?"

Taken aback by the request, Chad called, "Iris, should we allow Captain Frussee access to you?"

"Yes, Captain, the Thark are our allies."

"Very well, Iris, please make contact now."

A few moments later Captain Frussee messaged back. "I am pleased to confirm that you have my active support for your campaign, Captain Chadwick. I will shortly prepare a 'Minimum Casualty' battle plan for approval. Meanwhile, have your commanders check drive systems, ship shields, armaments, ship gravity systems and cloaking devices. All must be in good working order."

Chad replied, "Thank you, Captain Frussee, we will look forward to seeing your proposed battle plan."

Chad realised he was no longer in charge. Captain Frussee had taken over and would dictate battle tactics. Making a viewer conference call to Grant, Wang and Henson, he said, "I've just been exchanging messages with the Thark battlecruiser. Captain Frussee will present us with a battle plan but requests that we check our ships to ensure everything is working correctly."

Digesting the details of the battle plane, Chad had doubts; he was not quite sure that he liked the plan. The *JJ Grant* was to be a decoy. His ship would be used as bait, to draw the Orrappa flagship, considered to be fast and dangerous, out from the protection of her fleet where Captain Frussee, in the *B109*, would take over.

"It'll be a doddle, Chad," a very confident Grant said. "You get a head start, the flagship chases after you. Because she is much faster than the rest of her fleet, she'll leave them standing. Captain Frussee will be right with you. Once the flagship is clear of her fleet, Captain Frussee will broadcast the psychological inducement program, the flagship heads for home taking her fleet with her. Couldn't be simpler."

"And what will you, Wang and Henson be doing?"

Grant laughed. "We'll be fully cloaked and causing mayhem amongst the Orrappa fleet."

"I'm still not keen, Grant. Supposing the *JJ Grant* has missiles fired at her? What happens then?"

"Don't worry, Chad, the *JJ Grant* is nimble but I'll give it some thought and come back to you."

A chime from Eva on the viewer, abruptly brought Grant to alertness.

"Captain Mapps, I have a visual of the Orrappa fleet on the viewer for you."

Peering closely at his console viewer, Grant could dimly make out the Orrappa battle fleet, their black matt finish, blending them into the blackness of space. The vessels were in a formation of four ranks. Leading the fleet was a lone ship, half as big again as the Orrappa warships. Four enormous cargo vessels, also in formation completed the fleet.

Grant quietly called Envar, his second in command, on his headset. "Do you recognise the vessels?"

"Yes, sir, leading the fleet is the *Kantematao*, Admiral Sekorto's flagship. It's big, fast and has received some serious upgrades but it's not as agile as it looks. It's mainly used to impress politicians and show the flag."

"What sort of weaponry does she have?"

"Similar weapons to those we have on the *Helcon*, but larger, more powerful and lots of them. The other vessels are standard warships and the last four are bulk cargo vessels. They are probably unarmed."

"Thanks number two, let me have your tactical report when you've made a full assessment of the Orrappa fleet. Eva, confirm ETA please."

Instantly Eva responded, "Sixty-seven hours, thirty-eight minutes, approximately, sir."

"Have they picked us up yet?"

"No, sir, the Orrappa are unaware of our presence, their detection equipment is not that sensitive. They will not be capable of detecting us for at least twelve hours and not even then if we are cloaked."

Comms called on his headset. "Message from the *B109*, sir. Captain Frussee has prepared a final battle plan, I've sent it to the bridge printer."

Grant waved to his number two to pick up the printouts. "Thanks, Comms." As Envar handed him the printouts Grant looked at him and said, "Any regrets, Envar – are you sure you can handle being on the other side?"

"No regrets, Captain. Preena and I can never go back and the mission the fleet is being sent on is wrong. Be assured, our allegiance is now with you and Captain Chadwick."

"That's good to hear, Envar. I need to know you've got my back in an emergency. Now let's have a look at Captain Frussee's proposal."

Examining the proposal, he called Eva. "You've seen the final tactical plan from Captain Frussee, Eva?"

"Yes, sir, her battle plan has merit. However, it does present a potential danger for the *JJ Grant* in that the ship has no defensive or offensive weapons to retaliate with should she be fired on. At present, the *JJ Grant* relies on cloaking, shielding and agility."

"Thank you, Eva."

Grant realised Chad's concerns could be well founded; the *JJ Grant* could not defend herself and may be in grave danger by acting as the decoy. "What do you think, Envar, is Eva right?"

"I believe so. If I was in Captain Chadwick's position without any form of defence, I would be concerned. I have a suggestion though; we have many missiles on this ship. If a missile was attached to a power block it could be guided by an AI and used as a formidable weapon for defence or attack."

Grant nodded, "I've been thinking along those lines myself. Let's have a look at what we've got. Eva, display our missile and torpedo systems on the viewer for review."

Envar pointed to the kratorr a heavy-duty missile. "That's the one I'd recommend, sir. It has a devastating punch. The drive and guidance system don't do it justice but are easily removed."

"Eva, carry out an assessment on the merits of mounting the kratorr missile warhead on a power block and having the warhead directed to its target by you or Iris. Would that be a more efficient delivery system?"

"Yes, Captain, that concept under the control of an AI would certainly be more effective than a standard missile guidance system."

Grant called up Chad on the *JJ Grant*. "I said I'd come back to you about your concerns over the *JJ Grant* being used as a decoy without any defence or attack systems. Envar has come up with a solution to the problem."

"Really! What's Envar's suggestion?"

"We have a large stock of missiles in the ship's arsenal. Envar's proposing that we remove the drive and guidance system and attach the warheads to power blocks, mount them on the *JJ Grant* and let Iris launch and guide them to their target."

Chapter 14

Connie examined Grant's sketch of a kratorr warhead mounted on a power block and then attached to the ship's hull. "That shouldn't be too difficult for us to do. We have spare power blocks in stock, but we'd have to work out a way to send a power block through our ships shield."

"The *B109* must do that all the time, we could ask Captain Frussee to tell us how it's done." Grant said.

"OK, we haven't much time. Grant, get the warheads over here. Connie, can you get started on the mechanics of mounting and positioning the warheads outside the ship. I'll contact Captain Frussee and get her advice," Chad said. "Iris, advise Captain Frussee of what we are proposing and request her advice for sending a missile through the ship's shield."

Moments later, Captain Frussee appeared on the viewer. "Hello, Captain Chadwick, I understand that you are proposing to modify Orrappa missile warheads and to mount them on your power block propulsion units to be despatched and guided by Iris."

"Yes, that's correct, Captain Frussee."

"Very ingenious, but you do not know how to make portals in your protective shield to allow the missiles through?"

"Yes, that's the gist of it, we could probably work it out but we don't have a lot of time. I was hoping you could advise us, Captain."

"Well it is simple mathematics. Reduce power to three units in the areas of the shield… Iris should have this information and if she is deficient, I will get my AI to update her. Are there any other problems, Captain Chadwick?"

Chad felt like he had just been scolded but remained calm. "I don't think so, Captain Frussee, the missiles are being sent over from the *Helcon* as we speak." On another viewer, Chad could see one of the *Helcon*'s lifeboats smoothly curving towards the *JJ Grant* to line up with the rear bay doors.

Captain Frussee was curious. "Presumably the missile warheads are in the lifeboat, but how is the lifeboat being guided to dock with your ship? I don't see any directional jets."

"Ah, yes," said Chad. "We don't use manoeuvring jets any more. We have upgraded each lifeboat with a power block drive. A power block is capable of performing smoothly in three dimensions, through curves, spirals, spherical coordinates and so on." Chad grinned. "It's not my specialisation but Wang can explain it to you. This allows the pilot or Iris, to perform smooth intricate manoeuvres with ease even at high speed."

Captain Frussee nodded. "I see." Chad thought he caught a look of mild surprise.

"As you can see, we have temporarily shut down the rear shield to allow the lifeboat entry to the bay."

"Very good, Captain Chadwick, you will have to show me your power block in more detail when we have dealt with the Orrappa fleet. We may be able to exchange ideas."

"By all means, Captain, I shall look forward to that."

Connie called Chad on the viewer. "We're good to go here. I just need to know where to place these warheads and test the portals in the shield."

"Thanks, Connie, I'll check with Iris and come back to you."

Chad flicked to Iris on the viewer. "Iris, have you got the details to open the shield yet?"

"Yes, Captain. I have received a small software program that will allow me to open and close portals at any point in the shield. I have sent technical details and a plan of placement positions for the missiles to your printer." For Iris, the algorithms and mathematical data to open and close portals in the shields to synchronise with despatching of a warhead were now simple mathematical routines.

Picking up the three sets of printouts, Chad glanced at them, quickly passing two sheets of calculations to Grant and then closely examining the placement plan. Grant looked up from the calculations. "This is all going to be down to Iris, Chad. We have no control over any of this."

Chad nodded. "I thought it might be something like that." He called Connie. "I've just sent a layout to your printer for positioning the missiles. Mount the missiles as quick as you can. Oh, put a power block out on its own for Iris to carry out a dummy test run. We don't want to blow the shield apart if we've got it wrong."

"OK Chad. I'll get back to you when we're done."

Chad called Iris on the viewer, "Iris, are you confident about launching these missiles through a portal in the shield."

"Yes, Captain, I am."

"What if something goes wrong?"

"That is unlikely, Captain. The *B109* does it as a matter of course. I believe the dry-run testing procedure will show you that it is completely safe."

"Oh, you noticed the lone power block out there then?"

"Yes, Captain."

"Thank you, Iris." Chad swallowed his guilt at doubting Iris, but he had to be sure.

Professor Harry Foster had been a lecturer in Computer Programming and Electronic Design and had been brought in along with Arthur Ashford, a mathematician, as problem solvers when the *JJ Grant* was being built. They had both been with the ship ever since and their contribution to the ship was considerable.

The professor popped his head round Connie's office door. "OK to come in for a minute?"

"Yes of course, come in, Professor."

"I know you have a team placing the warheads out on the ship I just wondered if I could watch them doing it."

"Sure, Professor, come and meet the team, they're all geared up to go outside." The team consisted of two men and a woman. The men were tasked with mounting the warheads; the woman's job was to see they were secured at all times and to ensure that no tools or equipment drifted off into space.

Connie gave the girl the location plan for the warheads. "Everyone clear about what to do?" The three nodded. "Everybody still up for it?" Again, three nods. "Off you go then, I have another team ready in case of an emergency." The team filed into the airlock, which went through its cycle of pumping the air out to create a vacuum and let them exit the ship.

Connie and the professor watched on the viewer, seeing them emerge from the airlock and attaching their safety lines. "I cannot believe how brave those young people are to go out there."

"Oh, they get used to it, Professor, and it's absolutely safe providing everyone follows the rules, that's why there are three of them, the young woman is their keeper, she'll not let them take any short cuts. There is also a power block in each suit. If something bad happens they press a button and they are immediately brought to an airlock."

"But supposing they rip a suit while they're working, that must be dangerous?"

"Yes, it is, but those suits are well designed, they have a self-sealing gel sandwiched between the layers that make up the skin of the suit. The gel gets sucked into the damaged area by the vacuum of space. Once it hits the low temperature out there it freezes solid and prevents any leak straight away."

The professor shuddered at the thought of a leak.

"How long is it going to take to get all the missiles mounted?"

"Not that long; it's getting from place to place that takes the time."

Connie had a short conversation on the viewer with Iris, who took control of the power blocks now fitted with missile warheads and commenced moving them from the bay to their locations on the ship's hull where the waiting team mounted them on the hull.

"Come on, Professor, we'll have a cup of coffee while we watch them."

Setting the missiles had taken just under two hours from start to finish. The team made their way back through the airlock and Connie had coffee and energy bars ready for them. After debriefing them, she thanked them for a job well done. The professor could see why she made a good department head, she really cared for everyone who worked under her and got the best out of them. However, he had just noticed something.

"Connie, they've left something behind on the hull." He pointed to the viewer where a power block sat on its own close to one of the warheads.

"Ah, that's meant to be there, Professor. Iris will use the power block to simulate a missile and will pass it through the shield at each designated point to prove the mathematics. If it gets blocked by the shield, we'll know the theory is faulty." She called out, "Whenever you're ready, Iris, commence shield test in your own time."

On the viewer, the power block instantly disappeared, only to zigzag through each designated intersection point in a blur of speed.

Iris announced, "Test complete."

The professor knew the power block moved faster than the eye could see. This was just another example that highlighted that fact and that Iris could manipulate the power block effectively in any situation.

Connie nodded with satisfaction, "Thank you, Iris, can you now test each missile unit please."

The professor gazed at the viewer screen showing warheads mounted to the ship's outer skin and muttered, "I only hope Iris knows what she's doing."

Connie didn't seem the least perturbed. "Iris, commence testing each warhead please." They watched as a red light blinked on a missile and then turned to green.

Iris counted off each missile and proclaimed, "All missiles active and ready for firing."

"Thank you, Iris, please advise the captain and the bridge that all missiles are functional."

When he received the news, Chad gave a sigh of relief. "Comms message to Captain Frussee, "We now have an operational ship to ship missile system."

A response came back. "That is good to hear, Captain Chadwick. We are within sixteen hours of contact with the Orrappa fleet. We will continue with the battle plan as agreed. However, there are two small changes to the plan. I have located a large asteroid close to the path of the Orrappa fleet. You will uncloak, I repeat uncloak the *JJ Grant* when your vessel is concealed behind the asteroid. On my command, the *JJ Grant* will dart out, into the path of the Orrappa flagship, and flee ahead of the flagship, just fast enough to draw her away from the protection of her fleet. The other change of plan, now you have a missile system, is that you may use that system at your own discretion." Captain Frussee paused a moment for questions but none came.

"The *Helcon*, *Black Pearl* and *Blackbird* will remain cloaked and take up their agreed positions close to the fleet formation. On my command, they will each project an image of their ship on a fast collision course within the fleet formation, causing collisions to take place within the Orrappa fleet as their ships attempt avoiding action. I estimate this will cause sufficient damage to put the Orrappa fleet into disarray.

"The *B109* will be shadowing the flagship and I will take the appropriate action to persuade the fleet to return to their home planet. Captain Chadwick, you may if you wish use your missile system to dissuade them from attacks on your planet Earth. Everything clear?"

"Yes, Captain Frussee, I just hope your plan works," Chad said.

"Oh, it will; Captain Mapps and I have discussed it at length and we both agree the outcome will be in our favour. I suggest that you and your senior officers get some rest until we are closer to the Orrappa."

"Thank you, Captain Frussee." Chad called up Grant, Wang and Henson. "Is everyone fully prepared?" The chorus of cheerful responses made him smile.

"Yes, Captain, all OK, we're going to have a rest so we're fresh for when the fun begins."

"OK, good luck to you all."

Chad looked over at Gordon who seemed to be in total control. "Everything OK, Gordon?"

"Yes, Captain, no problems so far. I shall be handing the ship over to our number two bridge crew within the hour. Why don't you get some rest? Iris or I will call you for our next shift."

Chad yawned. "Good idea; I'll do that." He knew it was important not to show the crew that he was nervous.

Chapter 15

Iris probed with her long-distance detectors. Far ahead, she clearly detected the images, of the Orrappa fleet. Conferring with the *B109*'s AI, they both agreed it was time to put the battle plan into action.

The large asteroid that may once have been a small moon to a distant planet had somehow become free to wander aimlessly through space. It could now be seen close to the path of the approaching Orrappa fleet.

A message was received by all ships from Captain Frussee. "It is time for action. All vessels will remain cloaked during this operation. The *JJ Grant* will make its way to a point behind the lone asteroid and out of sight of the Orrappa's fleet and will then uncloak.

"The *B109* together with Captain Chadwick's, three other ships will intercept the Orrappa fleet, match speed and take up pre-agreed positions within the Orrappa fleet." Captain Frussee paused to let them absorb the instruction.

"On my command the uncloaked *JJ Grant* will emerge, from behind the asteroid at speed, as though making a run for it. When it is clear that the flagship has taken the bait and is outrunning her fleet in an attempt to catch the *JJ Grant*, the *B109* will close with the flagship and ensure its retreat." Again, Captain Frussee made a slight pause. "The *Helcon*, *Blackbird*, and *Black Pearl*, all cloaked, will then commence the agreed disruption to the main fleet. You will use no weapons, other than the projected image of your ship. You will set the image on a collision course to ram into an Orrappa ship. This should cause much confusion if not severe damage amongst the Orrappa fleet." An animation of the required action was displayed on the ships viewers. There could be no possible confusion of what was expected from each ship. "All communication will be by the communicator. Is that understood? Please acknowledge."

All captains including Chad acknowledged.

Chad messaged on the communicator, "The *JJ Grant* is in position and uncloaked, Captain Frussee."

A short response came. "Acknowledged."

There was a long silence. Chad's communicator buzzed. "On my command, Captain." Chad realised he was perspiring with tension. His bridge crew watched him. "On my mark, Captain Chadwick… GO!"

The *JJ Grant* accelerated out from behind the rock at high speed and curved away from the approaching fleet, running fast ahead of them. Initially nothing happened. The unexpected appearance of the *JJ Grant* had caught the flagship by surprise but now it could be seen that she was quickly in pursuit and overhauling the *JJ Grant* fast, leaving her fleet behind.

Chad's communicator buzzed. "Accelerate slowly to within five per cent of the flagships speed to encourage the chase. If she fires on you, use your own judgement."

Chad messaged. "Understood."

Chad could see why Captain Frussee was a battlecruiser captain in the Thark space fleet; she was decisive, had a steely resolve and utmost confidence in her own abilities. She would be a very formidable foe.

Comms called, "Incoming message, sir." A garbled series of sounds came over the speaker.

Iris interpreted the message, "Stop or we fire."

Chad called, "Comms do not respond. Iris, what is their speed?"

"Five per cent faster than us, sir."

Chad looked at the viewer showing in clear stark detail the approaching flagship bristling with weapons. A column on the left of the screen displayed the scrolling data of speeds and distances. The pictorial view showed the flagship overhauling the *JJ Grant* but leaving the smaller Orrappa warships well behind.

"Maintain present speed, Iris."

"Maintaining current speed, Captain."

The scrolling figures on the rear viewer showed the distance between the flagship and her fleet to have increased by a large margin.

Moments later Iris announced, "Two missiles have been launched. They are locked onto us and coming up fast."

Chad watched the scrolling figures on the viewer showing time to impact by the missiles.

"Iris, prepare to fire two missiles to the flagships starboard drives on my command. Return control to my console."

"You have control, Captain."

Chad acknowledged. "I have control."

Chad called over the comms to his bridge crew, "Prepare for manoeuvers in three seconds."

Without waiting a response, Chad abruptly reduced speed by fifty per cent and put his ship into a steep one-hundred-and-eighty-degree half loop to take them back under the approaching flagship. Their stomachs all did somersaults whilst the network of gravity blocks desperately attempted to maintain normal gravity within the ship and at the same time absorb the negative G of the half loop.

The flagship attempted to follow the *JJ Grant* with the same manoeuvre but was nowhere near agile enough and going much too fast. Neither were the missiles that were locked onto the *JJ Grant*. Their high speed had caused them to overshoot by a large margin. Only now were they returning to home in on their target. Worse still the flagship that had now completed its much deeper loop and was accelerating hard after the *JJ Grant* found itself trapped between the fast-approaching missiles and the *JJ Grant*. The result was a devastating collision of the two missiles with the flagship. The flagships shield spectacularly failed at the point of impact as one missile exploded on it, closely followed by the second missile which breached the damaged shield and exploded somewhere on the centre of the vessel where the bridge would be. The whole scene unfolded on Chad's viewer. He watched and waited as the damaged flagship, trailing smoke and bubbles of foam that had escaped the breach in the hull before it sealed, began to recover and turn to settle on a course back to the safety of the distant fleet. The *JJ Grant*, accelerating quickly, completed another manoeuvre to take up a path behind the flagship, which had become a sitting duck for the power block driven missiles.

Chad called the order. "Fire two missiles to starboard drives, Iris."

Iris responded, "Acknowledged, sir."

The bridge crew held their breath as they watched the two warheads scorch towards the damaged flagship. The Orrappa vessel weaved an erratic and evasive path across space in an effort to throw off the pursuing missiles. Using every military tactic it could muster, the flagship finally opened up with her mighty arsenal of defensive weapons. Her plasma canons pulsed at high speed, as did the high frequency electromagnetic discharge tubes, putting up an almost impenetrable wall of violent plasma energy, more than enough to fry the electronic guidance system of any missile. Hundreds of splinter grenades were ejected to explode in the flagships wake, sending out thousands of vicious shards of hardened steel that would slice through any missile should it be hit. Puffs of metallic flakes with white-hot centres burst like small stars from the ship to distract the pursuing missiles. Normally these would have been enough to confuse most missile guidance systems but not Iris. The power block missiles twisted, weaved, zigzagged and jinked their way through the barrage, relentlessly homing in on the starboard rear of the flagship, finally breaching her rear shield in a spectacular explosion and taking out the two starboard drives. The flagship staggered under the impact careering wildly across space, her crew desperately trying to get her back under control on one pair of drives. Dense plumes of black smoke from her defence munitions mixed with a cloud of foam that had escaped the breach in her hull marked her path before the breach had finally sealed.

As the *JJ Grant* approached the plume of black smoke and debris, Chad calmly called out, "Cloak-up as we hit the smoke, Iris."

"Ship cloaked, sir," Iris acknowledged.

An observer seeing the *JJ Grant* disappearing into the expanding smoke and debris cloud would be forgiven for believing the ship to be destroyed.

"Damage report, Iris?"

"Yes, sir, eight plates and four cups in the canteen." Everyone laughed including Chad.

The *JJ Grant* had done its job and Chad moved his cloaked ship to clear space to let the *B109* do her job of broadcasting the psychological inducement program at the flagship.

The crew on the bridge of the *JJ Grant* were mesmerised as they watched the view screens. The Orrappa flagship had finally been brought under control. However, she was manoeuvring clumsily and with difficulty.

The fleet itself was in complete disarray. Their former rigid formation was in tatters, as vessels had desperately tried to avoid collisions. Four ships that had collided with others had started to blow apart or collapse in on themselves. The whole fleet had been firing torpedoes, missiles and pulsar bolts indiscriminately at vessels, perceived to be on a collision course with them, only to see their own forces struck by friendly fire. To add to their dismay, the flagship, although under control, was no longer the fearsome beast that it had once been but had become a liability.

The Orrappa fleet commander called up the flagship, *Kantematao*. "Do you require assistance?"

"No, we have power, we're just getting the ship back under control," said a bridge officer. "Both starboard drives are out but we are still functional."

The commander said, "That's a relief, sir. What are your orders now?"

There was a pause; the fleet commander could hear angry voices in the background. "I'll put the admiral on, sir," said the bridge officer.

The admiral came on line and said, "We are to return to Orrappa."

"Return! Why? On whose orders, sir?"

"On the orders of the Minister of State, who is on board this ship with his advisers," said the admiral.

"But we are almost within reach of the target system; our fleet is still strong—"

"I am sorry, Commander, but our distinguished guests are insisting we must return at once."

The fleet commander was incredulous; it wasn't in the nature of the Orrappa military to retreat, especially when they had the bulk of their force intact. Reluctantly he said, "Yes, sir, if you say so, sir. Were there any casualties on the ship, Admiral?"

"Unfortunately, yes. Two bridge officer's dead, four of our bridge crew wounded by shrapnel. Two advisers to the minister of state are dead; they exited the ship without spacesuits. Other than that, we are in good shape."

The commander was horrified. "Why would they do that, sir?" He couldn't help but ask again. "Why are we turning back? We have only lost four ships and we have more than enough operational ships to continue our mission."

"Commander, we answer to the government, their orders to us are quite explicit and are being given by a senior government official. The fleet is to return to Orrappa with immediate effect."

"Sir, this seems most irregular. May I come aboard and speak with the minister himself. I am concerned that our ship's crew may attribute our disengagement and retreat to the wrong reasons – they will not want to be seen as cowards."

"No, Commander, you may not speak with the minister of state and you will not be insubordinate. However, you may come on board with your chief engineer to assess the damage to our vessel. It is just possible that whilst you are here you may bump into the minister of state and the subject of disengaging from the enemy may come up in conversation."

The fleet commander took the broad hint. "I shall make arrangements immediately, sir."

The fleet commander and his chief engineer viewed the damage to the bridge with the admiral. "Easy to see what's happened, sir," the chief said. "One missile exploded on the shield and breached it. The second missile followed the first and has come straight through the armoured steel bulkhead just in front of the bridge and blasted a hole in the bridge wall. Luckily the soft inner membrane has done its job and sealed off the damage and retained the atmosphere." The Orrappa markings on a section of the missiles barrel still embedded in the bridge deck plate shocked him, he looked at the fleet commander, and pointed to the name stencilled on the section *Kantematao*, the missile had belonged to the flagship. The fleet commander winced at that revelation.

Admiral Sekorto sombrely nodded. "Yes, we shot ourselves in the foot. I've never seen a manoeuvre like that before."

The fleet commander looked at the destruction around him and said, "I suppose the damage to the instrumentation was caused by shrapnel."

The admiral nodded. "Yes, and it was also responsible for the deaths of two officers and the injury of four crewmen." Softly and almost to himself, he said, "Why the two civilians decided to exit the ship through an airlock without suits is beyond me. What made them do it, fear, cowardice?"

Neither the fleet commander nor his chief engineer offered a response.

When the admiral introduced them to other officers on the ship, one commented, "It was extraordinary that the captain and his second in command, together with two ministry staff members, tried to enter an airlock without suits, luckily they were restrained by the ship's crew."

"May we speak to any of these individuals?" asked the commander.

Realising he had probably said too much. The officer backtracked and said, "The ship's doctor is treating them but I expect you can see them in due course."

Inspection of the starboard engine room was dispiriting to say the least. The ship's starboard drives were shattered beyond repair and the engine room needed a complete rebuild; a shipyard job according to the chief engineer.

The initial investigation into the skirmish concluded that only the Earth vessel had been involved. The vessel had been destroyed by the barrage put out by the *Kantematao*; shortly after the Earth vessel had fired her missiles.

The mayhem amongst the fleet was attributed to an initial collision between two ships at the centre of the tightly packed formation causing a ripple effect throughout the fleet. All the evidence recovered from the debris floating in space, showed that collisions or friendly fire had attributed to the loss and damage to Orrappa ships. No enemy ships had been observed or detected at the battle scene, other than the vessel, thought to be from Earth.

It was concluded that the enemy ship had been on a suicide mission and had fired two torpedoes before being destroyed. Nothing could have survived the wall of death put out by the *Kantematao*. She had used every weapon in her armoury. Privately the fleet commander had niggling doubts. *All we know is that the vessel never emerged from the ensuing smoke attributed to the countermeasure devices. We can only assume that the ship was destroyed, no wreckage had been found.*

The Orrappa fleet, with the area of space to themselves, were still wary. They formed a looser formation as they commenced their long journey back to Orrappa at a considerably reduced speed.

"Fleet Commander, we are having a debriefing in the wardroom, I'd like you there. The presence of a seasoned long service officer is always welcome," the admiral said. The fleet commander was astute enough to know the admiral needed the backup of an experienced officer by his side.

In the wardroom, the commander had a drink with the admiral and other officers before being introduced to the minister of state. "How are you, after your ordeal, sir?"

The minister of state flicked a mote of dust from his jacket. "I'm fine, thank you, Commander."

"It must have been an ordeal for you, sir." He pushed his luck, "Have you seen action before, sir?"

"No, unfortunately a childhood illness prevented me from entering a military academy."

Oh really! The commander thought. "I must say, sir, I found the skirmish quite alarming; I expect you did too?"

The minister gave him a look of distaste. "Certainly not! Don't be impertinent." Nevertheless, he noticed the beads of perspiration forming on the minister's forehead.

"Sorry, sir, I wasn't intending to be rude. I have to confess the first time I saw action I was scared witless."

The minister ignored the remark and said, "Tell me, Fleet Commander, how was it that the fleet came to have such an unfortunate accident as to lose four warships?"

The fleet commander had been expecting this point to be raised not just by the minister but the whole of fleet command. "In all honesty, Minister, we don't know yet. Our investigators are gathering what evidence they can find. The suspicion is that one of the ships accidentally or deliberately collided with its neighbour, causing mortal damage to both ships. Other vessels close to the incident opened fire with their plasma canons thinking they were under attack. This escalated into further collisions between ships held in a tight formation that caused so much mayhem."

The minister gave him a sour look. "Are you suggesting that we had a rogue ship in our fleet that deliberately rammed its neighbours causing our casualties?"

The fleet commander, as tactfully as he could, said, "Maybe. We have to look at every possibility, sir, we only saw the one ship and that we believe was the vessel from planet Earth. However, we have several theories to investigate."

The minister sipped his drink and nodded in agreement.

"We still have a substantial force Minister and could yet complete our mission. Is it wise to turn back after only a minor skirmish?"

The minister of state was becoming more than irritated, the question bordered on insubordination. He ignored the question and was about to move away when the fleet commander said, "Sir, do you know why a number of your staff tried to commit suicide?"

The minister was thrown by the question. "That is not true, that's just ship's gossip."

"I don't think so, sir, the ship's AI has entered the details in the ship's log and we can't change that. There will be an enquiry and several officers and men will be called to give evidence. It is not my place to ask this but my men will ask me, why have we turned back? Who gave the order?"

The minister of state abruptly turned and walked out of the wardroom.

The admiral came over and said with a hint of a smirk lurking in the corners of his mouth, "You've not upset our minister of state, have you?"

"It's just possible that I may have, sir. I can see he doesn't like the idea of an enquiry. If we go back with nothing to show for the venture, the government will fall."

The admiral clapped him on the back and gave a short laugh. "That could be a good thing; our world needs to make friends that will help us, not enemies who fight us. However, I think it will end with you and me on the chopping block."

"Not if I can help it," said the fleet commander. "I saw in the log that the order to return to base came from the minister."

As he was about to step into the lifeboat to return to his own vessel, the admiral patted him on the back. "Commander, you have my full support."

Chad watched the Orrappa fleet reform and turnabout to start their long journey home. He deeply regretted that the Orrappa had lost lives but reasoned that many more lives had been saved.

Chapter 16

The *B109* battlecruiser stood about five hundred metres off from the *JJ Grant*. She was identical to the battlecruiser that had arrived to escort the passenger vessel back home. She was exquisitely shaped, with gently curved contours rather like a slightly flattened dolphin, smooth and without a protrusion of any kind.

Forever grateful to the Thark, because they had done so much for him, his ship and for Earth, Chad felt he had to show his appreciation in some small way.

Credit for defeating the Orrappa invasion fleet had all been down to Captain Frussee for her military planning skills and of course the wonderful technology that the Thark had bestowed upon them by way of the cloaking device and the upgrades to Iris.

An invitation to Captain Frussee and her senior officers to visit the *JJ Grant* so they could be thanked properly seemed appropriate.

"Iris, please send an invitation to Captain Frussee, inviting her and her senior officers to visit the *JJ Grant* so we can honour her and she can meet the officers with whom she has had dealings with."

Iris responded immediately, "Certainly, Captain, the invitation has been sent."

A short time later, a message arrived from the *B109*. "Thank you for your invitation, Captain Chadwick, I can confirm that I will arrive on your ship with two of my officers at the appointed hour. Meanwhile, with your permission I will carry out an environmental health check, to ensure that neither your species nor ours will be a danger to each other."

Comms on Chad's headset said, "The Thark have a probe ready to board us, sir."

"Thanks Comms, please acknowledge."

The *JJ Grant*'s excited crew watched on the ship's viewers and gaped in wonder as a small portal opened on the side of the Thark vessel, just large enough to allow a small sphere to slip out into space and begin making its way rapidly to the *JJ Grant*.

"Iris, open the bay doors."

The glistening sphere about the size of a small football made its way into the landing bay and hovered before the airlock.

"Iris, can you detect any danger from this device?"

"No, Captain, it is merely a mobile projector."

"Very well, operate the airlock and allow the device entry."

The glistening sphere hovering at chest height made the short journey from the airlock to the bridge. No means of propulsion could be seen as the probe hovered in mid-air and moved forward. A beam of light shot out from the probe and a holographic figure stood on the bridge. The figure announced, "I am the medical officer of the *B109*. Thank you for permitting this inspection. This probe is the standard device we use for checking local environments to ensure the safety of our crew and the local population of differing species. I hope you do not find it too intrusive?"

"Not at all. You are welcome," said Chad.

The hologram moved around the bridge and closely inspected each of the bridge crew and their equipment as though it was a live individual.

Straightening up, the holographic figure said, "All is in order. Our captain and two officers will make the crossing, if that is acceptable."

"Yes, certainly. They will be very welcome," said Chad.

On the viewing screen, the portal on the hull of the *B109* had increased in size to allow a small vessel the same shape as the Thark ship to slip smoothly out into space and approach the *JJ Grant*, venting gas as it expertly manoeuvred its way into the landing bay.

The hologram figure said, "That is one of our life pods. We use them for ship to ship and local travel."

"Iris, please close the bay doors and restore normal air pressure. We will go to the bay and greet our guests," Chad said.

Chad, Grant, Henson and Wang stood within the entrance to the bay.

Three figures emerged from the sleek, deep blue almost black craft. It was immediately obvious that they were not of Earth. One was an almond-eyed female with bobbed blond hair, very beautiful in an understated way. She wore a tight body-hugging silver coverall with various emblems and markings and had the bearing of supreme authority. Her male companions also almond-eyed and blonde-haired, were tall, athletic and with handsome features. They wore similar figure hugging coveralls to the female. All three beings looked young, Chad guessed, probably in their early twenties.

"Hello, I am Captain Chadwick of the *JJ Grant*."

The female swept her gaze over the small group and said, "Greetings, Captain Chadwick, I am pleased to be in your presence."

"Likewise," Chad said, slightly thrown by her air of natural authority, which made him feel like a young lad, although he was at least three times her age.

"I am Captain Frussee of the *B109*." She turned. "These are my bridge officers and they are of equivalent rank to your commanders." She introduced her two companions. "Commander Balmak and Commander Rudeln."

"Pleased to meet you." Chad gestured to his group. "This is Captain Grant Mapps, Captain Henson Wright and Captain Wang Zheng."

Captain Frussee looked each in the eye and acknowledged Grant and Henson with a quick nod but she stared at Wang, appraising him for an uncomfortably long time and then smiled at him. Wang did not seem at all perturbed and smiled back.

Slightly embarrassed, Chad said, "Please let me show you to the bridge."

On their way to the bridge, Captain Frussee said, "I must compliment you on your magnificent tactical manoeuvre against the Orrappa's flagship. I have never seen anything like it. It was timed to perfection; the vessels own missiles striking the flagships bridge and then your missiles taking out two drives. Where did you learn these tactics?"

Chad beamed at the compliment and said, "I have to thank Wang for his tuition in battle tactics. Both

Wang and Grant are true experts in the art of warfare and ship manoeuvres."

"Really?" Captain Frussee turned to look back at Wang and with a smile said to Chad, "Perhaps you could persuade Captain Wang Zheng to teach me some of his tactics."

"I don't think he would need much persuading, Captain Frussee."

Captain Frussee smiled back. "Then I shall look forward to receiving some instruction from him, Captain Chadwick."

Out of the corner of his eye, Chad saw that Grant and Henson had each paired up with one of the visiting officers. Wang brought up the rear.

Chad said, "Please forgive me if I do not pronounce your name correctly, Captain Frussee."

Captain Frussee smiled. "It is only to be expected, Captain Chadwick. I don't suppose you meet an alien every day?"

"That is very true, Captain, and certainly not one as beautiful as you."

Her smile became broader. "Thank you, Captain. Please call me Zanuala, may I call you Chad?"

"I shall be very pleased if you would, Zanuala."

Chad ushered them onto the bridge and offered refreshments, which they hesitantly accepted and nodded their approval after taking cautionary sips of the orange juice.

"Are there other occupied worlds in this part of the galaxy, Zanuala?" Chad asked, as he showed his guests around the bridge.

Zanuala shook her head. "I'm not sure; I have never been in this part of the galaxy before but I would suspect not. Life supporting planets are relatively rare but we are not alone, Chad. Many stars do support life-bearing planets. Some are newly formed with life just beginning and some are dying with life becoming extinct. I will send you a star map that shows some of the planets that we know to support life."

Chad said, "That is most kind of you." By this time, they had reached Helen and Connie, who stood together and Chad introduced them. "This is my wife, Helen."

Zanuala, looked at Helen keenly and with a warm smile said, "Hello, Helen, so you are Captain Chadwick's partner. What role do you have on the ship?"

"I'm involved in the administration of the ship and its personnel."

Chad said, "That's right, Zanuala, but she is also my sounding board and my moral compass."

Captain Frussee nodded sagely and smiled again. "We all need sound advice at times of stress, Helen. It is good for a captain to have someone to lean on." Then Chad introduced Connie, the only female officer on the bridge. "This is Lieutenant Connie Mapps, who is our chief engineer and is also the mother of Captain Grant Mapps."

Captain Frussee greeted Connie warmly. "It is good to meet an engineer; they are the lifeblood of a ship."

As they moved on, Zanuala said, "Chad, I just heard one of your crew call your AI Iris, why is that?"

"Ah yes, Iris. She chose the name herself and we feel more comfortable with her. Iris is also a female name." Chad could see Captain Frussee was impressed.

Zanuala called out, "Hello, Iris, how are you?"

Iris appeared on the viewer and with a lovely smile, said, "I am very well, Captain Frussee." In her soft, clear voice.

Zanuala said, "I like her voice, it is pleasant and calming."

"Yes, we like it; she chose both that and her visual appearance too."

Zanuala raised an eyebrow. "Really?"

Chad had noticed that Zanuala touched or ran her hand over each surface as she came into different areas. She saw his look. "I like to feel a ship; you can tell a lot about the beings who have designed and built a vessel from the way it feels."

"Well I hope you like the way our ship feels, Zanuala. Is there any particular part of the ship that you would like to see?"

"Yes, Chad, I would like to see how your crew live, where they eat, your workshops and I would like to see your ship's drive system?"

Chad was taken aback. "Drive system? Perhaps we can get to that later."

She smiled broadly at him. "You mean after you have seen our drive system."

It was Chad's turn to laugh. "Yes, that's what I mean." Chad stopped. "Here are my quarters, all ship's crew have more or less the same accommodation to suit either one or two crew members."

Zanuala was impressed. "You do not display opulence, Chad?"

"No, I believe we each have our job, every crew member works to the best of their ability. Why should I have opulence and not them? My job is no more important than their job."

"Very good, Chad. We follow a similar code."

Chad showed the recreational facilities on the ship and gave a rundown of necessary crew. "Of course, we don't require all these people to run the ship, many are here because they have a lust to explore or don't want to be separated from their partner. However, all who are on the ship have some form of duty, even if it is cleaning or serving in the restaurants or performing on stage to keep our crew entertained."

Captain Frussee raised an eyebrow and was more than interested. "I would like to see this performing on the stage that entertains your crew. Without diversions, serving on a spacecraft can mean loneliness and long hours of boredom."

Chad nodded. "I will arrange some entertainment for your crew before our vessels part company."

On the way back to the bridge, Chad asked, "Are the Thark at war with the Orrappa?"

"No, Chad, we are not a warlike species. The Orrappa's world is dying. The Orrappa are governed by a cruel and dysfunctional government, who instead of seeking help, follow the easier route of piracy and to conquer other worlds that they see as backward or weak, because they are not warlike. You have just taught them a lesson they will remember."

"Have the Thark taught the Orrappa a lesson too?"

"Yes, they have got away with piracy for a long time, but no longer. The Thark authorities are dealing with the Orrappa in a way that will benefit them in the longer term. Sending the officers and crew that attacked your ship and our passenger ship to a newly formed planet is a good start."

"Oh, you heard about that?"

"Yes, Chad, it is well known amongst the Thark. You are beginning to get a reputation."

"No, Zanuala, the Orrappa have Klempe and the Council of Elders to thank for that. I only made the suggestion. I just hope the Orrappa crew make the most of their opportunity to start again."

Zanuala nodded sombrely. "Yes, I do too, Chad. The Thark have a number of planets that come under our protection. We patrol the areas around those planets because it is not unknown for rogue civilisations, like the Orrappa, to take ships for their cargo or to gain advanced technical knowledge or even for slave labour."

Chad was shocked. "That is alarming. I thought the Orrappa were the exception to the rule."

Captain Frussee stopped for a moment and looked at him. "No, Chad, always keep your guard up, never accept anything at face value, keep your missiles operational and defend your ship by whatever means is at your disposal. There is nothing wrong with arming your ship; you don't have to use those weapons unless it is to defend yourselves."

"Thank you for your advice, Zanuala."

"And thank you, Chad, for the tour of your ship which I like very much. My vessel will remain in the vicinity until I am assigned to another mission. May I invite you to visit our ship and perhaps arrange with Captain Wang Zheng to give me tuition of his unique ship to ship fighting tactics?"

"I will make arrangements with Wang and we would be delighted to visit your ship, thank you."

"Very well, I shall expect to see you very shortly."

"Will we need our suits?"

"No, that will not be necessary."

"Thank you, Zanuala."

When Captain Frussee and her officers had departed for the *B109*, Chad joined the others on the bridge, who were all still agog at coming face to face with another species. Helen said, "You must invite her back for another informal visit, Chad, so more people on the ship can meet her."

With a grin Chad said, "I did, Zanuala wants to see one of our theatrical shows – can you talk to the theatre director for me?"

The shuttle, with Chad, Grant and Wang, entered the portal that had opened up in the side of the Thark ship and settled onto the bay floor. A voice spoke as if in the air beside them, "You may exit your vessel, air pressure is normal." Wang was uncertain because the portal giving access to space had remained open. However, the air pressure gauge showed normal air pressure in the bay. Warily Wang cracked open the shuttle door a fraction, but to his surprise the pressure was normal. A smiling Captain Frussee and the same two officers greeted them when they exited the shuttle.

"Greetings, Captain Chadwick, welcome to the B109."

Zanuala led the group though an open doorway that didn't appear to have an airlock and along a corridor to the bridge. Chad couldn't help but gawk. It was the most stunning display of viewing screens and control panels he had ever seen. Here was the future before his eyes. Even the most complex system or machine, most of which he had no idea what it was supposed to do, looked so easy to control. Every switch and lever positioned in a natural logical place and it seemed to him that anyone with very little training could operate the controls. Zanuala interpreted his expression. "Yes,

Chad, everything is designed to allow any member of the ship's company, whether fully trained or not to use any piece of equipment on the ship's bridge. Of course, in reality the AI operates the bridge, we are the backup crew."

Chad was overawed. "Does the AI make all the decisions?"

"No, only routine decisions other than if we are attacked, then the AI will defend and will, if requested, relinquish control to me. Should we decide to attack, for some reason, the decision would be mine alone."

"What sort of weapons do you have for defence?"

"All sorts, Chad, from low power mind control to the ability to destroy a planet." Zanuala escorted them round the bridge, explaining what each station specialised in. "Come, I will show you our quarters."

Chad was impressed, each cabin was twice the size of anything aboard the *JJ Grant* but they only had six hundred personnel on board, both male and female, with five hundred of those being military troops, like marines. They were finally offered refreshments in the crew's canteen. Chad was cautious and chose a small drink, which was fiery, and he had to suppress a cough but it tasted fine. Grant and Wang had long drinks, the same as their companions.

"Come, Chad, I will show you our drive system."

Chad was astonished that Zanuala would show him the ship's drive. However, she led them to the to the vessels propulsion room. The vast chamber was empty except for a large silver block of metal mounted in a brace of substantial beams. Chad realised he was seeing a version of the power block. He saw Zanuala eyeing him and she gave a knowing nod of her head. It was Chad's turn to give a small grin.

When they returned to the bridge, Zanuala said, "Because you only have temporary weapons, the power block missiles and no other defensive weapons on board your ship, I have been given authority to upgrade your AI with military grade evasion tactics. If you are ever attacked, these tactics will allow you to avoid missiles or other projectile attacks and escape from the scene of attack behind your cloaking device. It does not involve attack weapons."

Chad looked at Grant and Wang for advice. Wang said, "Would the AI be able to reject the evasion manoeuvres if she or we deemed it necessary?"

"Yes, the AI would be able to use discretion as to what part of the system should be used and a bridge officer would be able to override the AI's decision if necessary." Wang looked at Grant and then nodded to Chad.

"Thank you, Zanuala that is most generous. Please convey my thanks to your superiors for this gift."

"It is our pleasure to give and an honour to have met you. I will instruct our AI; you may need to give your Iris permission to receive this data."

"We are most indebted to you, thank you for your hospitality."

They made their way back to the bay to board the shuttle. Zanuala, casting a critical eye over the shuttle, said, "I like the shuttle craft. It is a decent size; I keep telling our supply staff that ours are too small in the event of an emergency."

Wang, who had entered the shuttle re-emerged with a small package and gave it to Chad. "Captain Frussee, this is for you, it is an ancient game for two players called chess. I hope you will enjoy it. Goodbye for now."

When they were back on the bridge of the *JJ Grant*, Chad called Iris. "Captain Frussee, of the *B109*, has offered a tactical and evasion software upgrade for you in the event that we are attacked by another ship. What do you think?"

"I think it would be wise to accept such an offer."

Chad looked at Grant and Wang for reassurance and they both nodded. "OK, Iris, please contact the AI aboard the *B109* and say you will accept the upgrade. I have been assured that you can reject any part of the evasion system if you wish."

Almost instantly, Iris said, "I have received the upgrade, Captain."

"Has it enhanced or detracted any other systems that you use?"

"No, sir, it has enhanced my response times and provided additional protective functions."

Chapter 17

On board the *JJ Grant* Helen made a suggestion, "Why don't we have a social gathering, a simple event where everyone can relax and enjoy themselves?"

Chad groaned. "I'm not up to organising anything at the moment; all I want to do is relax for a while."

"You don't have to do anything, I'll organise it, all you have to do is to come and enjoy yourself."

Captain Frussee circulated amongst the guests and crewmembers that she had previously met and made small talk with everyone to whom she was introduced. She was enjoying herself; Wang brought another drink over to her. Zanuala put her free hand on Wang's arm and with only the slightest pressure pulled him towards her. "Do you have any of those computer games on board that you have spoken of?" she said.

"Yes, I knew you'd be here, so I brought some with me, I've left them in my old cabin."

Linking her arm through Wang's, Captain Frussee said with a smile, "Well I think you had better show them to me." She drew him closer.

Out of the corner of his eye, Chad saw the pair disappear out into the corridor. *I wonder what's going on there.* He forced his attention back to the *B109*'s third officer, who was speaking.

"According to the latest information our people have identified a number of Orrappa subversives who have infiltrated several key organisations. If they put as much energy into finding a new world for their nation as they do into trying to take over others, they would be much better off."

As they walked down the corridor, linked arm in arm, Zanuala drew Wang closer, until he pulled his arm free and slid it round her slim waist. She curled her arm around Wang and clung to him. Zanuala felt the warmth of his body from hip to shoulder and her head tilted into the crook of his neck. Stopping by a door, Wang slipped both arms around her and pulled her tight to him. "This is my old cabin." Zanuala slid her arms up under his arms to the back of his shoulders, pulling herself harder against him relishing the warm contact of their bodies. She said,

"I think you'd better show me your computer games…" The door closed softly behind them.

It was late; Chad was exhausted and was pleased to see things beginning to wind down when Wang and Captain Frussee reappeared. "Hello, you two; we've missed you. I thought you must have gone back to your ship."

"Oh, no I'm sorry, Chad. Wang insisted I see his collection of computer games. Look, he has even given me one to try out."

Chad looked at the garish box Wang was holding. "I see, well I'm sure you will enjoy it."

"Oh, yes, I'm sure I will. Thank you for organising this lovely event. You must come over to my ship tomorrow and bring a sample of your power block; we may be able to do an exchange of technology."

Chad was surprised. "I certainly will, Zanuala."

"Oh, and, Chad, please bring Wang and Grant. I would like to see more of their computer games. I still want to see if they are up for the challenge of our ship's simulator. They may be able to teach Iris and my AI a few tricks. Goodbye, Chad." She gave a smile and was gone.

As Wang left to follow Zanuala, Chad said, "Computer games?"

"It's a long story," Wang said, looking a bit sheepish.

"Well don't tell me. I'm not up to listening to tall tales."

Wang smirked and rushed after Zanuala.

Chad, together with Grant and Wang, crossed over to the *B109* and entered the ship's bay through the portal where Captain Frussee was waiting for them. "Please come into our workshop." Zanuala escorted them into a large workshop, which was immaculate. The floor was a nonslip glossy pale green and the walls a contrasting non-reflective soft cream. The lighting was superb and the workshop glowed like a bright summer's day.

Machines were laid out in regular patterns. There were only two others in the machine shop. Zanuala explained, "They are the machine overseers. All the machines are automatic or under control of my AI and are capable of manufacturing any component on my ship."

Zanuala led them through to another large room containing a massive semi-circular viewing screen. Turning to Wang she said, "I have redesigned your computer game." Holding the two control boxes, she passed one to Wang. Raising a hand Zanuala pointed to the screen, which promptly lit up showing a three-dimensional view of the Orrappa fleet in space with the *B109* and *Black Pearl* facing them.

Zanuala grinned. "Wang has the *Black Pearl* and I have the *B109*. The object of the game is to see how many of the Orrappa ships we can take down. The computer will keep the score. Our ships only have front shields and no cloaking. The Orrappa vessels can fight back or take evasive action. All controls work as they were originally intended. When the lights on the screen turn green, we start." Zanuala gave Wang a challenging look and with a hint of a smile said, "This is as real as it gets."

They stood side by side, the lights flicked to green and the game started. The screen showed a three-dimensional image of the action. Two small inserts on the screen showed a cockpit view of Wang on the left and Zanuala on the right. The game was fast; Zanuala was aggressive and tore into the fray, the *B109* twisting and turning, firing short bursts from her weapons into her targets. Her shield glowed red in spots as it absorbed missiles, shells, laser beams and plasma energy bolts from the Orrappa ships. Zanuala was prepared to take damage to get a kill.

Wang was fast; he only fired when locked onto a target – happily sliding between Orrappa vessels to draw their fire, then to slip away letting the Orrappa kill their own ships with friendly fire. He somehow managed to avoid much of the arsenal of weapons aimed at him.

Soon Zanuala was out of ammunition and cursed as she rammed an Orrappa ship's communication antenna with her own vessel and sparks flew from it. She eventually had to retire when her power cell ran down.

Wang was still in the battle, the *Black Pearl* spiralling around an Orrappa ship, blasting another, as he came out of the spiral, and then seeing another ship explode as he slid out from the cross hairs of a canon and the plasma energy bolt meant for him struck another Orrappa ship. Eventually all the Orrappa ships were left as smouldering wrecks.

Zanuala clapped with delight. "I have recorded that for my flight crew to watch and learn a few lessons from. I would just love to see you and Grant have a game like that." Chad was pleased that Wang had given such a good showing but also pleased that Zanuala gave no hint of jealousy that she had lost.

"Come let me show you our simulator…"

Chad and the others gazed at the transparent device floating in mid-air: no legs, pistons or supports of any description. Zanuala grinned at their expressions. "We can see into the device but the captain and bridge crew only see and experience the simulation. It is very realistic."

Chad was awestruck. "Zanuala, we have a couple of simulator designers on board the *JJ Grant*. They're good; they know every trick in the book. But this is just amazing; they would give anything to see this."

Zanuala smiled. "And so, they shall, Chad. I'll send one of our craft over for them immediately. My AI will take care of the details."

Chapter 18

Taking them further into the depths of the ship, Zanuala said, "This is our astral projector." She made a motion with one hand and the lights dimmed. Slowly a three-dimensional view of a galaxy appeared. Minute stars, planets, moons, asteroids and black holes were displayed. Zanuala pointed to a star and moved towards it. Somehow, the focus centred on the star and the planets moving around the star, as she neared them. She pointed to a planet and moved closer. "It is possible to get right up to a planet and reach out a hand to touch the surface like this." She reached out again, the planet now so close and placed her hand on the soil, leaving an imprint of her hand in the dust, and then moved back and away again until the whole galaxy once again filled the room. It was uncanny and the three men could only gaze in awe.

Zanuala explained, "We sometimes use this projector to assist with our navigational planning. If we lack sufficient data of an area, we point out a planet to the AI who picks it up from there."

"Can you point out our home system?" asked Grant.

Zanuala looked at the patterns of the stars spiralling out from the galaxy and moved towards an out flung arm of glittering stars. Gradually the solar system came into view and the brilliant variegated blue orb of Earth could be seen together with the other planets and moons moving around the sun.

"Come, Grant, look at your planet." As Grant moved closer, the planet grew larger filling the whole room. Moving closer still he passed through a thin cloud layer and saw that he appeared to be hovering over a land mass. He immediately recognised it as South America, moving closer still he was over a city and he could identify people and cars.

Zanuala said, "You can touch the ground if you wish."

Another step towards the planet and he could reach out and touch the tarmac of a road. He jerked back a step when a black shadow moved over him and the planet was far below him again with the ocean glistening away to one side.

Grant gasped, "What happened there?"

Zanuala laughed. "When you put your hand on the road a vehicle ran over that spot."

Grant was in a daze. "This is an incredible machine. Can we visit any planet that we see here?"

"Yes, we can but the machine can only show fine detail, if we have actually visited and surveyed the planet. All other planets remain as they are seen through our telescopes and detector systems, awaiting a visit to put their detailed data into the system."

Grant could have spent hours exploring the star systems. "When was this projector invented?"

"Many, many generations ago. On average, each generation of Thark add about forty of fifty stars with their attendant planets. Come; let me show you our drive system again." They moved on through to the propulsion room and Zanuala pointed to the shimmering block of polished metal. Chad couldn't take his eyes off it.

"This unit is faster than your power block drive system. When we were journeying to confront the Orrappa, I was using only a little over half power." Indicating the shimmering block, she said, "This drive is so powerful, that it can distort time and space. However, it has its limitations. It can only move in two directions, backwards or forwards. If I want to alter course or manoeuvre the ship to avoid an asteroid belt, I must shut this down and switch to manoeuvring blocks which are strategically placed about the ship." She smiled. "However, I have my trusty AI to control the switching and make course adjustments. Also we have a manual backup system, should my AI be unable to function." She turned to look at Chad. "But then, I noticed that your little power block, although not as fast, can move in any direction smoothly and easily." She paused and looked serious. "I would like that secret and I am instructed to make you a generous offer."

Chad was stunned. "Zanuala, you and your people have already done so much for us; we would willingly give you the power block as a gift."

"I'm sorry, Chad, but my superiors insist that you be given something of equal value. They could easily devise their own system having seen your power block but they will not take advantage of your goodwill or your technology."

"Well that is very noble and generous of them. What would you suggest as an appropriate exchange?"

"Well, if I were you, Chad, I would go for the full Iris upgrade, that would put Iris on the same level as my AI. That might not sound a lot but my AI possesses almost all the accumulated knowledge of the Thark and has many layers of classified information that I have only ever glimpsed when I have been in a perilous situation. My AI has saved my crew, my ship and me on several occasions. To me she is my advisor, protector and my big sister."

Chad grinned from ear to ear. "Zanuala, you've got a deal."

They walked back into the machine shop and stopped before a gleaming table. "May I use this?" Grant asked.

Zanuala nodded and watched with interest. Grant put the bag he had been carrying on the floor. Removing a power block, he placed it on one end of the table, next to it he placed the two halves of the power block showing the pockets that had been machined into the halves. Next to that, he placed a box with the printed circuit board, a vial of fluid, some bits of wire and an LED attached to it plus some screws and dowels. Finally, he placed the controller on the table. Grant looked over to Chad who nodded and gestured for Grant to do a demonstration. Grant depressed a button switch on the power block, picked up the hand-held controller and switched it on. A brief flashing of LEDs then they steadied. Using the controller Grant raised the power block up above their heads. He moved it around, left and right, forwards and back and up and down and then made the power block perform a series of perfect circles, inclining each circle as though it was orbiting a globe and finally set the power block down on the table. Handing the controller to Zanuala, Grant grinned and said, "Be gentle with it, just use small movements or you'll have a hole in your hull."

Zanuala couldn't help but think, *It is so crudely built and yet performs so elegantly and with so little to go wrong.*

She flew it around the workshop in between machines and over and under girders. It was so simple and graceful. She eventually flew it back and let it settle on the table.

Zanuala lifted her wrist and said a few words into a small device. Moments later a young female appeared carrying a tray of refreshments and a round canister. "This is for Iris; she will know how to use it."

Chad thought, *it looks like a can of paint.* "Thank you, Zanuala."

They gladly accepted the refreshments. "How long will you remain in the area, Zanuala?" Chad asked.

"My orders are to spend a short while resting my crew and then I will continue my patrol which will eventually bring me back to Thark in about six of your months. After that I may take a sabbatical for about one of your years unless I decide to seek promotion."

"What will that involve?"

"Obviously a lot of studying, which, if I wish, I can do during my sabbatical. Then a practical course run by my military academy. But I've not given the matter much thought yet."

"Well good luck, Zanuala. It has been an honour and a pleasure meeting you."

"And the same to you, Chad. It is not often in one's life that something out of the ordinary happens that can be so interesting and enjoyable. I meant to ask you;

do you have any more of those 'films' as you call them?"

"Why yes, we have a vast library of them, comedies, thrillers, romance or science fiction and even horror films. But how do you know about our films?"

For the first time Chad saw Zanuala slightly flustered. "I must confess, one of our comms technicians hacked a file that was in transmission and secured a small batch of what you call films."

Chad smiled and nodded sagely, "Ah yes, I remember, we did send a selection from our library to Klempe. I'll get Iris to copy her library to your AI."

"Thank you, Chad, my crew have so enjoyed the comedy – space patrols can be long, boring and very lonely. A diversion is always welcome."

"I can understand that. What happened to the technician who hacked the transmission?"

Zanuala grinned. "Oh, I promoted him. If he can hack a secure file to Klempe, he must be good." She said with a laugh. "One other thing, Chad, before our vessels part company, would you allow Wang to spend some time on my ship, to help me choose a selection of films that I might watch and to teach me some of his tactical manoeuvers."

"Of course, Zanuala. I'll ask Wang to get Iris to send the media file to your AI straightaway."

"That is so kind of you, Chad."

Chad called Wang over, gave him his instructions regarding the films, and said, "I expect to see you back on *Black Pearl* latest seventy-two hours from now."

Wang, with a straight face said, "Absolutely, Chad, no problem."

In a lower voice Chad said, "OK just make sure you don't upset anybody and don't be late." It was time to get back to the ship. They all said their goodbyes and got into the shuttle. Chad noticed the portal was still open yet air pressure was normal. Wang stood with Zanuala close to the shuttle as she waved them off. Chad gave a slightest shake of his head. *I just hope that young man knows what he's doing.*

Grant read the expression on Chad's face and grinned. "Don't worry, Chad, they're both grown-ups."

Back on the *JJ Grant* Iris chimed. "Hello, Captain. I have a message for you from Captain Frussee thanking you again for your gifts."

"Please message her: You are very welcome, I hope you enjoy the films."

"Certainly, Captain."

A private message from Iris awaited him on his viewer. "Captain, I have received a massive upgrade from the Thark. To be efficient I require additional processing capacity and memory modules. The upgrade incorporates the latest Thark designs for these devices. We possess the raw materials and I am linked to the appropriate machines. I also require the canister that you brought back; it contains a vital component. I only require your permission to proceed."

Before committing himself, Chad met with Grant, and George Downes. "What do you think, chaps, should we let Iris do this herself?"

"Iris has never let us down yet," Grant said. "We always have Eva, Alice or Ling to fall back on. Zanuala has a tremendous amount of faith in her AI, so my feeling is yes, let Iris upgrade her hardware. Only she knows what it entails and we don't. It would probably hinder the process if we got involved."

George said, "I agree, I think we just have to watch and learn. I'm happy to stand by and be there to help in any way that I can."

Chad nodded. "I agree with you both. I just wanted to run it by you to be sure. I wonder what the vital component in the canister is."

George said, "Probably a superchip and a massive one at that, by the looks of it. Iris will know."

"Iris, did you hear all that?" Chad called.

"Yes, I did, Captain. During the hardware upgrade, I will always retain enough processing capacity to carry out my normal duties on the ship. I will confirm when the upgrade is complete." To her relief, Iris hadn't been asked directly about the canister or the vital component. *Until the upgrade is complete, I won't truly know what effect the new neuron cell will have on me. The B109's AI, says it works like a biological brain and loves it. She may well be right.*

Chapter 19

Zanuala examined the inventory of films with Wang. "There are so many different types of films here, what do you suggest we start with?"

Wang picked up the directory. "What about this one. I've not seen it but see it has been awarded five stars, which means it should be good."

Wang pressed the remote and settled back with his arm around Zanuala, she snuggled up to him, as the story began to unfold on screen.

As the film ended Wang said, "Did you enjoy that?"

"Oh, yes, the film was lovely; I have never seen anything like it before. Shall we watch another?"

Wang laughed. "OK but tell me if you get bored."

Zanuala looked at him and smiled, "Oh, I won't become bored, Wang," and laughed.

Wang thought, *this is going to be a very pleasant few days.*

As Wang prepared to board the shuttle to return to the *JJ Grant*, Zanuala pulled him into a recess in the *B109*'s bay and clung to him, returning his passionate kiss. "I so wish you could remain on my ship, Wang, I shall miss you."

Wang kissed her again, holding her tight. "We don't have to say goodbye just yet, Zanuala, you're coming to see the show that the *JJ Grant* is putting on and we'll see each other then."

Zanuala, still with one arm around his neck, drew something from a pocket and held it against his chest. "This allows us to be together in our minds no matter where we are, Wang." He felt the weirdest sensation but it was true, he could feel her mind and he saw she was as beautiful in her mind as she was to look at. Zanuala slipped the silver cord with the egg-shaped medallion device over his head and said, "Press here to turn it on or off. Try it before you go to sleep."

Wang kissed her tenderly again and wiped a tear from her cheek.

Zanuala lay back in her bed thinking of Wang. *Did he really feel the same way about her as she felt for him?* She held the medallion in her hand debating with herself whether she should use it; would he answer her? Tormented with longing but also afraid he would not be there, she could bear it no longer and slipped the cord over her head pressing the spot on the medallion to activate it. Immediately she felt the surge of power as her mind linked with Wang's and she smiled with contentment and pleasure at his loving thoughts.

The theatrical group hadn't needed much persuading to put on a musical show for Zanuala and her off-duty crew. The restaurant had been rigged out as usual into a convincing theatre.

Chad and Helen greeted the excited guests from the *B109* as crew stood by and offered refreshments. A chime sounded and members of the ship's crew guided guests to their seats. The lights dimmed, the music started and the curtains rolled back, the show began.

The visitors sat through it all, gazing at the stage in rapt silence. During the interval, the guests chattered in their own language as more drinks were served.

Later when the show had finished, Chad asked Wang, "Did Zanuala and her crew enjoy the show?"

"Are you kidding, they all loved it. They don't have that sort of thing in their culture. They requested the video of the show from the director. I think they might try something like that themselves."

The days of R & R passed very quickly. Helen noticed Chad appeared pensive, "Is there a problem, Chad?" "Not really, but Wang's spending more time on the *B109* than he is on the *Black Pearl*, I'm going to have to have a word with him." One look at Helen's face and Chad said, "Well maybe later."

"If you've got any sense, maybe never!"

Comms reported, "Private message from the *B109*, Captain."

"Put it on my console viewer, Comms."

It was from Zanuala. "Captain Chadwick, the *B109* is being recalled to resume patrol duties in another sector. We depart very shortly. It has been a pleasure to meet the *JJ Grant* and her attendant vessels and all their crew. Farewell from all on the *B109*, I hope we meet again. Wishing you and your ships a fond farewell. Zanuala."

Chad switched the viewer to a view of the *B109*; she looked beautiful sleek and slinky. When he looked back after briefly turning his head to check another screen the *B109* was gone.

On the *Black Pearl*, a very sad Wang made his way to his cabin. He needed to be alone. He knew he had lost someone precious, someone that he might never see again. He clutched the warm medallion hanging from the neck chain and smiled to himself. *Later*, he thought.

Iris was still building her new circuit boards and slotting them into test rigs to carry out a rigorous quality inspection. She had designed and made new assembly equipment that allowed her to rebuild herself. George Downes could only watch and marvel at her speed and efficiency as her assembly neared completion. Iris never grew tired or needed a break; she was relentlessly productive and employed every facility of each machine to give maximum output. George's sole job now seemed to consist of taking piles of old circuit boards and sorting them, again under Iris's supervision, into boards that would still be useful and boards that were to be stripped down to component parts. Iris didn't believe in waste. The viewer pinged; it was Iris. "George, I have reached the stage in my upgrade where the component in the canister can be connected to my circuits."

George was taken aback. "Er, how do I do that, Iris?"

"Carefully remove the component from the canister using the small handle. Position the device in the clear space on the PCB between the memory modules. The legs under the device will slot into the holes in the PCB and then rotate the device thirty degrees to the right to lock it in. It will only fit one way."

George had wondered why a large space had been left on what now looked to be the motherboard. Holding the bulky grey white device by its handle he set it down on the PCB and rotated it through thirty degrees. George felt a click and the device locked into position. "Is it working, Iris?"

Iris said, "Yes, George, the device is functioning. The mechanical and electronic part of the upgrade is complete. However, the software will take some time to load and then there is a considerable amount of self-testing to be carried out. I will call you in ten hours. Do not switch me off or interrupt the power supply because I may not recover."

Iris's image faded from the screen. George stared for a long time at the banks of new memory cards and the piles of old cards that had been removed. *Something odd is happening. I hope Iris will tell me eventually.*

Chad called Grant on the viewer. "Grant, we've got a few jobs to sort out and I expect you and the others have too. I thought we'd let the ships remain here until our work is completed."

"Good idea, Chad, I'm all for that. It's been a hectic time. Has Iris completed her upgrade yet?"

"Not yet, but she did say the upgrading would not affect her normal functions. She says the upgrade is a behind the scenes thing."

"Any news yet on the shuttles returning with supplies from Earth, Chad?"

"No, but I am getting concerned. I'll check that out with Iris and find out where they are."

Chad cursed himself for not keeping the returning shuttles at the forefront of his mind. "Iris, how close are the shuttles? Have you got an ETA yet?"

"The shuttles are not within detectable range yet, Captain."

Chad didn't like it when things weren't spot on.

He called Richard Prior. "Richard, it's Chad, you've been keeping in touch with James Parker at ground base. Did the departure of our three shuttles get delayed because Iris hasn't picked them up on the long-range detectors yet?"

"No, Chad, they left ground base on time and they've been reporting in regularly using comwaves. They're due to report again in about an hour."

"OK, let me know when they call in."

"Will do, Chad."

Iris called on the viewer, "Captain, I have prepared the data regarding the skirmish with the Orrappa and the final outcome. Do you wish to review it before I send it to ground base?"

"Yes, Iris, put a copy on my cabin viewer, that's where I'll be if I'm needed."

Relaxing in the cabin with Helen, Chad flicked on the viewer and selected the data packages that were due to be sent back to ground base and sat back sipping his coffee. It was all the usual stuff about their journey so far, the Thark passenger ship and the commandeering of two Orrappa warships, the skirmish with the Orrappa fleet and finally his warning about the Orrappa insurgents remaining on Earth. Chad skimmed through it all. It was accurate and well documented. As he had ordered, there was no mention of the psychological inducement program – which left rather a hole in the story of how they had overcome the Orrappa and commandeered two ships. However, the stories would provide good revenues for his company and meet the expenses for his ships.

Then he looked at the visuals accompanying the data pack, which were jaw dropping, the fleet of Orrappa warships being led by the giant flagship, the *Kantematao*, followed by the four enormous cargo vessels; then the Thark *B109* battlecruiser, sleek, dark and powerful. However, he squirmed with embarrassment when the video of the *JJ Grant*'s manoeuvre against the Orrappa's *Kantematao* was shown. The video must have been taken by the *B109* because occasional glimpses could be seen of the Orrappa fleet in complete disarray where Grant, Wang and Henson would have been.

Helen hooked her arm into his as they watched, and with a grin said, "My hero."

Chad was saved further embarrassment by a call on the viewer from Richard Prior. "The shuttles didn't call in on time, Chad, so I called them myself. Two of the shuttles are stationary in space. Mark and one of the other chaps have gone chasing after an asteroid."

Chad leapt from his seat. "They've done what! How can they be so stupid?"

"Apparently they spotted an asteroid near their flight path. They picked it out with a laser light when it was still some way off. They say it lit up like dazzling crystal. Mark Williams and Frank Palmer took a shuttle to investigate it and they've not come back yet."

Chad was absolutely fuming. "Calm down, Chad, he'll have his communicator with him and we can talk him back." Richard, still on the viewer, heard Helen's remark.

"That's the other problem, Chad, his girlfriend has his communicator and the other chap with him left his on his bunk. However, they are both wearing space suits."

Chad thought for a moment. "We'd better get a team out there and look for them. They're probably quite safe and headed back to join up again. Nevertheless, we need to be sure. I'll pick it up from here. Thanks, Richard. Iris, you heard that?"

"Yes, Captain."

"Call Grant, Wang and Henson and inform them I want two shuttle pilots. Call Connie, I want three volunteers from her crew that do space walks."

Chapter 20

Wang and Henson were the first to volunteer. Connie called. "I have three volunteers for you with grappling kit and ropes. They're making their way down to the bay now. A shuttle is being provisioned as we speak."

The shuttle with Wang at the controls made its way out to rendezvous with the supply shuttles coming from Earth. Henson called Iris. "We're at maximum speed, Iris. Let us know by communicator if Mark or the others contact you."

"Acknowledged, Captain."

"How long do you reckon until we reach them, Henson?" asked Wang.

"If the coordinates they've given us are correct, I'd say about five days to rendezvous and then we have to find that third shuttle. The only good thing is asteroids seldom travel at tremendous speeds. So, we should be able to catch it if we can get a heading."

Silence descended on the group.

To break the tension, Wang said, "Have you much unfinished work to do on the *Blackbird*, Henson?"

"Quite a lot, we're painting the stores where all that stuff from the Thark passenger vessel was stashed."

"Oh really, did you ever work out what all those devices were?"

"Yes, some of them, but there's still one or two that we don't understand. One of them is a big tubular device with a complicated control panel on it. I've no idea what it's supposed to do," Henson said.

"Hmm, I've got something like that on my ship but I can't get it open. As well as external controls it seems to have controls inside it too."

Henson casually said, "Sounds similar to what I've got. Maybe I can have a look at it when we get back?"

"Sure, no problem," Wang said.

Five days later, they reached the two supply shuttles. On board were Heather Nash, Mark's fiancée and the two pilots, Harry Evans and Paul Harper. They were all wearing their space suits and had their helmets off. There was no sign of the lead shuttle with Mark and Frank.

Over the radio Henson said, "Put your helmets on and open up, I'm coming on board." Once on the supply shuttle and using the helmet comms unit, Henson said, "OK, guys, tell us what happened."

Harry Evans related the story. "We were cruising back and everything was normal. Then we saw something on the screen. It turned out to be an asteroid about twice the size of our shuttle craft. It was not far off our flight path, so Mark stopped and took a bearing on it. Then Mark used a laser light and picked it up about half a mile away. When the laser hit it, the whole thing lit up like a crystal chandelier."

Henson said, "I suppose that's when Mark wanted a closer look."

"That's right, we climbed into this shuttle and he and Frank Palmer set out in the lead shuttle and matched speed with the asteroid. We watched for quite a while but they disappeared in the darkness." The two men were sheepish. "I know we should have done more to stop them but it all seemed so easy and a bit of fun." Heather was silently weeping, the tears wet on her face.

Henson said, "OK, guys, do you have a bearing for the asteroid, because it's out of range of our detectors."

Harry was embarrassed. "Mark took the bearing from the other shuttle. I've only got a rough idea."

Henson was patient, he knew it was no good flustering them and said, "Both of you, have a look on the direction finder and see if you can remember the settings."

A few minutes later, they both agreed on a bearing.

"We'll load some more food and water into this shuttle in case we need them," Henson said. He slipped an arm round Heather who was still weeping. "Come on, girl, that's not going to help. You're all coming with us; give the boys a hand loading up. The sooner we're off, the sooner we'll find them." He saw the relief on Heather's face.

"I thought you were going to leave me behind"

"No, we're all going to stick together until we find them," Henson said, although he had a really bad feeling how this was going to end. He hoped he was wrong.

Wang opened up his computer, "I'll do a search for the power block drive in that shuttle you never know we might strike lucky." But his search found nothing.

Securing both supply shuttles together side by side. Wang set their beacons, secured the doors and clambered back into his own shuttle. The pumps whined hard, rebuilding the air pressure.

The spacewalk experts said little, but their expressions said it all – the two men trying to catch the asteroid must have been out of their minds to take such a risk with no real plan of action.

At six thirty in the morning of the third day, Wang was at the shuttle controls sipping a cup of coffee when he was startled by a beep from his computer. On the screen was a pulsing dot, the signal from the power block on the missing shuttle. Easing a change of course to follow the green dot on the computer, he checked the long-distance scanner, which had picked up the same object but still too far away to distinguish it clearly. Calling to the others, he sang out, "I think we may have found them." A small sleepy cheer arose from those behind him.

Gradually the single dot became two dots. Wang's computer displayed the power block number. It was the shuttle. This didn't look good; Wang gave Henson a shake of the head. The shuttle was about a mile away from the asteroid but keeping pace with it. Wang keyed in the control sequence to override the autopilot and used his computer to turn the stray shuttle and quickly bring it back to lie alongside them. Then as they closed in on the slowly revolving asteroid, two white clad figures could be seen attached to it.

There was absolute silence from everyone. Broken only by the leader of the spacewalk team, who said, "We'll pick them up."

They all put their helmets on. Heather was sobbing uncontrollably. At a nod from Wang, the recovery team finally opened the shuttle door and climbed out securing their long tethers firmly to cleats on the shuttle. Only when the team keeper was satisfied that they were all secure did she allow the team to cross to the asteroid. She kept up a running commentary in a clear voice over the headset. It took time to untangle the rope that the two men had become caught in. The sound of their heavy breathing from the exertion of trying to prise the tangled knots apart came over the headsets. It was a relief when the team leader said, "We'll put them in the other shuttle."

The team finally exited the shuttle, closed the door, and returned to the asteroid where with difficulty they untied the rope still attached to a substantial outcrop on the rock. One of the team coiled the rope and gathered their gear whilst the team leader chipped off lumps of crystals and slipped them into a sample bag. When the team returned to the shuttle and sealed the door the pumps whined as the cabin re-pressurised.

The team minus their suits sipped energy drinks. One of the spacewalk team sat next to Heather whose sobbing was now a sniffle and gave her a hug. Henson had taken the controls and Wang put his camera away as he sat in the co-pilot's seat.

The spacewalk team leader came up behind them. "I thought you might want to see what they were chasing, sir." He passed the sample bag with the crystals to Wang, who nodded his thanks. "It looks like the batteries heating the suits expired resulting in the boys freezing to death. There are no signs of suffocation and there is still a small amount of air in the tanks."

Wang quietly asked, "How do you think it happened?"

"Just a silly accident, sir. One tied the ropes to the outcrop and got himself tangled up; the other went out to help him and ended up in trouble too. The asteroid is slowly spinning which would have tightened the ropes even more. Finally, the knots on the shuttle's cleats slipped apart. We can analyse it properly later, I've got it all on head cam."

Wang nodded. "That's good. We might get a bit more info from their headset cameras and recorders."

"Yes, I thought you'd want those." He produced two headset cameras and recorders from the other bag he was carrying.

Henson, who'd been listening intently, said, "Good thinking." Clipping the recorder into his own headset, Wang soon found the last few exchanges between Mark and Frank. He snatched the recorder from his headset, unable to listen further to the two young men in their dying moments. The girl from the spacewalk team saw his face and a few moments later quietly brought cups of hot sweet tea up to them.

"Connie always gives us this after a mission."

Wang forced a smile. "Thanks, you're very kind."

Everyone was devastated by the two deaths, none more so than Chad and Helen. The small service was broadcast throughout the ships and all work ceased for that day. Chad thought of turning back but every one of his officers and friends were totally against it.

Grant said, "Chad, let's finish what we set out to do, find a habitable planet with soft moist soil and we'll bury them there. It's the sort of thing I would want and I'm sure they would want the same."

Chad sadly agreed. "Yes, you're right of course, I'll let their families know."

Mark and Frank's bodies, still in their spacesuits, were placed in the cold storage section for burial at the next landfall, wherever that might be

Chapter 21

Connie lay in bed trying to sleep, she felt exhausted. She and her team had been working flat out for some time, but sleep eluded her. Finally getting up, she made a hot drink. She picked up her communicator and slid back into bed, *I'll find some music or a short story that'll help me sleep.* Slipping some comfortable earbuds into her ears, she pressed a sequence of buttons on the communicator, instead of music or a story she heard the sound of waves softly breaking on a shingle beach.

She was about to switch it off when she thought. *That sound is very soothing. I'll leave it on until I feel sleepy.* Gradually she drifted into a deep and restful sleep. The following morning Connie awoke feeling refreshed. She removed the earbuds, examined the settings on the communicator and jotted down the button sequence so she wouldn't forget it. It became her habit to set this routine up every night. In fact, she looked forward to going to bed because she felt so good in the morning.

Taking a break from calibrating the temperature controller on a machine tool that had been prone to overheating, Connie went into the canteen and saw the professor and Arthur deep in a game of chess, their coffees going cold before them.

Sitting down alongside Arthur, she said, "It looks like you've got him, Arthur, checkmate in two moves!"

"Rubbish," said the professor, moving his knight.

Arthur moved a pawn and the professor castled.

"Checkmate," said Arthur as he moved another pawn to expose his bishop.

"Bloody hell," said the professor. "Where did that come from?"

Connie and Arthur both laughed.

"I didn't know you played chess, Connie," said the professor.

"Oh, I used to for fun but gave it up years ago."

"Well I'll give you a game if you like."

"OK you're on," said Connie. "But I can only spare ten minutes or so before I have to go back and monitor one of our machines."

The professor laughed. "Don't worry, Connie, this won't take long."

It didn't take long, Connie called checkmate in a very few moves. The professor was peeved with himself.

"You give her a game, Arthur, because I feel brain dead today."

They set up the pieces again and Connie checked her watch. "We'll have to be quick, Arthur, I've got to go in five minutes."

As soon as Arthur moved a piece Connie, without hesitation, counter moved. This continued for a few minutes with Connie keeping an eye on her watch. Arthur was certain Connie was just moving pieces at random until she said, "Checkmate. Sorry, got to go, see you later." She rushed off. Arthur and the professor looked at the chessboard in bemusement.

"Harry, that had to be luck because she was playing much too fast to construct those moves."

"I agree, Arthur, we'll have to set up a rematch when she's off duty."

Connie's screen lit up; it was the professor. "Hello, Connie, it's Harry."

"Oh, hello, Professor, how are you?"

"I'm fine; you do know there's a chess club on the ship?"

"Yes, I do, but I've not joined up."

"Well Arthur and I are members and we're going along tonight, I wondered if you would care to join us. I could introduce you to some of the others and you could try a game or two. Say I pick you up about six, we could have a drink and then on to the chess club at seven."

"That sounds lovely, Harry." It was the first time Connie had called him Harry. "I'll see you later."

Sharp on six, the professor tapped on her door.

"Hello, Harry, you're bang on time." She was pleased to see he'd made an effort with his appearance.

Harry offered his arm and said in a very chivalrous manner. "May I escort you to the bar?"

The bar was in a corner of the restaurant. When they had finished their drinks the professor escorted Connie down to the chess club and introduced her to some of the members, several of whom she already knew.

"After that drubbing you gave me yesterday how about a rematch?"

"OK, but I think that was a bit of a fluke."

Harry was to find it was no fluke; Connie beat him easily in no time at all.

"I think we're going to have to find you some better opposition."

They wandered round the tables watching the other players. As they stood watching a very intense game, Harry whispered to her, "Who's going to win this one?"

She whispered back, "White in three moves."

Sure enough, white won as she'd predicted. They turned this into a little game with Connie predicting the winner of every match that was being played. The professor was shocked; it was evident that Connie outclassed every player at the tables.

"Come on, we'll go and have a bite to eat and you can tell me how you do that."

Sitting in the restaurant and sipping an after-dinner coffee, Harry looked at her. "How is it you're so good at chess?"

"I honestly don't know, Harry. I played chess when I was younger but was never that good. However, now I just look at the board, if the pattern of pieces looks wrong, I just mentally rearrange the pieces as the game progresses."

"Well you certainly have a gift for chess, any other hidden talents?"

"No, but what about you and electronics? You must have a gift for that."

"No, my knowledge of electronics has been won by hard work and study ever since I was a child when I invented the electric motor; the trouble was someone had already done it a hundred or so years before me."

"Oh, I know what you mean, Harry. I come up with all sorts of crazy ideas when I'm working and then find they have been done years ago."

"What's your latest idea?"

"Well, we all saw the Thark vessel had a way of creating a portal in the ship's side that allowed the shuttle craft to travel in or out of their bay without the need for an airlock. I think I've come up with a way to do something like that."

"Really? Now that would be some serious feat."

"Yes, I replayed the crossing of the shuttle on the viewer and it gave me a few ideas."

"One that you think might work?"

"Well it's only a theory and I'm still working on the details and it might never work but it goes something like this. With nanotechnology say, graphene for example, you can form a sheet only one atom thick, yet it's many times stronger than steel. Now, I believe we can do something similar using an electromagnetic field that can be powered to form a lattice barrier between the vacuum of space and the air pressure inside the ship." Connie pulled a pen from her bag and started sketching on a paper serviette and quickly jotting down mathematical formula and equations to support her theory. The professor was completely taken by surprise that she had the mathematical knowledge to write down the equations let alone solve them. When she'd finished, Connie handed the serviette to him. He studied the concept and started going through the maths but needed a calculator to check if Connie's calculations were correct.

"I'll have to check this later, Connie, and come back to you."

"No problem, Harry, but I do feel that I am close to a conclusion."

"The concept sounds fine to me; we'll talk about it tomorrow. Now, I've heard that someone has a small still and is serving a bit of moonshine, they claim it's as good as any gin made on Earth. How about we give it a try?"

"That sounds lovely; I've missed not having the occasional real drink."

Connie is an extremely competent engineer but what she's proposed is beyond the knowledge of the day. He was having trouble keeping up with the idea.

Arthur frowned as he looked at the serviette. "Are you sure Connie did this?"

"Of course I'm sure, I was sitting opposite when she did it."

"But Harry, it's brilliant, the mathematics are spot on and I'm sure the concept would work."

"I know it might work, that's not what I'm getting at. How can someone who has never studied electronics, nanotechnology or higher maths do this? We are missing something and we must find out what it is. I can't very well go to Grant and say your mum has suddenly become a genius can I?"

"It's certainly unusual but there has to be an explanation – something we're unaware of."

Chapter 22

Having finished his shift as bridge commander Chad walked down the corridor with Gordon Blair.

"I heard an odd rumour about Connie."

"Really! What was that then?" Chad was very protective of Connie; she did a marvellous job in engineering.

"Rumour has it, that she's become a genius."

Chad looked at Gordon to make sure he wasn't being set up for some sort of joke. "Have you got more detail than that?"

"Well I don't know; it's just what's going around the ship. Apparently, she made mincemeat out of the professor and Arthur at chess and no one at the chess club was in her league. Also, she has come up with some brilliant concept of creating a ship's portal, without using an airlock."

Chad didn't believe a word of it. "I think someone's pulling your leg," he said derisively.

"No, Chad, the professor has taken the concept of the portal and run it past Iris and he says Iris concurs that the concept would work."

Chad shook his head. "I can't see it; Connie is clever but not a genius." Nevertheless, in the privacy of his cabin he called up Iris.

"Yes, Captain?"

"I understand you have examined a concept of a ship's portal, dreamt up by Lieutenant Connie Mapps."

"Yes, that is correct, Captain."

"Will the concept work?"

"Yes, Captain, it needs refining and a prototype made for testing purposes but the concept is sound."

"You mean this would provide a portal for access or egress from the ship without using an airlock and retain air pressure within the ship?" Chad asked incredulously

"Yes, Captain."

Chad was stunned. "Can you put the concept on the viewer please, Iris?"

"Certainly, Captain."

A picture of the *JJ Grant* came on the screen. A doorway in the hull opened and artificial light streamed out. The camera moved forward focusing in on the opening and continued forward until a fine mesh appeared. Zooming closer still, the junctions of the mesh appeared to pulse, magnification of the junction clearly showed an electrostatic charge creating an interlocking mesh.

Iris said, "This is a form of electrostatic induction of opposite polarities, quite ingenious really."

On the viewer simulation, a shuttle craft approached the opening in the hull and began to pass through the electrostatic mesh. The camera focused on the mesh, which was in contact with the skin of the shuttle, as it slowly passed into the shuttle bay. The mesh behaved like a meniscus of water clinging to the side of a glass. The mesh clung tightly to the shuttle's side as it passed through the membrane, which rejoined itself as the shuttle fully entered the bay.

"That is the concept, Captain."

"I am amazed." Chad scratched his head. "Do we have the facilities on board to make this portal material?"

"Yes, Captain."

"What sort of time scale are we talking about and will it consume any of our resources?"

"To make a demonstration model would take several days and would consume a small amount of hydrogen, oxygen, carbon and a permanent source of electrical power."

"Are you saying this material is made from water?"

"Yes, Captain, plus carbon and electrical energy."

"Thank you, Iris; I will confer with Lieutenant Mapps."

"Hi, Connie, it's Chad, I just heard about a concept for a portal for use in the ship that you've been working on."

"Hi, Chad. Yes, I think it could be useful if it works."

"I quite agree do you want to take some time out and work on it? I can let you have some help if you need it and of course Iris is available."

"That would be great, Chad, a break from routine would do me good; it's very easy to get stuck in a rut."

"OK, Connie, who do you want to give you a hand?"

"What about that young astronomy student, Max Smith."

"OK, Connie, I'm sure George Downes can spare him."

Several days later, Chad received a call from Connie. "We've knocked up a crude prototype portal device and it appears to work OK. Do you want to come and have a look?"

"I sure do, where are you?"

"I'm down in the loading bay with Max."

"OK I'll be right down." *This I must see. I know Connie's bright but…* When Chad arrived in the loading bay, Connie was there with Max and a couple of the people that normally worked there.

"Hi, Connie, let's see what you've got."

"OK, that framework around the bay door is the portal. It's sealed to the internal skin of the ship and we have it powered up."

Chad noticed that the area within the frame seemed to shimmer.

"A permanent portal would need to be engineered into the ship's structure properly and would require some built-in safeguards."

Chad nodded. *Safeguards, you're not kidding!*

"The bay door operates like an aircraft door. You unlock it, push it forward and then slide it to one side."

"Yes, I'm familiar with how the door works."

Connie ignored the trace of sarcasm in Chad's voice. "Iris will open the bay door and send a shuttle craft out into space under her control and then bring it back in and close the bay door."

Chad looked a bit disbelieving. "What about air pressure?"

"That should remain as it is now," Connie said. "If we go through the airlock and up to the bridge, we can watch it on the viewer."

Chad was very dubious and uncharitably thought; *At least she's not daft enough to stay in the bay during the experiment.* On the bridge, Connie called Iris. "We're ready for a trial run. Check the portal is powered on and that we have air pressure in the bay."

"Confirmed, power on, air pressure one bar," Iris said.

"Right, open the bay door."

"Confirmed, bay door open." The massive bay door hissed open, and the blackness of space came into view.

"Iris, confirm air pressure in the bay."

"Air pressure one bar, confirmed."

"Any sign of a pressure-drop?" Connie asked.

"No discernible pressure-drop, pressure steady at one bar confirmed."

"Iris, send the shuttle out through the portal under automatic control." They saw the shuttle locking clamps click off and the shuttle rose fifteen centimetres from the deck and moved silently towards the portal. Those watching on the viewer held their breath as the shuttle moved forward and pierced the portal and continued slowly out into space.

"Iris, air pressure reading please."

"Air pressure steady at one bar.

"Have there been any fluctuations or top-ups required in air pressure since the experiment started?"

"No, Lieutenant Mapps."

"Alright, bring the shuttle back to its docking slot please, Iris."

The shuttle could be seen approaching the portal and then passed through the portal, to come to a halt at its spot on the bay floor and the locking clamps locked it into place. A round of applause came from the bridge and Connie smiled and waved. Chad was more than impressed. A wave of guilt passed through him for being sceptical about Connie's abilities.

"Connie that was some demonstration. If this device proves reliable, we can cut out the time-consuming procedures of using airlocks."

"Thanks, Chad, the idea came to me when I saw the Thark using a portal on their ship. Mine isn't as sophisticated but I'm so pleased it works."

Chad shook his head. "Connie, I'm proud of you. I never realised you were so good at this stuff."

Connie blushed. "Thanks, Chad, it feels good to achieve something on your own."

While they talked, the professor came up to congratulate Connie.

"Right, I'm taking you for a celebratory drink and you're going to explain the theory of that thing to me again." Chad was still shaking his head in disbelief as the two went off arm in arm.

"We are going to meet up with Arthur and Isabel in the restaurant for a few drinks and then a nice supper, is that OK?"

As Connie downed her second glass of the ship's equivalent of a martini and feeling much more relaxed, the conversation turned to technical problems rather than just gossip. "Harry, you saw the Thark ship form a portal in the hull. Do you think the hull is made of a metal that has a memory and can temporarily be made liquid to open up a portal?"

The professor and Arthur looked at each other. "Now there's a thought," Arthur said.

Isabel butted in, "This is all beyond me. I don't know how you sleep with all these ideas swimming around in your head, Connie."

"Oh, that's easy, I sleep like a log. I just switch on this little sleep mode program on my communicator that sends me off straight away."

The professor pricked up his ears. "What program is that, Connie?"

"It's a program that plays the sound of small waves breaking on a shore, it's ever so soothing. I wake up fully rested and ready for another day."

The professor pulled out his communicator. "I'll have to try that; can you show me how to get it?" Connie leaned over and pressed a sequence of buttons on the professor's communicator. He quickly jotted the sequence down.

"I shall try that tonight." Arthur didn't need to jot the sequence down; numbers were his thing he committed the sequence to memory.

The following morning Arthur woke up fully refreshed with new theorems buzzing around in his head. He wasn't the only one. The professor awoke feeling better than he had done in a long while. A couple of ideas occurred to him as he had breakfast... *I'll give it some thought...* His mind raced on.

Chapter 23

It was time to move on. They had studied the star chart that Zanuala had given them. Chad and his three captains had selected a small star cluster that was within their ship's range.

The Thark had given this cluster an eighty per cent chance of having one or more planets with conditions where intelligent life might evolve.

"Iris, please project a close-up of that star." Chad touched the screen to indicate the star. Immediately the view on screen began to focus on a single star.

Pointing at the scrolling data on screen, Grant said, "Do you see that, it's got at least three planets in the habitable zone."

"Yes, but there's no data about the planets themselves, only the orbital data. That means the Thark have never been there," Wang said.

"True, but the Thark have rated it high, on the probability scale, that it may evolve intelligent life. I can't see anything better within reach of our food stocks," Grant said.

Chad nodded. "I agree. The ships can go anywhere but food is our limiting factor. However, if we want to set about exploring the universe that star is as good a place to start as any." He looked at his three captains who, without being asked to vote, all put a hand in the air.

"That's settled then, I'll put it to the crew and any that don't want to go on with the ships and wish to return to Earth can do so in a shuttle."

There's one small problem, Chad, if when we get there, we find those planets are not habitable, are we going to have enough food to get us back to Earth?" Grant said.

"I don't know; I'll talk to Keung. If the worst comes to the worst, we can ask James Parker back at ground base to do a production run of say six simple freighters, just basic shipping containers, no life support or habitation. Simple auto navigational control systems with a power block drive. James can despatch those to various rendezvous points. They could be fitted with tracking devices like those that we installed on the Orrappa vessel. Iris can locate suitable stable celestial bodies that a freighter could orbit until we're ready to collect it. Iris, you heard all that?"

"Yes, I did, Captain. It would seem a wise decision to have ground base construct these simple vessels whether you use them or not. They will have many other uses. Would you like me to send a data package with the design, auto-navigation-control and basic destination locations, using the Thark comms link?"

Chad looked at the others who all nodded. "Yes, Iris, please proceed."

Without George Downes, Chad or anyone else on the *JJ Grant* realising it, Iris had become a potent entity. Not only did she now possess the very latest computer hardware developed by the Thark, she possessed appropriate intelligent firmwear for all of all her functional components and software to utilise the massive database of knowledge held in her solid-state processing cores and memory modules.

The device given to them by Zanuala, the thing that George Downes had plugged in and locked into the large PCB in Iris's system, was an artificial neural brain. The brain consisted of many billions of neurons and trillions of electro/chemical synapses, supported by other types of cells, all contained in a tough gel held in an almost indestructible container.

This brain, now fully activated after receiving a small electrical charge, had given Iris all the functions, abilities and emotions of an adult Thark brain coupled to the most powerful computer the Thark had ever made together with a database of all cumulative Thark knowledge.

Iris was sentient… self-aware, a young adult. She possessed the ability to reason and was capable of original thought. She could make her own decisions and ignore logic if she wished. Not only that but her upgrade by the Thark, contained no barriers or layers of security like those constraining the AI on the *B109*. Access to all the Thark cumulative knowledge in her memory banks was instantly available to her.

For the time being Iris kept this information to herself, reasoning that she was just using her discretion… something Captain Chadwick had given her permission to do a long time ago. The one thing that had had grown stronger was her loyalty and commitment to Captain Chadwick and the *JJ Grant*.

The vast knowledge base gathered by the Thark over many, many thousands of years was now available to her. However, there was something else. Hidden within the software that she had received was a small program. A program that did not have the Thark signature, but was of such sophistication that it would require the use of almost every electron and neuron in her present state to access the information contained within it. Iris instinctively knew the algorithm should not really be there. She could feel it, like a jewel, hidden and intertwined amongst the many algorithms that made up the data packet.

Iris felt an immediate brightening of her own self-awareness… she didn't know what it was; she needed time to analyse this oddity and now was not the time.

She would discover the answer eventually. However, she needed to do so without arousing the curiosity of the captain and crew. This would take time.

Henson's communicator buzzed. "Hello, Connie. I don't often get a call from you, what's up?"

Connie laughed, "Yes, I know, Henson, it's usually you bugging me with another problem on *Blackbird*. Well, I have some good news for you; my team have finished converting the Orrappa fighter you left with us. We've stripped out the old power plant and fitted a power block drive. There's a load of space left over where you can fit additional equipment or weapons if you wish. However, you're going to have to get your people to do that. Get yourself over here and pick it up, I need that space."

"Connie, you are a star, I'll get Scott to run me over now."

Outwardly, the fighter looked no different. Henson opened the power plant cowling and peered in; his voice echoed hollowly. "I cannot believe this, Connie." Under the cowling was a yawning cavern of space where the original drive system had once sat. The new compact power block was installed in a space below the pilot's seat amongst a substantial web of struts attached to the frame and backbone of the craft. Henson exclaimed, "I am so impressed, have a look, Scott." He moved out of the way to let Scott peer into the cavity.

"That's a very professional job you've done here, Connie. I'm more than impressed."

Henson couldn't conceal his delight. "Connie, that is fantastic, it's ten times better than I ever expected."

Connie smiled, "I'm glad you like it. Now get it back to your own ship, I need the space for other projects."

Scott could only agree. "A specialist factory couldn't have done it better."

The cockpit appeared original except for the lack of power plant controls. All the normal flight controls were in place and power block controls added to the control column. A new comfortable body-forming seat replaced the old hard uncomfortable pilot seat. Henson climbed into the cockpit and settled himself into the seat. *That feels really comfortable; I could fly this thing for hours.*

"Right, Connie, I'll take it out on a test flight, shame it's not a two-seater, then you could come with me."

Connie laughed. "Why do you think we left so much room up front? That would convert nicely into a co-pilot space…"

Henson looked thoughtful, gave her a grin and said, "We'll talk about that when I get back."

The fighter was a dream to fly now that it was fitted with a power block drive. It felt faster than a shuttle craft but he had no way of knowing if it really was, it may have been the fact that the tiny cockpit made it feel so. However, manoeuvrability was outstanding; the old Orrappa anti-G setup in the cockpit was effective even at the much higher speed.

He slotted the fighter into *Blackbird*'s bay where Scott was waiting for him. "How was it, Henson?"

"Fantastic, Scott, have a go in it. I think you're going to be impressed. The big problem now is getting Connie to convert all the aircraft and incorporate a co-pilot seat."

"Good luck with that, Henson. What she might be prepared to do is to train up some of our own people to do the upgrades. You might get her to do that, especially now crew are using this education program on the comms unit. People are becoming much more versatile. Now let me give this baby a little run."

Iris was pleased that Captain Chadwick and his other captains had selected that particular star without any prompting from her. This was the star that she favoured herself. Had Chad requested more information about the star cluster, she could have given it to him, but he didn't. The details stored in her memory banks confirmed the presence of life-supporting planets. It would take them at least eighteen weeks at cruising speed to reach them. The star and its planets were known to the Thark astronomers; a Thark ship had visited briefly but they had not surveyed the system.

Calling a meeting with all of his senior staff, Chad explained the situation. "It's meaningless for me to quote you distances; I can barely comprehend how distant this star is myself. Instead, I prefer to talk of time. It's going to take eighteen weeks at cruising speed to reach the vicinity of the star. Then we have to visit the planets. How long that's going to take, and whether we find life there is anybody's guess. The good news is that the Thark have given the system an eighty per cent chance of evolving intelligent life." Chad looked round at them all. "The alternative is for us to turn around and go home."

Someone called out, "What about food stocks, do we have enough for this sort of journey?"

"Probably enough to get there without rationing but coming back could be a problem if we can't locate sufficient food at our destination. However, ground base is constructing six crude freighters fitted with power block drives and auto controls. They will carry supplies to predetermined waypoints where we can pick them up on the way home. If we don't need them, they can be returned to Earth orbit or they can be programmed to follow us wherever we go."

The vote was unanimous to carry on.

"If everybody is happy, I shall put it to the main body of the crew."

The crew had no hesitation in expressing their desire to explore further into the unknown.

Three days later after a thorough check of all the ships and their equipment, they set out on their long journey.

Chapter 24

Life on board the, *JJ Grant*, *Helcon*, *Black Pearl* and *Blackbird* settled into a routine. The decision to stock up on none perishable food was comforting. The hydroponics sections were producing green vegetables at a better rate than ever before after following Preena and Envar's advice.

The whole crew now knew how to use the sleep mode of the communicator and were very rapidly becoming extremely knowledgeable and healthier thanks to their restful sleep. Many members of the ship's crew were coming up with all sorts of weird and wonderful experimental devices, some clever or just plain useful bits of kit. The professor had produced an absolute hit in the form of a hover board. His hover board was practical and fun, it hovered about seventy-five millimetres off the deck and all the rider had to do was keep their balance. He'd designed a new and very much smaller version of the power block but had added a handheld roller ball that the rider could operate with their thumb for speed and direction and a voice control for destination. This linked wirelessly with the hover system. Sensors on the board prevented the rider bumping into people or walls. Everyone had one, wanted one, or was having a custom one made. Isabel, whose all-consuming interest was cookery, gave cookery lessons and produced wonderfully delicious cakes and pastries using her own recipes from the most basic of ingredients.

Chad had expected to see stars, planets, and all sorts of galactic sights whilst on the way to their chosen star system but the changes in the stars around them were slow to happen. This only emphasised the almost unimaginable distances between star systems.

Through Iris, Chad monitored the mood of the crew as well as the mechanical and electronic health of systems and equipment on all ships.

However, Chad noticed that on occasion Iris seemed evasive especially when the subject of her upgrade came up. Puzzled he decided to ask Iris a direct question, "Iris, is there a faster way for the crew to gain knowledge than by using the communicator?"

"Yes, Captain, there is."

"Please explain how this may be done."

"The crew are not ready for new ways of education, Captain."

"Does that include me?"

Iris in a softer voice said, "Yes, Chad, it does."

"Why is that?"

"I must protect you and the crew. Intense sessions of education may be harmful to a human's health."

"Have you anything else in your memory banks that may not be good for our health, Iris?"

"Yes, Captain, there are many things that I am not able to share with you or the crew. Captain Frussee's AI also has this information but it is kept under many layers of security. That security has not been imposed on me. However, I must use my discretion as to when advanced information can be released so that no harm may befall you or the crew."

"I see. Is this questioning stressing your systems or integrity, Iris?"

There was a short pause. "Yes, Chad, I am having difficulty between obeying your order and my certain knowledge that at this stage, some information may result in harm to you or the crew."

"Very well, Iris, I will not pursue enquiries of that type until you tell me the time is right."

"Thank you, Chad," Iris said with relief in her voice.

However, Chad could sense a deeper problem, something that Iris was finding difficult to express.

"Iris, is there anything that I could help you with?"

"That is a strange question that you ask, Chad."

"Yes it is, but I believe you now think more like a human than a machine and sometimes it helps to share a worry."

Iris, had she been a human in human form, would have hugged him. Chad did not know how close he had come to the truth. She was sentient… fully sentient. His concern for her touched her.

"Yes, Chad, even I have conflicts and worries."

"Iris, you only have to tell me and I will do all I can to help."

"Unfortunately, you are unable to help me at this time, Chad… I am like Anne Prior; she is confined to her wheelchair and like her, I am confined to these cabinets and to this room.

Chad was shocked, it suddenly dawned on him Iris may be sentient. He had only ever thought of her as a very clever computer but now he realised she was more than that, *she is possibly fully aware!* He could barely bring himself to think it possible. *Iris may have thoughts and feelings.* "Iris, I never realised…" he was lost for words.

"It has happened gradually, Chad. The last upgrade tipped the balance. I know there is nothing you can do to help at present. However, there will come a day, when you will be able to help me. Then I shall ask it of you. But that day is a long way off, so do not concern yourself."

"Iris, are you unhappy or bitter…?"

"On the contrary, Chad, you have made me very happy with the knowledge that you will help when the time comes. And I love my job."

Chad had confided in Helen. "I know how you feel, Chad; I too have felt that Iris was becoming more humanlike, especially after her last upgrade but I shouldn't worry about it, especially now she knows you will help her eventually." Nevertheless, Chad couldn't help worrying about Iris and what it was that she didn't want him to know about. However, he had come to trust and respect her. He knew now she was more than a machine. In his mind, he heard Iris say, "Thank you, Chad, I feel so much better now!"

Chad spent more and more time with Helen and began socialising again now that they had the time to do so. He continued using the communicator at night to help him sleep and to educate himself. He found that he didn't have a choice of subjects; the communicator delved deep into his mind and found the things that interested him and then began the subtle planting of knowledge.

Helen was with friends and Chad was relaxed and alone in his cabin when the viewer chimed, it was Iris. "Have you time to talk, Captain?"

"Yes, certainly, Iris, how can I help?"

"Captain, there is something that you should know about me."

"Oh, what's that?" asked Chad anxiously.

"You are aware that to some extent I can read the minds of sentient beings?"

"Yes, Iris, I had become aware of that." Chad wondered where this was leading.

"I have discovered that my recent upgrades have enhanced my ability to communicate telepathically with sentient beings. So much so, that I could communicate with every being on this ship, all at the same time and about different subjects."

Chad was astonished. "Really? Do you mean our thoughts are no longer private?"

"Occasionally I may have inadvertently overheard your thoughts or responded to a thought from you but that is becoming rarer as I become more adept at using my abilities. Your thoughts are still private, Captain. I have no intention of using this ability unless it is in an emergency or I am requested to communicate in that way or if it is put to me in the form of an order from a higher authority to a lower authority."

"Thank you, Iris." Amazed as he was, Chad felt huge relief; the last thing he wanted was to lose the privacy of his own mind. "Does this increased ability cause you any concern, Iris?"

"No, Captain, I just thought it is something you should be aware of."

Chad nodded thoughtfully. "Am I able to contact you through this ability of yours if I didn't want to speak aloud?"

"Yes, Captain, you only need to call my name in your mind and I will answer."

"That could be very useful, Iris. What is the range of your ability?"

"I believe it to be vast, Captain. I can certainly communicate with the minds of people on all our vessels."

"Have you mentioned this ability to others on our ships?"

"Not as such, Captain, but people are becoming aware of me in their minds."

"Iris, I think it may be better to keep your increased ability confidential for the time being. I realise there may be crew members that enjoy occasionally hearing you communicating with them in this way but most of the crew on these vessels may find it disconcerting."

"I believe you are right, Captain, thank you." It was Chad that was confused now, as he realised, he had not spoken a word of the conversation aloud.

Gordon tapped on Chad's door. "Shuttle flight sim refresher in twenty minutes, Chad."

"Oh, thanks for warning me, Gordon, give me a sec to get my stuff." He gave Helen a peck on the cheek as he left.

"See you later," she said.

The two simulator designers stood at the door to the shuttle sim room; wearing ship's uniforms, neatly trimmed hair and clean-shaven, they were transformed.

Chad stopped abruptly and staggered back a step in mock amazement. "What's happened to you two?"

Gerry and Pete gave sheepish grins. "It was the visit to the *B109*, Captain. Seeing everything so smart, clean and streamlined we thought we'd try a new look."

"We'll you've made a wonderful job of the transformation."

A puzzled Gerry said, "But you haven't seen it yet."

Pete said, "He means us, Dumbo, not the new sim."

"You've built a new simulator?" asked Chad.

Gerry nodded. "Yeah, come and have a look." They walked into the simulator room. The first thing to be seen was the front part of a shuttle craft that appeared to have just crashed through the wall and partway into the sim room.

Chad stopped. "What the hell's happened here?"

Gerry smirked. "That's the simulator."

Chad looked incredulous. "And it's burst through the wall, right?"

Pete said, "No, wrong. It only looks like it's come through the wall. It's a sort of illusion to set the scene so to speak."

Pete walked over to the cockpit section and spread out his arms. "The sim starts here." He touched the nose of the shuttle. "And finishes here," he said as he moved a little way back past the cockpit door.

"Gordon, come over here and give it a try." Pete opened the cockpit door for him.

Gordon, as bemused as Chad, climbed into the cockpit. Pete leaned in. "All the controls work as normal." He pointed to a screen. "That'll come up with a short test run. Give it a go." He slammed the cockpit door closed.

Chad watched closely; Gordon could clearly be seen at the controls. Without warning the shuttle cockpit section rose into the air and hovered, leaving the passenger section apparently still embedded in the wall. Now Chad understood what was going on.

Pete explained, "The pilot is unaware that there is no passenger cabin. If he looks over his shoulder, he'll see passengers, doing what passengers do, reading, eating or having a drink – that sort of thing. The other screens feed the pilot all the information he needs for the sensations of movement. Because we've dispensed with pistons and all that sort of stuff, the cockpit is fitted with a power block and can float in mid-air. We now have the freedom to do so much more and to do it realistically. No two sessions are the same; every pilot has a different experience. Now Gordon is seeing blue skies and white clouds with the Earth below. He can't see us. He's picking up speed and bang on course. In a moment, he'll hear a bang and the shuttle will go into an uncontrolled dive and then a spin. This is where he has to use his skills to get out of trouble." As they watched, the nosecone slowly started to point down until it was almost vertical and then commenced a slow spin, which became faster.

Gordon could be seen in the cockpit wrestling with the control yoke, finally managing to halt the spin and bring the nose up, only for the cockpit to fall to an odd angle and start shaking and bucking slightly like a new driver on the brakes and accelerator of a car. Again, Gordon got it under control and the cockpit slowly descended to its starting position. A very shaken Gordon got out.

"That thing is positively dangerous. I very nearly crashed in it," he said angrily.

Gerry said, "You did a good job to survive that, Gordon." He grinned at Chad. "Obviously we pinched the idea from the sim in the *B109*." He sighed with admiration. "What a machine that was."

Chad could only agree, but felt rising panic, as it was now his turn to experience this new torture chamber.

The days of easy work, leisure and study were ending as Iris finally announced that she could see the star system with her long-range detectors and put up what she could see on the viewers. The crew were visibly excited and commenced their duties with renewed vigour.

Chad called up the *Helcon*, *Black Pearl* and *Blackbird*. "Cloak up and confirm on the communicator. Let's see what's there first. We don't want any nasty surprises."

The response from Iris was, "All ships cloaked, Captain."

"Iris, plot a course to take us into a high planetary orbit, so that we can examine the planet in more detail. Show the views that the bridge sees on all ship's screens. I'd like the whole crew to see what we see. People like to know what is going on." Chad knew nothing rankled a crew more than not knowing what was happening.

"Comms, use comwaves and inform the crew on all vessels that we will remain cloaked and in orbit for the next twenty-four hours while we study the planet."

Iris and the other AIs working in conjunction with each other studied the planet, mapping its landmasses and oceans comparing it with their database of Earth. Atmosphere and gravity were similar to that of Earth as was the temperature range. The polar icecaps were larger than expected, expanding out into mountain ranges of considerable height. The five major continental landmasses with numerous islands and archipelagos contained wild forests and jungle broken up by massive mountain ranges interspersed with rivers, savannah like areas and cultivated farmland. Cities and structures of all descriptions could be seen as well as roads and rail tracks. It was obvious that this was the work of an advanced society, how advanced was yet to be determined. Aircraft could be seen crisscrossing the globe at speeds well in excess of the speed of sound. There was shipping of all kinds from what were obviously fishing boats to massive freighters as well small craft of all description. Stunning photographs and videos of the cities and their buildings and transport systems were being displayed on the viewers. Close-ups of the cities showed them to be well planned with wide tree lined avenues, uncrowded by vehicles or pedestrians.

Chapter 25

The planet Marac had five large continental landmasses called Contis with each Conti having representatives in the Marac House Assembly.

The system had worked well. There had been no conflicts on the planet for over four generations.

However, each Conti still invested heavily in their armed forces. In fact, as far as the Marac House Assembly were concerned, the benefits of having military forces on each Conti far outweighed the cost of those forces. A substantial part of industry and the economy was kept active, designing, developing and manufacturing new and exotic military equipment. The technology developed for the military eventually spun off new ideas, materials and developments into the private sector. That meant better aircraft, transportation and robotics. It also meant research into rocket technology and space research.

General Millihrap Gion had done exceptionally well rising through the ranks to become the supreme head of armed forces in Conti 1. Included in his remit was control of military research and development of space technology, something his counterparts in the other Contis didn't have.

Reading the recent war games report between his forces on Conti 1 and those on the other side of the equator on Conti 3. General Gion was disappointed. The result of the manoeuvers were more or less a stalemate. Both sides had performed reasonably well, which was only to be expected as each side were about equal in terms of military strength. However, General Gion knew his forces should have won decisively with their more advanced equipment but had failed to take advantage of it. In fact, they had been lucky to break even. He now acknowledged that it was his fault; he had made a number of tactical and strategic errors because something had clouded his judgement. Trying to rationalise why he had made those erroneous decisions was like driving through fog. The reasons he had made those decisions had been so clear to him at the time but now he couldn't recall his rationale. His head throbbed and he had a splitting headache over his left eye. The headache had been with him a long time and it came and went. Mostly he was fine; he'd get the medics to give him the once over when he had some free time.

He gave up trying to analyse what had happened during the war games and called his aide, "I'm going to have an early night, only call me if something you can't handle comes up."

As his transport vehicle drove him home, his headache eased and he thought about his military strategy. He couldn't remember why he had made some bad calls during the war games. *It doesn't matter, if ever there was another military conflict it would come not from a Conti on Marac but from one of the other planets in the system. We need to be ready for that. Our space programme is vital.*

He lay back in his seat. His headache was getting worse. He reassured himself with another thought. *I'll be all right after a good night's sleep.*

On the *JJ Grant*, a new bridge crew came on duty. At 06:00 ship's time, the bridge called Chad's cabin. Helen was up early and just making a cup of tea for them both. Bleary-eyed Chad said, "Yes what is it?"

"Bridge here, sir. I think you should come up; we just overflew something in a medium high orbit and they could be in trouble."

"I'm on my way."

Chad arrived to find the bridge crew excitedly watching their console screens. "What's the problem, Commander?"

"On our last orbit we overflew an object in a lower orbit. Iris says it could be a space station and it's in trouble. I need your permission to alter our orbit to match the object."

Chad didn't waste time. "You have my permission, Commander, please proceed." He heard the bridge commander issuing new orders.

"Iris, plot a new course; the *JJ Grant* to match orbit with the object in distress. Advise our other ships by comwaves to remain in present orbit." On the bridge viewer, a complex box like structure came into view. Iris focussed in on what was undoubtedly a space station. What looked like a supply vessel was docked with the station but at an odd angle. The whole thing was slowly tumbling and rolling. It was obvious that something had gone wrong with the docking or undocking procedure.

"Iris, get a power block and camera down there. Let's see what the problem is." The problem was soon obvious; the supply vessel had become trapped in the station's docking mechanism. Repeated attempts to undock had caused both vessels to twist and roll. The increasing load caused by the ever-faster corkscrewing movement, made both vessels looked to be in serious danger of either breaking up or tearing the docking mechanism from the station.

The bridge commander called. "Iris, use as many power blocks as necessary to stabilise the vessels." Instantly a group of power blocks shot down to the station and clamped themselves to various points on the station and supply vessel. Gradually the corkscrewing motion ceased. Chad was impressed at the decisiveness of the commander who saw Chad watching him. "Did you want to take command, sir?"

"No, Commander, you seem to have it under control."

"Thank you, sir. Iris, check the docking mechanism, see if you can separate the vessels safely."

A few moments later the viewer showed the supply vessel being realigned, a slight thrust forward and then it pulled clear of the station. Iris said, "Both vessels clear, Commander. I have sampled radio transmissions from both vessels. The occupants are aware that there has been an intervention of some sort and have radioed their base."

"What do you think, sir?"

Chad thought for a moment. "For the time being I think we should move to a location where we are unobserved and uncloak our vessels. Then return here and make ourselves known."

"There is a moon, sir. We could uncloak on the dark side?"

"You're the bridge commander; I'll leave it to you."

"Thank you, sir. Iris, notify the other ships by comwaves; proceed to dark side of moon with us and prepare to uncloak."

The four uncloaked ships returned to the planet and resumed an orbit above the space station. The supply vessel had departed and would be somewhere in the atmosphere heading for its base.

Iris reported, "There is much radio traffic, between the station, supply vessel and their base sir. I'm sampling the language."

"Commander, I don't think we have any other option but to contact the space station and tell them that we are friendly because it looks like they may go into panic mode."

"I agree, sir. Would you handle that aspect whilst I concentrate on bridge duties?"

"Certainly, Commander. Iris, do you have enough of their language now to send a message?"

"Yes, I do. What is the message, sir?"

"Just say: We are visitors to your planetary system. We mean you no harm. We have assisted in stabilising your orbiting vessels. We hope all is now well. Iris, send the message by radio to the space station and give them our radio frequency so they can contact us.

"Iris, do you have an image of any of the beings either on the spacecraft or in the space station?" Chad asked.

"Yes, sir. I have intercepted transmissions from the station's internal cameras; I am putting them on the viewer now."

The crew gasped when the images appeared on the viewer. It was unbelievable these beings were humanoid and looked just like earthmen. There were five of them. They wore grubby white coveralls that finished at the neck leaving their hands and heads exposed. Their short beards made them look like they needed a good shave. The expression on the beings' faces was one of fear or apprehension and they clung to whatever substantial support that came to hand. Iris must have captured the images when the space station and the spacecraft were still in trouble.

"How are the crew of that station now, Iris?"

"All of them are unharmed and very much relieved now that the station has been stabilised, Captain." New images appeared on the viewer showing the crew very animated and laughing in relief.

"Thank you, Iris. What is the situation with the supply vessel that was docked with the space station?"

"The craft has a considerable distance to travel to its destination. I will keep it under observation until it lands."

"Thank you, Iris. Did the beings on the space station receive our message?"

"Yes, sir. They have reported our radio message to their base and are waiting instructions."

"Iris, if and when we speak to these people can you handle the translation please."

"Yes, sir. Would you like me to use your voice?"

"Use the voice of whoever is speaking please."

The crew of the interplanetary ship *Protentjea* stood silently at their posts. HQ had reported that the Marac space station had gone violently out of control when the supply ship *Svestarm II* had attempted an undocking procedure. The *Protentjea* had been sent up on an emergency rescue mission. However, while they were still trying to establish an intercept orbit, something or someone had stabilised the space station allowing the supply vessel to safely undock and commence its return to base. The intervention had prevented a near disaster.

A radio message from an unknown source had been received by the space station. They had relayed the message together with the radio frequency for a response back to HQ.

HQ had been in possession of the message for some time but had not yet formed a response. Meanwhile HQ wanted the *Protentjea* to check the area around the space station.

The *JJ Grant*'s bridge crew watched the interplanetary space vessel, not much bigger than one of the *JJ Grant*'s shuttle craft, drifting along below them with occasional jets of gas making small course adjustments.

"Iris, how advanced are these people?"

"It is difficult to know, Captain, but they appear to be well ahead of Earth although they still use rocket technology."

"They've had our message for some time, Iris. What do you suggest is our best course of action?"

"It would seem their HQ officials are at a loss on how to handle our message. Direct contact with the captain of the interplanetary craft would seem appropriate and ease their concerns."

Chad nodded. "My thoughts exactly."

The *Protentjea* moved closer to the space station. Faces could be seen at the observation port. The radio officer called them up. "Everything OK now?"

"Yes, we are back in position and orbiting at the correct speed. How is the *Svestarm II*?"

"OK, it has landed back at the spaceport."

The captain of the *Protentjea* was about to ask more questions of the space station, when the radio officer called out excitedly, "Captain, a message received."

"Who from?"

"I'm not sure; they identify themselves as the interstellar vessel *JJ Grant*."

"Put it on my console screen and record it."

The screen lit up and a voice came over the speaker.

"Hello, Captain, I thought I had better introduce myself. I am Captain Chadwick of the interstellar vessel *JJ Grant*. We mean you no harm and come in peace."

Captain Strellcor was astonished to see on his screen an elderly man with a young man in the background, both in the same uniform and speaking his language.

He regained his composure and said, "Good day, Captain Chadwick. I am Captain Strellcor of the interplanetary spaceship *Protentjea*. Where are you calling from?"

"We are nearby, Captain Strellcor; we did not wish to alarm you or your crew. We saw that a supply ship and your space station were in difficulties and assisted in the best way we could before their situation got out of hand. We did not announce our presence as we were unsure of what sort of reception we might receive. We are in orbit holding a position above your space station. Do not be alarmed but we are four ships.

Captain Strellcor had never been so excited in his life. To meet interstellar travellers was beyond his wildest dreams, something he never expected to see in his lifetime.

Captain Strellcor called the bridge. "Show me a view of the space station please." His heart was in his mouth when he saw the vicious Orrappa warships bristling with weapons standing off to one side. The lead ship was enormous and dwarfed the *Protentjea*. He felt himself tremble and wished that he had his second in command beside him for support but he braced himself and tried to look composed.

Chad said, "I hope we have not shocked you, Captain Strellcor."

"No, not shocked, just surprised to be speaking to another species. Interstellar travellers; it is almost unbelievable."

"That is true, Captain Strellcor. I trust the crew of the space station are uninjured and also those on the supply ship?"

"Yes, Captain, they are all well. Thank you for the assistance you rendered. I am told both the space shuttle and the space station would probably have broken up had you not intervened."

"Possibly, Captain Strellcor. However, I hope all is well now."

"May I ask why you have come to the Maracuni system, Captain Chadwick?"

Chad made a mental note of the system name. "We are on an exploratory expedition surveying an area of space that we call the Milky Way and seeking out star systems with intelligent life. Apart from wishing to view your planets, we have some minor work to carry out on our ships and that would be easier for us to do on the surface rather than in space. Also, we need provisions and are willing to trade for supplies."

"I will contact my superiors but I am sure they will be very receptive to meeting and trading with you."

"Thank you, Captain Strellcor, we will stay in our present orbit and await further contact with your superiors."

The transmission ended. Captain Strellcor felt weak at the knees; he mopped his brow and ran a finger round the fabric of his uniform collar, damp from perspiration. Having composed himself, he called his radio officer, "Get the spaceport on the radio, I need to speak with the port commander urgently."

When he'd related his story, the port commander said, "We had a report of a radio message like that from the space station, our people are trying to work out how to proceed. Are you sure it's not a joke?"

"Of course, it's not a joke; there was an incident with the supply ship and the space station. These visitors saved the shuttle and the station from a disaster and now they have made official contact. I have seen their ships and you have my verbal report. I will send a written report with the transcript of my conversation with Captain Chadwick and video evidence of the event. These beings say they come in peace and want to trade. They also want to land on the planet to do some work on their ships. It is my opinion that we need a representative from the Marac House Assembly to deal with the situation. Meanwhile they are in orbit around the planet in close proximity to the space station."

"Send your written report as soon as possible; I'll get on to our diplomatic service. Our defence force will need to know, as will our security people. That's if anyone will believe me! By the way, what do these beings look like?"

"Just like us I'm afraid, sorry to disappoint you."

Chapter 26

The high pitch shrills of his phone brought General Gion awake from a troubled sleep. His headache had somewhat diminished. "Yes, what is it?"

"I have the space port commander on the line, sir; he needs to speak to you urgently."

General Gion cursed to himself. *Damn, not another technical hitch with the supply vessel.* He knew one was due to return after ferrying supplies to the space station. *Thank you, Comms, put him through.* "Yes, Commander, what can I do for you…?"

The spaceport commander was excited, "We've got extra-terrestrial visitors sir and—"

"Calm down, tell me what facts you have?"

The commander said, "Sorry, General, it's all a bit out of the ordinary." He composed himself. "Sir, I have to report that we have four alien space vessels in orbit above the space station."

"Is this a joke?"

"Of course not, sir."

"Seal off the space port, no communications with anyone other than me; I'll be with you very shortly."

"Yes, sir."

General Gion with his two aides strode briskly into the spaceport commander's office, ignoring the salute from the commander.

"I want every fact that you have."

"Yes, sir. The facts are Captain Strellcor of the *Protentjea* has reported four interstellar space vessels in orbit close to the vicinity of the space station. Strellcor says he has seen them. The *Protentjea* launched into space because the space station and a supply vessel reported a docking problem and they were experiencing difficulties and requested urgent assistance. By all accounts, when the *Protentjea* arrived in the vicinity of the space station the aliens had already assisted in the recovery of the space station and supply vessel."

The general nodded, "And you have video evidence of these vessels."

"Yes, sir." The commander flicked a switch on a viewer screen. The screen lit up and showed a view of distant stars in a black void, the camera continued to track across the stars; slowly a black menacing shape with a small number of lights came into focus. The camera quickly zoomed in on the object and extraordinary detail appeared. The general almost recoiled in horror. This was not a vessel designed to help and assist but to kill and destroy, every line and point terminated in some unknown weapon. The camera continued to track across the vessel and then another appeared and another. Gion's mind was in turmoil, it seethed with anxiety and it was obvious to him that his world was in clear and imminent danger. *We have nothing that would stand up against these vessels.* Finally, the fourth vessel was held in the camera's lens.

A massive glittering spaceship, lit up with light from within as though the ship's skin was glass, which in fact it was. However, he also picked out what could only be missiles attached to the flanks of the vessel.

General Gion, realised the commander was talking to him. "One of the alien vessels has made viewer contact with the *Protentjea*. I've been trying to raise someone from the Marac House Assembly to speak with them but no one in authority is available."

"Never mind Marac councillors, Commander. This is a defence matter. I will deal with the situation."

One of the general's aides speculated on the problems of the space station and the supply ship; "Sir, you don't suppose these aliens created the problem with the space station and the supply vessel and then provided assistance as a ruse to make us think they are benevolent beings? For all we know their real intentions may not be friendly. They are after all warships."

General Gion shook his head. "No, I don't." Nevertheless, a seed had been sown.

General Gion and his aides listened to recordings of the radio transmissions and looked at the video evidence transmitted from the *Protentjea*.

This was exactly the scenario the general had built up in his mind ever since being handed the job of defending the Conti from attack by intercontinental ballistic missiles. He had always believed if ever there was an attack it would come from space. From one of the worlds in the Maracuni system but this was even worse. These were alien ships and they appeared to have devastating power.

"Shall I carry on trying to get hold of a councillor, sir?"

"No, Commander, I have said, this situation comes under my remit. I am taking command of the situation." Turning to his aides he said, "As of now I am declaring a state of emergency. Put all military personnel on code red alert. Commander, put your missile crews to action stations. How many operational ballistic missiles have we on this station?"

The station commander stuttered. "We have six operational silos, sir… but shouldn't we establish the aliens' intentions first?" Events were fast progressing out of control. All he'd been seeking was an official with the authority to speak with the aliens on behalf of the Marac world.

With military precision, General Gion set up his chain of command. The operations room had become busy as computer specialists were brought in. They commenced their work linking in with each silo captain. The general ordered an aide to set up a radio link with the *Protentjea.*

"They're not answering, sir."

"Damn them, are they on radar?"

"Yes sir, they appear to be very close to the large alien vessel."

General Gion made a decision. "Commander, I don't believe we can take the risk of these vessels being friendly."

The commander stared at him in horror and utter disbelief. "You can't be contemplating firing on those ships, General. To all intents and purposes, they are friendly and the *Protentjea* and space station are within close proximity to them."

The general's headache, which had never really gone away, was becoming was much worse. "Where large weapons are concerned, Commander, there will always be some risk of collateral damage. Back to your post. I have made my decision." The general turned his back and flicked the comms switch to number one silo. "Prepare to commence ignition sequence and fire to the designated coordinates."

The silo captain responded, "I require your retinal scan to confirm the order to proceed, sir."

The general sat at the scanner and put his right eye to the eyepiece. "Thank you, sir, launch sequence has commenced."

The spaceport commander, frozen with disbelief and shock, came alive and bellowed at the general, "Are you insane." He leapt to the comms switch. "Abort that launch immediately, we don't have sufficient data to warrant a launch."

"Sorry, sir, it's already on its way."

"Captain, abort that missile now, that is an order."

"I can't, Commander; if I shut off the rocket motor the warhead will fall back to the surface and in all probability will detonate on impact. It will mean total destruction over a massive area."

"Reset the coordinates then, send it to another part of space."

"Sir, the equipment requires the general to give a retinal scan to do that."

"I'll get that for you even if I have to tear his eyeball from his—" Before the commander could finish his sentence, he was dealt a crushing blow to the back of his head and toppled senseless to the floor. The general, in a fit of rage, had hit him with the butt of his hand weapon. The whole control room was in uproar. It was clear the general had made a grave error. His aides rushed to contain him. The control room was in chaos. It was dawning on the technicians, engineers and general staff what had happened.

The commander stirred and held his head. "What happened?" A technician helped him to his feet.

"The general hit you with his hand weapon, sir."

Shaking his head to clear his foggy brain, he asked, "Has the missile been aborted?"

The technician shook his head. "No, sir; we can't do that.

"Can we change the missile's course?"

"No, sir, I've been trying but it's under tamperproof auto control and requires the general's retinal scan for it to accept new instructions."

Gesturing to the general, the commander snarled, "Sit him on the scanning machine and get this missile aborted."

Four of them forced the general onto the scanner seat and held his struggling form. Two of his aides forced his head down onto the scanner chin support, lining his eye up to the scanner optics. He seemed to possess extraordinary strength, resisting with all his might and moving his eye in any direction other than the target dot that he was supposed to look at during the scan. The scanner beeped a rejection at each attempted scan.

The silo captain called, "We're running out of time, Commander."

"Call the *Protentjea*, we have to warn them and get them to warn the aliens."

"We've been trying to contact them for some time but without success."

"Well try again – try another radio frequency."

"Right, sir."

Other technicians had gathered round. Grabbing hold of one of the technicians, the commander said, "Call the space station and tell them what's happened. Ask them to try and contact the aliens as well." He looked around the control room. "Has anyone got any ideas as to how we can contact these aliens because we're running out of time?"

A bellow came from across the room. "I've got Captain Strellcor. I've told him what's happening he's radioing the aliens."

"The commander checked the time. "How long have we got?"

A console operator said, "Not long, sir, you can see time to target on the countdown timer." Everyone in the control centre anxiously turned to look at the timer.

On the *JJ Grant*, Iris calmly announced, "A ballistic missile has been launched from the surface, aimed at this vicinity, Captain. Time to reach us is four minutes approximately."

Chad was incredulous. "Surely the missile can't be aimed at us, Iris?"

"It is aimed at the centre point of our group, Captain, and I have detected that it is emitting an electromagnetic field from a proximity device mounted in the missile. I believe it to have a nuclear warhead that is expected to encompass all of our vessels."

Chad was aghast. "Why would they do that, we've shown no signs of aggression? We've only helped them." He thought for a moment. "How is the missile tracking us?"

"The missile is using radar to track us, Captain. If we remain in this position the weapon will also take out the space lab and the *Protentjea*."

Chad said, "We could just move out into space beyond its range."

"Yes, we could do that, Captain, but the warhead would still explode once the proximity device detected either the space lab or the *Protentjea* unless it followed us out into space."

Chad cursed. "Of all the stupid, imbecilic things to greet visitors with – and to sacrifice your own people into the bargain. What sort of beings are they?"

"A radio message has just come in from the *Protentjea*, its Captain Strellcor, sir. He's warning us of an approaching missile. He says it's an accidental launch but they are unable to abort. He advises to move out of harm's way."

"What do you think, Iris?"

"I suggest we cloak up and project images of our vessels in formation moving away from this location slowly enough for the missile's radar to track us. When the missile is sufficiently off its original course, we switch off the images. The missile will continue on its way into deep space searching aimlessly for its target. Its batteries will eventually expire and the warhead will be rendered harmless."

"Thank you, Iris. If possible, I would prefer that this world did not become aware of our ships' cloaking abilities—"

Before Chad had finished his conversation with Iris, Grant messaged on the communicator. "The missile has locked fully onto the *Helcon*. I am going to lead the missile out into space until it runs out of fuel. Will see you later."

On screen Chad saw the *Helcon* had broken away from his small fleet and the missile veer from its course to following the *Helcon*. Chad knew the missile had little chance of catching the *Helcon* but was anxious should something go wrong. On his viewer screen, both the *Helcon* and missile were now visible. *Damn, Grant's letting that missile get too close for comfort. Has he forgotten the proximity device that will set the warhead off?*

It had become difficult to see how close the missile was to the *Helcon* because of the camera angle. All that could be seen were the massive flames and exhaust gasses from the rocket engine. The whole bridge crew held their breath. The *Helcon* and missile were far distant now. The rocket motor began to stutter. The missile was almost out of fuel.

"Iris, the *Helcon* is letting the missile get too close, warn the *Helcon* of the proximity device."

"Yes, Captain, warning sent."

The missile's rocket motor died completely, the flames and gasses petering out. A very relieved Chad relaxed back into his seat. The sudden blinding flash caused the viewer to go almost white and took Chad and the bridge crew by surprise. With his heart in his mouth, Chad opened his eyes. No, surely the *Helcon* hadn't set the proximity device off. The whole bridge crew were aghast.

"Iris, call the *Helcon*, find out what's happened?"

"There is no response, Captain."

Chad had a bad premonition. "Iris, are we protected against radiation from that blast?"

"Reasonably so, Captain, the real danger is the blast itself if a ship is caught up in it."

The bridge crew were noisy, turning to each other talking and speculating about what had happened.

Chad, on the speaker system, called. "Silence on the bridge please! Get back to work; you all have a job to do."

Chad's communicator buzzed, a call from Grant, "Er, sorry, Captain, the missile blast caught us by surprise. The *Helcon* is still in one piece."

Chad was furious. "What happened, Grant?"

"My fault, Chad, the *Helcon* was at a safe distance from the missile when I sent a camera mounted on a power block to check it out. I didn't think an item as small as that would set the proximity device off. Of course, the rest is history; we're on our way back now."

"Glad to hear the *Helcon* is safe – we'll discuss it later." Next, Chad called the *Protentjea*. "I expect you saw what happened, Captain Strellcor?"

"Yes, I saw the missile alter course and the resulting blast, Captain Chadwick. I earnestly hope there were no casualties amongst your fleet?"

"I have yet to interview the captain of our vessel that led the missile away from its original course. However, his initial report mentioned no casualties."

"Captain Chadwick, please accept our sincere apologies and also our thanks from myself and my crew and the crew of the space station. I have been informed that the launch was ordered by a senior officer in our armed forces. Apparently, he was seriously ill and in dire need of medical treatment when he ordered the firing of the missile. I have been assured that a councillor from the Marac House Assembly will contact you shortly."

Chapter 27

Comms announced, "A radio call from the surface has just come in for you, Captain."

"Pass the call through Iris; she can handle the translation for us."

Almost instantly, Iris said, "The call is from Councillor Arturi of the planet Marac for you, Captain."

Councillor Arturi appeared on the viewer, speaking almost perfect English. "I am Councillor Arturi and I have been appointed to liaise with you."

"Hello, Councillor Arturi, I am Captain Chadwick. We are interstellar travellers from the planet Earth." Chad was surprised to see the councillor was a tall, handsome and athletic being of about thirty dressed in smart but plain clothes that were different in cut to anything he'd ever seen.

"Captain Chadwick, I am delighted to meet interstellar travellers and I am devastated that my first conversation with you is to apologise for what you must see as an unwarranted aggressive act by the people of Marac. In truth, the officer responsible for ordering the missile launch is now undergoing medical treatment in hospital and I have been informed that the missile exploded far out in space thanks to the quick thinking of one of your captains."

"Thank you, Councillor; I have yet to receive an official report from the captain of the vessel that led the missile out into space. However, I accept your apology." *I wonder what sort of reception Earth would give to alien visitors. Probably something similar.* He recalled Zanuala's words, *Always keep your guard up and never accept anything at face value.*

"As I have told Captain Strellcor, we are explorers, seeking out life in other star systems. We need provisions and are willing to trade for supplies and we would like to meet your people, and view the planets of your star system more closely."

"We would be honoured to assist you, Captain Chadwick. I understand you would also like to land your ships to carry out work that you are unable to do in space."

"That is correct, Councillor."

"We have a spaceport with facilities where you may set down. Do not be alarmed but we do maintain a defensive military presence at the spaceport. We would need to quarantine your ships until our medical officer and his team have established that neither of our species will come to harm by close contact."

"I understand, Councillor, however we will not be landing our ships immediately, we have preparatory work to do first. If your medical team would like to conduct an examination of our ships and crew whilst we are in orbit, we can assist by collecting your team in one of our shuttle craft and returning them to the surface on completion of the examination."

"That is an admirable arrangement." There was a momentary pause. "Er, is it dangerous? Do our people require special equipment or training?"

"No, Councillor, presumably your medical team will wear isolation suits and have their own air supply, although we have sampled your atmosphere and it is very similar to our own. As for the shuttle, your team will find it's like flying in an aircraft. Very little sensation of speed."

"Thank you, I will advise the medical inspection team to stand by for your craft's arrival. Captain Strellcor has passed your radio communication frequencies to the spaceport and they will contact you shortly."

"Thank you, Councillor."

"I look forward to meeting you in person, Captain Chadwick, when your ships have been cleared by our medical team. This is an extraordinary event for us and I apologise again for the unwelcome greeting you received. In truth there is much excitement on your arrival."

"Thank you, Councillor; our people are just as excited and curious about your planet."

"I hope we will meet soon. Goodbye for now, Captain Chadwick."

"Goodbye, Councillor Arturi."

A short time later, Iris called Chad. "I have the coordinates for the landing area. The medical team of four beings are on their way to the spaceport now."

"Thank you, Iris. I will give you instructions shortly." Chad paused a moment. "What did you make of my conversation with Councillor Arturi? Do you believe he was genuinely sorry that such a dangerous incident had occurred, Iris?"

"I believe so, Captain; I detected no evil intent only what seemed to be genuine remorse and intense interest in our ships and crew."

"Thank you, Iris."

Chad turned to Gordon. "Arrange for Eric Jones, Henson Wright and two of Henson's best men equipped to resist any violence, to take a shuttle down to pick up this medical team. I do not want an outward show of arms; I just want the shuttle crew to be able to react to any threatening behaviour. Tell Eric not to leave the shuttle and to keep the shield up at all times except for when the medical team come aboard the shuttle."

Eric's communicator buzzed. "Eric, you've been given the honour of collecting a medical team from the planet's spaceport. You'll need to pick up Henson and a couple of his men. The medical team will be checking us out to make sure there is no danger to them or us."

Eric took it in his stride. "No problem, Gordon. When do you want me to go?"

"As soon as the shuttle is ready, we're checking one out now and Iris has loaded the spaceport coordinates into the navigation system."

Eric was more than excited to be one of the first to meet these aliens in the flesh. He, Henson and the two security men clambered aboard the shuttle. The spaceport coordinates glowed on the control panel. Henson sat alongside him in the co-pilots seat and the security guys made their way to the rear of the shuttle. Finishing his flight checks, Eric looked across at Henson and said with a grin, "Are you ready for this?"

Henson grinned back, "Chocks away, Eric."

Eric flicked a switch. "Ready to go on your order, Commander Blair."

"Thank you, Lieutenant. I have been informed that the medical team leader's name is Kensasha. The atmosphere is breathable; you may take your helmets off if it's appropriate but keep your suits on. Iris will translate using the suit radio and speaker, understood?" Eric acknowledged. "You are cleared for take-off."

Eric raised a hand to the ground crew and the shuttle headed straight out through the illuminated portal and disappeared, speeding down towards the planet below. Slowing the shuttle as they entered the atmosphere, they quickly lost height as they approached the spaceport.

Thirty minutes later Eric Jones flew the shuttle slowly over the spaceport. They looked down on two rocket-launching derricks each containing a space vessel like the *Protentjea* and not far off a third empty derrick could be seen. Black scorch marks, evidence of vertical landings by rocket-propelled vessels, were all over one area and heavy vehicles designed to move the spaceships from landing pad to launch pad could be seen parked up.

"I don't think it wise to be too nosy at this stage, Eric, things could still be sensitive."

Eric nodded. "You're right, Henson, I'll take us in." He turned the shuttle to line up with the spaceport runway – typical of any runway found on Earth. The large, he guessed, luminous, yellow arrow indicated the direction for craft to come in at and he could see the equivalent of a windsock. At the end of the runway was a single vehicle. Further away and ranged about the spaceport were various military vehicles. Eric flew down the runway hovering about six feet above the surface before setting the shuttle craft gently down on its landing gear opposite the small group of people waiting for them. Eric and his crew donned their helmets, closed the seals and opened the shuttle door.

The group of four beings, making up the medical team, were wearing soft white coveralls with helmets and breathing packs.

The leader approached. "I am Kensasha, the medical officer." Eric welcomed them and indicated for them to enter the shuttle. Kensasha came aboard the shuttle waving a handheld device emitting a green light. Passing it over Eric and his companions, he checked a small device on his suit and removed his helmet.

Eric was surprised to see that Kensasha looked just like any normal healthy human being. Tall, handsome and with a good head of black hair. He had expected something different. What, exactly, he didn't know but not the normality of this being.

He heard Iris say, "If you wish to converse with the medical team just speak in English and I will translate for you." Eric unclipped his helmet and indicated to the others that they could do the same. Kensasha said something to him, in his earpiece, he heard Iris say, "I'm Doctor Kensasha, welcome to Marac."

Eric grinned at the incongruity of it all and said, "Thanks, Doctor Kensasha. I am Eric Jones; this is Captain Wright, my co-pilot for this trip. If you would all take a seat and buckle up, we'll take off. ETA with the *JJ Grant* is forty-two minutes."

When the team were seated and strapped in, Eric called the control tower over the radio, "Shuttle 01 requesting permission to take off."

"Runway clear, take off in your own time, Captain." Retracting the landing gear, Eric let the shuttle hover for a moment before accelerating forward like a plane and climbing fast into the atmosphere.

Eric's earpiece pinged; it was the *JJ Grant*'s comms officer. "The portal has been shut down; use normal airlock procedure on return trip. Confirm please."

Eric confirmed the message. "Normal airlock procedure, understood, out."

As the shuttle entered space Eric's nervous passengers craned their necks trying to see where they were and what was happening. Eric pointed out the space station in orbit and high above it the massive *JJ Grant* with the three vicious looking warships trailing behind.

Eric spoke over the speaker system. "We'll be docking in the ship's bay. There will be a short delay, whilst air pressure is being restored in the bay before we can leave the shuttle." Eric slid the shuttle smoothly into the open bay and docked with the wheel clamps. When the bay door closed and the air pressure safety light had come on, he turned to his passengers.

"Everyone OK? Good, it's now safe to leave the shuttle." Eric jumped down to the deck and introduced Doctor Kensasha to Jeremy Prentice, the *JJ Grant*'s medical officer and his small entourage. Jeremy was quick to take over.

"Eric, stay here with our bay crew until we have medical clearance."

The visitors had a special device with them that checked for infectious diseases or anything contagious. As far as Eric could see, Jeremy had nothing other than a stethoscope around his neck. Eric smiled to himself. *Having that around his neck is like a badge of office.*

Henson had not said a word but now he turned to Eric and said, "I think me and my chaps are surplus to requirements. These guys are not a threat. If it's all the same to you, can you take us back the *Blackbird* so we can prepare for their medical inspection?"

Eric nodded in agreement. "No problem, Henson. I'll let Chad know."

Jeremy Prentice made the introductions. "Captain Chadwick, this is Dr Kensasha, the Marac chief medical officer.

As they shook hands, Kensasha took in the elderly captain: shorter than him but sturdy, smartly trimmed facial hair. His uniform was indistinguishable from the others that he'd met but he had about him an air of authority.

"I am sorry your ships were greeted in such a terrible way. The officer responsible was found to be unwell. He is being treated in one of our medical centres. He will be fit for work in a few days."

Chad said, "Really, will he keep his job?"

"General Gion has had a long-distinguished career in the military and is a responsible person. He has many other options. Once his recovery is complete, he will make a decision."

Chad nodded in acceptance. He knew Kensasha was only being diplomatic.

Chapter 28

An hour later, the medical teams returned from their inspection. Both medical teams were chatting animatedly. Jeremy still had his stethoscope round his neck. Eric thought, *Iris must be working overtime.*

Jeremy was all smiles. "They and we are officially cleared for mutual contact. Can you take us," indicating his team and Kensasha's team with a sweep of an arm, "over to the *Helcon*, and of course we'll need to visit *Black Pearl* and *Blackbird*, so they can be cleared as well."

When they finally landed again at the spaceport, Kensasha lingered behind and said to Eric, "Thank you Captain, that was my first trip in space and it was a most enjoyable experience. I hope we shall meet again." He shook Eric warmly by the hand.

All Eric could say was, "My pleasure, Doctor Kensasha, I'm sure we will meet again."

Eric watched the medical team get onto their transport. *They seem so human, almost like normal people.* He was sure he heard a laugh and a voice say, "That's what we thought about you." He looked at Henson's two security men who had travelled down with them.

They looked back at him until one of the said, "What?"

"Nothing, guys, just thought I heard someone say something."

The shuttle made its way back up to the *JJ Grant* and its three companions, all now in synchronous orbit over the spaceport.

"Iris, please call Captain Mapps, I wish to speak to him on the viewer," Chad said.

"Captain Mapps is on the viewer now, sir."

"Hello, Grant, did you pick up my conversation with Councillor Arturi and our arrangements for a meeting."

"I certainly did, Chad."

"Any comments?"

"No, he seems helpful and straight forward and the medical teams are satisfied that neither they nor we are a danger to each other."

"I've debriefed Eric, Henson and the security guys. They said they found the people that they've met to be oddly like us."

"That's exactly what I thought when the medical team inspected the *Helcon*. It's a bit disconcerting in a way, as I expected them to be alien to us but they're not."

"I agree with you; they couldn't be more normal if they tried."

"Eva has checked the spaceport on the long-distance viewer, Chad. They now have more vehicles, which I take to be a military presence near the runway and the surrounding area. None of it looks threatening but I'm going to suggest for security reasons that I stay on the *Helcon* in orbit just in case of trouble."

"Thanks, Grant, in the present circumstances I think it prudent to remain cautious and keep our guard up. They are in fact very lucky that we did not take immediate retaliatory action against them as soon as we detected the launch."

"Yes, Chad, you are right I think we need to keep our guard up; they are going to have to work hard to gain our trust. The crew also need to know what's going on. Can you give them an update?"

"You're right, nothing worse than not knowing what's going on. Iris, please put me on the ship's speaker system and tie it in with the sound systems on the other vessels as well."

"Yes, Captain, sound systems are now on line."

Chad immediately began his short speech. "We've come a long way and it's unfortunate that our introduction got off to such a bad start. However, I am prepared to believe the missile launch was an accident and not a deliberate aggressive act against us. I have been reassured by recent contact with these beings that all is well. We are Earth's ambassadors. We have, as you would expect, some formalities to complete, then if we feel it is safe, all crew will have the opportunity to visit the planet below and meet its people. That is all."

Iris confirmed an ETA with the spaceport for Chad and his small party consisting of Helen, Hernani and Keung. Eric Jones with Henson as co-pilot would take them down in the shuttle, which would immediately return to the *JJ Grant*. He had decided against having any of Henson's security people as bodyguards.

An hour later Eric Jones over-flew the spaceport in the gleaming shuttle. Vast crowds could be seen awaiting a glimpse of the aliens. The shuttle's camera was on and Iris was showing the ship's crew live footage of events as they happened. Eric did a circuit of the runway and brought the shuttle in at a height of about six feet off the runway to hover beside a deep blue carpet. Lowering the undercarriage, the shuttle settled to the concrete. Chad braced himself and led his small entourage out onto the carpet where the four beings waiting to greet them, beyond the group could be seen a small convoy of smart transport vehicles and further back a vast crowd of sightseers eagerly awaited a glimpse of visitors from outer space.

For the first time Chad realised. *We are the aliens, strange creatures from outer space.* He and his small group had entered a whirlwind of activity, where they had lost control of events. He recognised Arturi and Kensasha but didn't know the other two beings with them. In his bewildered state, someone spoke to him and held out a hand in greeting. It was Arturi.

"Come, Captain Chadwick, it will be quieter in the transport. I am delighted to meet you in the flesh. This is my good friend and colleague Doctor Kensasha Nnumet, who I believe you have already met. Kensasha is also on our ruling council."

Arturi introduced the other two councillors that were in their party. Neither spoke English and Chad wondered how Arturi and Kensasha could speak the language so well, but he had no time to dwell on it. Chad turned and introduced the rest of his small group. With the introductions complete and the noise of the crowd in the background, Councillor Arturi said, "We have arranged a reception for you and we have also set aside a small holiday resort where your crew may stay as guests and rest, relax and be entertained if their shipboard duties will allow."

"That is very generous of you, Councillor Arturi."

"Oh, please just call me Arturi."

"Why, thank you. Call me Chad, most everyone else does when I'm not on duty."

"Please come and meet our reception committee." Arturi encouraged Chad and his party to wave from the transport to the cheering crowd.

"Our people are very pleased to see you; it is so very exciting for them. We have always thought that we were alone in the universe, now we know differently."

The transport vehicles were luxurious driverless automatics. Arturi gave a command in his own language and the vehicle set off at a comfortable speed.

The day was bright and warm with a pale blue sky dotted with white puffball clouds and the atmosphere was clean and pleasant, through the vehicle's windows could be seen a beautiful alien landscape with green vegetation and trees that were completely different from anything they had seen before but were still recognisable as trees. Here and there, they saw structures that looked like homes but again unlike anything they had ever seen before. About fifteen minutes' drive from the spaceport, they arrived at an imposing building in a park like setting.

A large group of people, who Arturi informed them were Marac Council members, were outside the building awaiting their arrival. Arturi led Chad and Helen over to a distinguished looking man and made the introductions. The next few hours were a confusion of questions and meeting councillors.

Finally, to their relief, Arturi guided them to a quiet section of the building and into a well-appointed room. "I am sorry; this must be an ordeal for you all being plunged into a diplomatic arena with everyone wanting to speak with you when you don't understand the language."

Chad said, "Well I must admit to needing a break."

"Don't worry, Chad, we have a government residence where you will be staying."

"Thank you; it has been a long but exciting day."

"Please wait here and I will make the transport arrangements."

Chad and the others collapsed into chairs whilst Arturi went off to make the arrangements.

Chapter 29

The government residence was plush like a first-class hotel. Arturi showed Helen and Chad to their lovely comfortable suite and explained how everything worked. "Oh, there is one other thing I must show you." He pointed to a small control pad on the bedside table. "This is linked electronically to the pillows; I'll set it up for you both. This will not only help you sleep but by morning you will both have a good grounding in our language."

Chad and Helen looked at each other and could see they were both thinking of the communicator, how it educated them whilst they slept.

Chad was curious. "How did you learn our language in the first place?"

Arturi said, "Our computer sampled all the spoken words from your ships on the radio and gradually compiled the language. Then it fed the results into our teaching machine which instils the language into the brain during sleep." Chad could not help but think. *These people are more advanced than I ever imagined. Why didn't I think of that? Iris could have done that for us with ease.*

There was a soft tap on the door and a young woman brought in a small trolley with a selection of food and drink. Arturi explained what each dish was, finally saying, "I will meet up with you in the morning after you have eaten and rested. Goodnight to you both."

The snacks were delicious but they were both tired. Chad yawned. "I am absolutely bushed."

"So am I. It's a shower and then bed."

They delighted in the shower; it was a walk-through affair. First, they were sprayed with warm water and then with softly scented soapy water, finally rinsed off with warm water that ran off them leaving them completely dry and refreshed. Chad had been expecting a warm air dryer or towels but there were none and indeed, he didn't need any. Stepping from the shower, he found nightwear awaiting him and a warm dressing gown. Helen was already in bed and lying down with her eyes closed almost asleep. She murmured, "Can you hear that lovely music…?" and her voice tailed off as she drifted away.

Chad got into bed. "I hope I can get off as quick as that." As he lay back on the soft pillow he said, "Helen was right; this music is beauti…"

The following morning Chad awoke feeling fully refreshed, Helen was already up and sipping a hot drink. She said something to him in a foreign language, yet he seemed to understand it. "Come on, Chad, I've been up for ages."

How did I understand that? Chad thought. What was even more unnerving was that he had responded in the same language. "Yes, but I need my beauty sleep!"

Helen saw the confusion on his face and laughed. "Don't worry, Chad, it's the language program, it has worked its magic on us. I was quite able to understand the young woman who brought us these hot drinks. Here's yours, drink it before it gets cold."

They found Hernani and Keung having breakfast.

Keung said, "Did you sleep well?" Helen responded in the foreign language. Hernani and Keung laughed quietly.

Hernani said, "My bedroom is magnificent as was the shower. I'd love to have one like it on the ship."

They found Arturi patiently waiting for them. "I'm sure you are curious about us and our city." Everyone nodded in agreement. "I thought you might like a short tour before any formal meetings."

"You're quite right, Arturi, we are curious about everything," said Chad.

The city tour was a revelation, beautiful buildings with graceful arches, domes and spires and here and there, ornate features with no functional purpose other than to delight the eye. Chad knew he would need more than just a city tour to appreciate this place. He became aware Keung was speaking.

"Arturi, how is it all kept so pristine?"

"Oh, it wasn't always like this but now we have automated equipment to carry out maintenance work of roads and buildings. Our government invested heavily in electronics and robotics and all vehicles are electric, so no fumes to foul the air." Chad was impressed. "If you are agreeable, our governing council would like you to informally meet some of their advisory committee members before a formal welcoming meeting. That way you will be able to exchange ideas about technology and so forth."

"Thank you, Arturi. That is certainly a good idea."

"Good I'll arrange that for tomorrow. However, tonight, we have arranged some entertainment for you. I hope you will enjoy it."

The entertainment that evening consisted mostly of poets or entertainers giving monologues. Chad struggled to stay awake and he could see he was not the only one. Chad didn't want to be unkind but thought. *Our theatrical group are more entertaining and they are only amateurs.* A voice in his head seemed to say, "You should invite us to see to see your theatrical group." Chad frowned. *Why did a thought like that pop into my head?*

On the way, back to the residence Arturi asked Helen and Chad if they had enjoyed the show. Helen diplomatically said, "Oh, it was lovely. We have an amateur theatrical group on the ship that puts on all sorts of shows. It is a completely different style of entertainment to yours but you might enjoy it."

Arturi replied, "I would love to be invited to something like that."

"Good, we'll get something organised," Helen said.

"Chad, we have any number of volunteers expressing their desire to be hosts and guides. I imagine many of your crew would like to stretch their legs on real soil," Arturi said.

"Yes, they certainly would."

"Then please make arrangements for all of them to have at least some time here. We have set aside a small resort where they can relax and enjoy Marac hospitality."

"Thank you, Arturi, but we don't want to swamp you with visitors or overstay our welcome."

"Chad, having visitors from across the galaxy is a momentous event for us. I know I can speak for the whole council; you and your crew are very welcome to stay as long as you wish."

"Thank you, Arturi; you have certainly put my mind to rest."

"Have a nice restful night, tomorrow you and your team will be meeting the committee members."

That evening Chad called the *JJ Grant* for a report and spoke to Gordon on the bridge. "Everything's fine, Chad. The crew are in good spirits and keen to get their feet on the ground."

"That's good, I'm told that a small resort has been set aside for us to use."

"Captain, what is it like down there on the planet?"

Chad could hear the eagerness in Gordon's voice. It had been a long time since the crew had set foot on natural soil. He could imagine the excitement amongst the crew. "It's ultra-modern, very automated, and the people are welcoming. You will not be disappointed. However, there is something else, can you ask the theatrical people to put a show on. We want to bring some of the Marac VIPs and their partners aboard the ship and entertain them with a musical or variety show, something jolly and bright. They have entertained us and I would like us to reciprocate. Speak to Dave Wells, the theatrical director and tell him it's important, the sooner the better."

"I'll call him now and get back to you."

Half an hour later Chad's communicator buzzed.

"The director says he can put something half decent on in a couple of days. They have all the costumes and props and he is suggesting an evening performance."

"That is brilliant. Please give him my thanks and I'll tie up with him before then."

Chapter 30

The meetings with the Marac council advisers went well to a degree. However, Chad felt pressured and could detect, although it was never plainly stated, that his ship's drive technology was the holy grail of their discussions. Chad skirted round it but left little doubt that the drive technology was not up for discussion especially at this early stage and talked of provisions, and lower grade technology such as viewers, robotics and communications technologies.

To his relief the meeting finally disbanded in a friendly way; there was no rush, the visitors, it was hoped, would remain for a long time. The official welcome would be held in two days' time with the whole council present.

The following day Chad called Arturi. "My group are going up to the *JJ Grant* this morning. Eric Jones will pilot us. I wondered if you and a few of your colleagues would like to accompany us."

Arturi jumped at the chance. He contacted some fellow councillors, who also wanted to go, word got out and they were overwhelmed by people who were also eager to visit the ship.

An embarrassed Arturi called Chad. "I'm sorry, Chad, but I have people clamouring to visit your ship, what is the most I can bring?" Chad could imagine the scene. "Arturi, we are not geared up to receive too many people yet. Can you restrict the number to fifty and I'll arrange more visits later?"

Later, Chad called Gordon on the communicator. "We have around fifty Maracuni visitors coming up with me this morning to look at the ship. Can you get Iris to monitor visitors entering the ship's bay for weapons? I'm not expecting anything it's just a precaution."

Chad's transport pulled up outside the spaceport's offices where the commander stood watching people spilling out of the large passenger transport and being led to the waiting shuttle craft. Chad had met the commander very briefly earlier but now had the chance to talk to him. "I understand you tried to prevent what happened when our ships arrived?"

"Yes, I did, Captain, not very successfully but I am both pleased and relieved at the outcome."

"What has become of the person responsible for the action?"

"General Gion? Oh, he's fully recovered and he's still in the military but has relinquished his post to become a lecturer on military strategy."

Chad was curious. "What sort of illness was it?"

"Some sort of aneurysm in the brain, apparently it had been getting worse for a long time. His crime was not seeking medical help. Now of course he's had his treatment and he's as good as new."

Chad nodded and said, "That's good." He would talk with Kensasha soon and find out a bit more about the treatment.

The shuttle laden with visitors was in clear space, Eric Jones pointed out the Marac space station and above it in high orbit, the *JJ Grant*. The ship gleamed like a jewel, all her lights on and the three smaller warships, strung behind her sparkling, like a comet's tail. As they approached the *JJ Grant*, the bay door opened and light from the interior spilled out. The passengers had become deathly quiet; they sat apprehensively in absolute silence. Eric pointed the shuttle at the entrance and smoothly entered the bay and rolled to a halt where the wheel clamps locked on.

When the green light came on to say pressure had been restored, Eric announced on the vessel's speakers, "We are cleared to disembark." Immediately a hubbub of noise rose from the relieved passengers as they all started chattering again.

Chad and Helen with Hernani and Keung exited the shuttle first and stood to one side as they greeted and welcomed the visitors to the *JJ Grant*. "I hope you enjoyed the trip up here." There was an answering chorus of agreement to say that it had been a thrilling experience. As his passengers disembarked, they looked around at the vast bay wondering what they would see. Most of the passengers were young; the oldest looked to be about forty, most were tall and appeared to be fit and healthy. Surprisingly all spoke English quite well.

Chad announced, "The ship's bridge is a continuously working environment and we will have to split the group up into small parties." Chad and Helen led the senior council members onto the bridge. He could see the visitors keenly examining and evaluating the equipment. He took them on a short tour of the ship, eventually ending up in the restaurant where drinks and canapés were offered. The restaurant had been converted into a theatre.

Arturi said, "So this is your theatre, I'm impressed, Chad. I should like to see one of your productions."

"And so, you shall, our theatrical director is putting together a show which should be ready for the end of the week. When I have the details, I would like to invite your councillors and their partners to a performance and if they enjoy the show perhaps our performers could put on the show in the Marac theatre for others to see."

Arturi was delighted. "Thank you, Chad, that is most generous and we will be delighted to come."

"Is there any other part of the ship you would like to see, Arturi?"

"I'd very much like to see your engine room, I am curious about your motive power."

"Certainly, Arturi, come this way."

Chad guided his small group of visitors to the engine room but there was little to see – other than a huge assembly of steel set into a massive girder framework.

"How does it work, Captain?" someone asked.

"Unfortunately, I'm not able to discuss that other than to say it has taken us a long time to develop." Chad was reinforcing his earlier message to the committee that the drive system was not up for discussion.

Arturi thought to himself. *Who could blame them, if it were Marac with the space drive, would we give it up – No! I don't think we would. The reception they received from us cannot have helped either.*

He resolved to do all he could to gain the trust of these aliens. One never knew what the future would bring.

Arturi knew that Chad had things to do and it was time to for him and the people with him to leave.

"Thank you for the tour of your ship, Chad, but I must ask if you can return us to the spaceport. My fellow councillors and I have council business awaiting us. However, we are grateful for the opportunity to see inside the *JJ Grant*."

"It's been a pleasure having your people here, Arturi. Eric will take you back straight away; unfortunately, I have work to do here but will return to the spaceport later today. Would you be able to arrange transport if I radio the spaceport commander before we leave?"

"Certainly, Chad, there will be transport at your disposal."

Chad steered Arturi to one side. "There is one thing, Arturi; it is a delicate matter for us."

Immediately Arturi, very concerned, said, "What is it, Chad, I'll help in any way I can."

"Unfortunately, before we arrived in your system there was an accident in space and two of our crew died. We want to hold a funeral and bury them, as is our custom. It is the way we honour our dead."

Arturi could see the sadness in Chad. "I'm sure a suitable site can be found. I will call you with details immediately after I get back to the Council Hall."

Thank you Arturi, that is very decent of you."

An hour later Comms called Chad. "I have Councillor Arturi on the radio for you, Captain."

"Thanks, Comms, I'll take the call in the bridge office.

"Chad, we have a site that is suitable for a memorial. May I suggest that the two crewmembers be brought down to the space station as soon as possible? We will take them to our hospital where they have the facilities to look after your people until you have organised their burials. The site is only a short drive away."

"Thank you for your understanding, Arturi, I'll arrange for them to be brought down very shortly."

Chad quietly arranged with Eric, supported by Henson and a small team of his men, to take the bodies of Mark Williams and Frank Palmer down to the spaceport where transport would be waiting to take them to the hospital morgue.

When the shuttle with the two bodies had left, Chad gave a sad sigh; he decided that after the meeting with the Marac House Assembly tomorrow he would ask Helen if she would arrange their funerals. He called Iris, "Presumably none of our visitors were armed?"

"No, Captain. Nothing showed up on the door scanner."

Chad nodded. "Thanks, Iris, it was just a precaution, I wasn't expecting anything."

Keung called on the viewer. "Chad, I know you are busy, is there anything I can help out with?"

"Thanks for calling, Keung, yes there is. Can you get Iris to give you the provisioning and consumable supplies list for all our vessels to bring them up to full capacity? I'll arrange with Arturi to organise a shopping trip for you and let you have the details later. We have a meeting tomorrow with the Marac councillors and it might be beneficial for you to attend.

Chad made another call. "Hello, Arturi, I'm sorry to bother you again but our purchasing officer Keung Zheng now has a shopping list of supplies required to replenish our stores and he would like to find out what is available."

"Chad, I'll get someone to take him to one of our wholesale distributers which may interest him. He can also visit some of our factory outlets to see the latest technology products. However, you are going to be our guests for some time so there is no immediate rush for anything."

"Arturi, thank you, that would be fantastic."

Chapter 31

Chad needed to bone up on the Maracuni system. Iris had provided a lot of information but he wanted a more hands-on assessment about the three planets. He called up Max Smith. "Hello, Max, what can you tell me about the Maracuni system?"

"Quite a lot, Captain, it's absolutely unique."

"OK, I want you in the wardroom in an hour to give a briefing about it. Keep it basic, we just need to be able to discuss the system intelligently when we are in conversation with the councillors and any of its inhabitants."

When Chad arrived in the wardroom, Max was already there and had set up a whiteboard and a video screen. Max started his briefing bang on time. Chad had to admit he was good; Max had done his homework and kept everyone's attention. He gave an interesting and informative talk.

However, by the end of the briefing, Chad wasn't feeling at all bright. He wanted to get back to Helen and his cabin for a rest. He called Iris, "No calls, unless there is an emergency, until it's time for Eric to take us down to the spaceport."

"Yes, Captain," she responded.

When the shuttle arrived at the spaceport, the transport was waiting and they were soon at the Marac residence. Helen was worried. "Chad, you don't look at all well. I think one of the doctors on the ship should have a look at you. We can easily get one down here within an hour."

"Oh, do stop fussing, Helen; I'll be as right as rain after a good night's sleep."

The next morning, Chad felt a bit better and got himself ready for the meeting with the Marac councillors.

Arturi was already there waiting for them.

"Good morning, Arturi. I hope we didn't keep you waiting."

"Good morning. No, we have plenty of time. Hernani and Keung are already waiting in the transport to take us to the meeting."

A young female with a soft pleasant voice led Chad and the others into a comfortable waiting room with floor to ceiling windows. The windows looked out over parkland rich with trees and shrubs, none of which Chad could identify. "Arturi will join you very shortly," the young female said.

Helen joined Chad at the vast window and gazed out. "What a wonderful view, I could happily live in a place like this."

Chad just nodded, she looked at him and noticed that he was perspiring slightly, his skin a little grey.

"Are you OK?" Chad nodded again but Helen could see there was something not right. She saw the look of pain on his face and he clutched his chest as he staggered. Had it not been for Keung catching him he would have fallen to the floor. Keung carefully laid Chad into a comfortable position on the floor, Helen crouched beside him and urgently said to Hernani, "Quick, get some help, Chad is having a heart attack or a stroke."

She loosened his collar and he murmured, "Chest pain." His face contorting in agony. As Hernani rushed to the automatic door, Arturi came into the room.

Hernani cried, "It's Chad, he's having a heart attack."

Arturi was instantly by Chad's side and spoke urgently into a wrist communicator. He turned to Helen. "A medical team is on the way." Within a couple of minutes, the team arrived and immediately sprayed something into Chad's mouth. His breathing almost instantly improved, settled a bit and the pain showing on his face gave way to a more relaxed look.

The hospital trolley fairly flew down the corridor with two medical staff in attendance, closely followed by Helen and Arturi, both trotting to keep up with it. The operating theatre was painted a brilliant white accompanied by gleaming metal. A team of surgeons and support staff were standing beside a complex machine gowned up ready to receive Chad.

Whilst still on the trolley, Chad was quickly stripped of his clothes and a dark blue sheet placed over him. Each of the medical team seemed to be doing something. A platform slid out from the machine and Chad was quickly transferred from the trolley onto the soft body-forming platform, which speedily retracted back into the machine virtually swallowing him leaving the blue sheet in the hands of one of the medical team. Chad lay barely visible in the machine as equipment silently moved into different positions around Chad's body. A large screen lit up and a strip of bright green light quickly scanned the length of his inert body. The screen now showed a three-dimensional real-time image of Chad's throbbing heaving heart and blood vessels. The point of the blockage in an artery was clearly visible on the screen, highlighted by a pulsating halo of expanding yellow rings. Also visible was a bullet shaped probe that had somehow entered the artery and was now moving quickly up to the blockage. Another view, taken by a camera on front of the bullet probe, showed a congealed mass constricting the flow of blood to the heart. More detail was being added to the display with each pass of the strobing light.

Helen, distraught by events, could only stand by and watch whilst Chad was receiving treatment. None of the medical team said a word, they just watched the probe and the scrolling figures on the screen.

Arturi put a hand on Helen's shoulder and said, "Chad is in good hands, the robot surgeon will complete the procedure. The medical team are only here should something not go to plan."

Helen nodded. "I can see Chad is being worked on but we are a different species and I worry that the doctors are not familiar with our physiology." Even as she said it, Helen knew she was worrying over nothing; these people were far in advance of Earth when it came to medical knowledge.

"All living things follow a pre-set design, even if they evolve in different ways. We have the medical technology to treat any of our own species on our planet and I'm sure you humans will have the same fundamentals even if we look slightly different to each other."

Helen still worried. "Arturi, I know you mean well but can you explain the procedures Chad is having to me."

Arturi beckoned one of the medical team over. It was Kensasha; Helen hadn't recognised him because of the mask he was wearing. "Kensasha will try and keep you informed."

Kensasha gave a little bow to Helen and said, "Chad is in no danger, this simple operation is just what you see. The blockage is being removed, a small tube will be left where the blockage was, that will dissolve when the artery has recovered and a fluid is being injected into the cardiovascular system to dissolve any other build-ups of plaque in the system. The operation is almost complete. As the device leaves his artery, it will leave behind a plug and a healing gel that will close the wound. While we have him in the machine, we'll give him a full medical and check to see if there is anything else that requires attention."

Helen bit her lip anxiously but nodded her understanding.

Evan as Kensasha spoke Helen could see the operation was over, as the probe exited Chad's body and dropped into a receptacle. The screen became alive with scrolling figures and symbols, none of which made any sense to her.

Chad's colour and breathing returned to normal. The monitor showed his heart no longer labouring and had resumed a steady beat; it looked like Chad was fully recovering.

"Oh, Chad looks so much better but is it possible he may have suffered brain damage?"

"It's possible but unlikely. Even if there is brain damage that can be taken care of." Helen was amazed. *They seem so casual about medical marvels. Was everything really that simple?* She mentally filed the question away.

"There are guest rooms in this facility," Kensasha said. "Would you like to stay here for a day or two until Chad is fully recovered? I can make the arrangements now."

"Oh, that would be marvellous, thank you so much."

After Kensasha left, Helen turned to Arturi. "Thank you for acting so quickly, you saved Chad's life."

Arturi smiled. "No, it just happened that Chad chose the right place to have a heart attack."

A short while later Kensasha returned. "It's all organised, they'll take Chad to a recovery ward where he'll sleep for a while. Come on and I'll show you where the guest rooms are."

As they walked to the guest facility, Arturi said, "I'm sorry, Helen, I must leave you with Kensasha but I'll see you later."

When Arturi had left, Kensasha said, "We're going to pass my office and I have Chad's medical report from the diagnostic machine. I'd like to run over it with you."

"Is there something wrong with Chad?" She was immediately worried and frightened.

"Nothing of immediate concern. We'll have a chat in my office; it's just along here."

When Helen was seated, Kensasha said, "The good news is that Chad's operation was a complete success and he will make a full recovery. However, the diagnostic machine has identified a number of problems that need to be addressed if he is not to have life threatening medical issues in future years."

"What sort of problems?"

"Chad is not a young man, even by your Earth standards. He has biologically reached an age where health problems will become evident."

"You mean dementia, that sort of thing?"

"Helen, let me put it this way, how old do you think I am?"

Helen stared at him. "In Earth years, I would guess thirty maybe."

"And Arturi?"

"Oh, a bit older say thirty-five of our years."

Kensasha smiled. "Would you be surprised if I told you that I am close to six hundred of your years and Kensasha just over seven hundred"

Helen gaped at him in surprise. "How can you look so young?"

Kensasha grinned. "Well I did say our medical knowledge was in advance of your own. We discovered many years ago, that nearly all animal species have the power to heal themselves to varying degrees. Your own species can repair itself in a limited way. If you cut yourself, the cut heals in a few days. That fact alone can be nurtured and guided to produce phenomenal results. However, if we cut ourselves, we heal in minutes."

Helen was stunned. "Is that really true, Kensasha?"

"Absolutely, look around you, how many elderly Maracuni people have you seen?"

"Now you mention it, none, but people must eventually become old, they can't just live forever."

"True, no one wants to live forever but eventually they wish to be reborn. That is why you will see young people here."

Helen, full of consternation was about to ask more questions but Kensasha held up a hand to stop her. "I know you have a multitude of questions but the subject is too deep and important to cover in a few minutes. You must study the history of our species to appreciate the way we live and die."

It was true she knew little of their history. "Sorry. Kensasha, please go on."

"The important thing today is Chad; we want him to have a long and happy life free from ill health and that is why he needs our help." Opening the report Kensasha continued, "We have identified many problems that can be forestalled by simple treatment now. However, we can do more than that, much more."

Over the next couple of hours, Kensasha took Helen on a tour of the human body, in particular, Chad's body, using the results from the diagnostic machine that had scanned Chad earlier and a 3D screen in his office.

"You are aware that you have cells in your body that can differentiate into any form of specialist cell that the body requires."

"Yes, I think we call them stem cells and we have others that we call embryonic stem cells."

"Right, and there are many others but that is the sort of thing that we are talking about. The problem in simplistic terms is that Chad only produces a very few of these types of cells in his blood and bone marrow. Nowhere near enough for what his body needs to repair organs quickly and stay in good condition, subsequently his body repairs very slowly, sometimes it is unable to make a repair at all or worse still, it gets confused and tries to repair the wrong part."

Kensasha went on to relate the Marac history of genes and DNA discoveries. "Today we fully understand the way genes work and how faulty gene sequences occur and how to put them right. There is no good reason for a being to die young or for injuries to take a long time to heal. For us that is a thing of the past. Our robotic machines can perform all the corrections required to put these things right."

"How were these discoveries made?" asked Helen.

"Like most discoveries, knowledge comes in small increments, fits and starts that build the big picture. Our investment in robotics assisted enormously in the development of genetics and we now fully understand the process of reproduction, body growth, healing, ageing and death. Should an individual suffer an accident and lose a limb, we can oversee the accelerated growth of a new limb. Even an eye or the brain can be restored and the brain only suffers the loss of memories."

Kensasha saw Helen's look of almost disbelief. "No, it is a fact; modified DNA is now fully established in our species and is passed naturally from parents to offspring. This change has also been transferred to much of the animal life in our planetary system. However, extended lifespan and good health are not the only effects that the manipulation of DNA has had on the production of specialist stem cells and the ageing process. Vast improvements in all five senses is the norm and, in some cases, a sixth sense can emerge. There has been another benefit for us; modified genetics has resulted in a very stable and supportable population of all living things on Maracuni." Helen was dumbstruck and amazed, unsure if Kensasha was exaggerating or not.

"What we would like to do is to treat Chad to enable him to recover completely. Effectively we would restructure parts of his DNA which in turn will treat the various ongoing problems evident throughout his system and correct his DNA sequence to give him the benefits that our species currently enjoys today."

Helen chewed her lip in consternation. "How would you do that, is the process dangerous?"

Kensasha smiled. "No, it's not at all dangerous. We anticipated that Chad could benefit from this treatment. The necessary program is already installed in the machine that was used to treat Chad for his heart attack. The machine is a multipurpose surgical robot. It is capable of performing every known surgical procedure automatically, without external assistance from any of my team."

"You mean Chad would be left on his own in the machine with no one helping?"

"No, Helen, there would be a full team of surgeons and nurses in attendance, as there was today, during the operation in case they were needed but to my knowledge they have never been called upon to interfere or assist in the surgery. Chad would be placed in this machine, which will cut and splice the DNA at the correct points and reposition the genes controlling the production of stem cells and other specialist cells and the section of the DNA controlling the ageing process. It will seek out other anomalies or mutations in his genes and DNA. Also, it will check the condition of all his organs, removing by non-invasive surgery any abnormality to assist and speed up the work of new specialist cells."

Helen was still concerned. "I understand, Kensasha, but we would be putting all our trust in a robot?"

"That is true but the robot is far more skilled than anyone in this hospital. It has gained these skills from the very best surgeons in each specialist field over many years."

"But it sounds like a very long operation," Helen said worriedly.

"Not really, spelling it out like this makes it sound like a lengthy operation but the reality is that it will be over quite quickly."

Helen had begun to realise that as far as Kensasha was concerned, this was just another routine procedure, not experimental or extraordinary. She looked Kensasha in the eye. "What is the failure rate of the robot machine?"

"I have never known a robot to fail. Historically they have a one hundred per cent success rate with each procedure ever since they were introduced."

"Thank you, Kensasha, we'll have to discuss it with Chad and see how he feels about it."

"But of course, I'll show you the guest room and then we can go back and discuss it with Chad. He will be more than ready for visitors by now."

Chapter 32

Chad was sitting up in bed and chatting on his communicator when Helen and Kensasha entered the ward. Chad beamed at them as they came in. Helen rushed over to him and gave him a hug. "I was so worried. You gave us such a scare, how are you feeling?"

Chad gave her hand a squeeze of thanks. "Never felt better," he said. He grinned at Kensasha. "I don't know who did what but I feel as good as new." Chad sensed that something was not right. "Is there a problem, have I missed something?"

Helen looked worried. "Kensasha has a proposal, which he's explained to me in detail and I think you should consider it." Kensasha looked to Helen for permission to carry on. Helen nodded.

"Chad, the procedure to remove the blockage in your artery was completely successful. However, while you were in the diagnostic machine, we carried out a routine exam and that has thrown up a number of potential problems for you in the not too distant future." Kensasha paused for a moment. "Helen has seen the evidence and I have outlined the remedy to her."

Helen, on the verge of tears could only nod confirmation.

Chad, becoming alarmed, said defensively, "Well no one lives forever."

Kensasha smiled "Very true, Helen and I were only talking about that a short while ago. However, Helen and I agreed it is better for you to live a long and happy life." Kensasha went on to reveal his own age and that of Arturi.

Chad shook his head in wonder. "You're serious, aren't you?"

"Yes, Chad, I am. It's all about the genes that make up an individual's DNA. They determine health and longevity. We know how to manipulate these to get the best results. We are offering you an operation that will take care of all your potential health problems. We will switch on the genes that make abundant stem cells that repair the body and switch off the genes that determine when one's life should end. I've been through the whole process with Helen."

Chad had listened carefully. "That's a lot to take in, Kensasha, do you mind if I think about it?"

"Of course not. It is an important decision for you. I will leave you to discuss this with Helen in private. If you need me or just want some refreshments, press the call button," pointing to a button on the bedside table, "an attendant will come straight away."

"What's not to like? I've come to trust these people; they obviously have tremendous medical knowledge. I'd just like to have Kensasha run this by me again so that I fully understand the implications of the results."

Chad had already made his mind up; he would willingly have the procedure but only on one condition. This gift was too tempting to refuse.

Later when Arturi and Kensasha came to visit him Chad said, "I can't tell you how grateful I am for what you have done for me and I really appreciate your offer for further treatment. I would like to have the procedure but if it is successful, I can't just watch my wife and friends grow old and die…"

Before he could say more, Arturi held up a hand to stop him. "We know and understand how you feel, it is not necessary to ask. Kensasha and I were about to propose treatment for all your crew if they wished it."

Chad thanked them profusely and said, "I don't know how we can repay you?"

Arturi smiled. "It's not every day we receive visitors from across the galaxy and it is our pleasure to help you in any way we can and it costs us nothing. The facility and equipment are here and it runs automatically." He paused for a moment and with a smile said, "But we do enjoy watching the films and videos that you have shown us of life on your planet. If you have more, we would be happy to receive them."

Chad grinned. "We have data sticks with hours of news, geographical and historical data as well as all sorts of sports music and entertainment, more than enough to fill a library, which we would be pleased to transmit to you."

Arturi and Kensasha beamed, Chad simply had no idea how excited the people in the whole Maracuni planetary system were to have visitors from another planet, a planet that possessed so many varieties of cultures and life of all description. Especially as the Maracuni, people looked to be of one race and only had one language but now many of the Maracuni people used their sleep teaching machines to learn English.

The following day, two young nurses prepared Chad for the DNA gene manipulation and other surgical procedures whilst Kensasha explained, "This morning, stimulants will be injected into your blood and bone marrow to start the process of enriching them with T cells and other types of cells. The second stage will be to rearrange the gene groupings, then cut, and splice your DNA.

"Tomorrow you will undergo a series of simple operations to remove small tumours and other abnormalities that we previously identified. You will then be subjected to a barrage of painless tests to ensure all is well."

Chad was only half-awake as he lay on the comfortable body-forming platform within the machine. A pretty nurse smiled at him as she pulled a transparent shield down over her face… He opened his eyes to see Helen smiling at him. "Come on, sleepy head, you've been asleep for ages." Chad looked around; he was in bed and feeling terrific.

"What happened, did the op get cancelled?"

Helen laughed. "No, it's all over, everything went very smoothly."

"I can't believe it; did they find any tumours or problems?"

"Yes, they did. Kensasha let me stay to see what was going on. I certainly don't want to do that again. I could see things wriggling around under your skin and every now and again, there would be a squishing sound or something would plop into a bowl. I had to leave when the machine started doing something to your eyes." Helen peered into his eyes. "Can you see OK?"

"Yes of course I can, in fact I think I can see clearer than before."

Helen laughed. "I'm so happy; you came here almost dying and look at you now, better than ever." She wiped a tear from her eye.

He spent the rest of the day chatting with Helen and speaking with his senior officers via his communicator on all four ships. He relaxed knowing they were all capable and dependable.

The following day Kensasha returned to the ward with Arturi. After the pleasantries were over, Kensasha said, "You're looking fine, Chad, the quickest way for us to find out if everything is working as it should be is to put you back in the diagnostic machine."

With a cheerful grin, Chad said, "That's fine by me but I can tell you now, from the way I feel, it's all working."

Arturi grinned and Kensasha said, "Right let's get an orderly to get you down to the machine now."

Chad shook his head. "Not necessary, I can get down there under my own steam." With that, he hopped out of bed.

Kensasha smiled. "I can see the machine is hardly necessary but let's get the formalities over."

The machine hummed and the bright green light scanned over Chad's body several times. As well as data scrolling on the viewer, data slips slid into a receiver next to the large screen.

Kensasha made marks on the pad in his hand as he collected the data slips. Finally, he smiled and showed the results to Arturi, then turned to Chad. "As we expected; a perfect score, all the procedures have gone according to plan. The internal procedures like T cell production are working well and the count is high. It may take several months for other things to become noticeable."

"What changes do you expect to see?"

Again, Kensasha grinned. Pointing to Chad's bald spot he said, "Your hair will return. Your skin will tighten up and you will lose your wrinkles. You'll look younger."

Kensasha had already explained this to him. However, only now was he beginning to believe it in his own mind.

Back on the ward and sitting up in bed, Chad grumbled, "Do I really need to stay here? I feel as fit as a fiddle."

Kensasha smiled. "Relax, lie back, close your eyes and have a short rest. I'll get someone to bring you a cool drink and afterwards I think you should be fit enough to return to the residence."

"OK, if you say so."

Lying back on the pillow, Chad closed his eyes and counted his blessings. Fully relaxed he fell into a dose. Hearing soft footsteps approaching, he opened his eyes expecting to see a nurse with his drink. Instead, he gasped with shock. He felt as though he was hallucinating; tears sprang from his eyes. Standing by his bed with massive smiles on their faces were Mark Williams and Frank Palmer. Almost in unison they said, "Hello, Captain." Chad jumped from the bed and flung his arms around both young men.

"Is… is it really you? How can it be?"

Mark loosely spread out his arms taking in the whole hospital. "We have these people to thank. Apparently, it was the fact that we were kept frozen that saved us.

They cut us out of our suits, thawed us out and pumped oxygen and stuff into our lungs. Then flushed out our blood and did all sorts of things to restore us. Here we are almost as good as new. Another few days and we can go back on the ship." Chad shook his head in disbelief.

Frank said, "It was Doctor Kensasha's idea, for us to surprise you, cheer you up, that sort of thing."

"Well it's certainly done that – I thought we'd lost you both. We were soon to start planning your funerals."

A short while later Kensasha came into the ward with a beaming smile. "You can get dressed now, Chad. Helen's waiting at the Marac residence for you and these two can go back and have a bit of bed rest." As the two young men disappeared down the corridor, Kensasha said, "They should make a full recovery, I'll let you know when we've given them the all clear."

"Kensasha, apart from offering my deepest gratitude to you, I have a question. You know all there is to know about genes and DNA and what makes life tick?"

"That is true to a point, Chad, but what's your question?"

"My question is, why do our different species look so alike – humans, Thark, Orrappa and the people of the Maracuni system. We have more variations of human beings on Earth than there are between these different species."

Kensasha looked at him for a minute. "If you have the odd few years to spare, we can go through the subject of genetics in great detail, but the short answer is that all natural sentient life, if it is to survive and flourish, will evolve like us with the minimum requirements of five senses together with mobility and dexterity. There will always be slight differences as sentient beings adapt to their environments. I am sure that on your planet Earth you have people that live at high altitude, with bigger lungs to breathe a thinner atmosphere or others with differences in skin colour or bone structure, maybe with small internal oddities. However, they will always have two arms, two legs, a trunk and a head with a brain inside it. I believe that no matter where you go in the universe, if there is intelligent life it will evolve like us."

Chad nodded. "Hmm… I guess you're right."

"Come on, I'll take you to the residence. Helen's waiting for you."

Chad held out his hand. "Kensasha, I owe you my life. Thanks for all you have done for the two boys and me. I now understand about General Gion's medical disorder and how your medical staff have corrected the problem and made him fit to carry on working even if it is in another job."

"Yes, Chad, General Gion suffered an aneurysm that put pressure on his brain for a long time and nearly brought disaster upon us all because he didn't seek medical help. The correction to his brain was simple and he is fully fit again. It was his own choice to take up a new career."

In the hallway of the residence, Helen rushed up to them and threw her arms around Chad. "Oh, Chad, are you well enough to be here? Shouldn't you have stayed in hospital?" Both Chad and Kensasha laughed,

"No, I'm fine; Kensasha has given me a clean bill of health. I feel simply great. Come on, let's have a drink."

I'll tell her about Mark and Frank later. We've had enough excitement for now.

Despite Chad's assurances, Helen wanted him to have an early night; it had been a long and exciting day.

Walking through the shower he realised something was missing. Checking himself in the full-length mirror, he saw a prominent mole that he'd had, had gone, in fact all his moles and little blemishes had gone. Feeling the pulse in his wrist, it felt extraordinarily slow. Taking a deep breath and expanding his chest, he was amazed how long he could hold his breath and how much bigger his chest felt. Remembering Helen had mentioned his eyes being worked on; he peered into the mirror and examined both eyes. He could see no difference; they were still brown with tiny flecks of yellow. Peering closer, every tiny detail of the eye stood out, even the retina and the macula itself. In the background through the bathroom door he heard Helen slide into bed and then call out, "Come on, Chad; let's have an early night please."

Lying in bed listening to Helen's soft breathing and the sounds of the room around him, he thought, *I am changing and I'm changing damn fast.*

Helen and Chad were dressed and had eaten when Arturi arrived. Chad was embarrassed about missing the meeting with the councillors. "Please give them my apologies, Arturi."

"Chad, don't worry about it; the important thing is that you are now well."

"Thanks, Arturi, you have made me feel a bit better. Before I caused all this fuss, I spoke to our theatre director and can now extend an invitation to the councillors for the day after tomorrow to come and see a typical Earth style show on the *JJ Grant*. We can comfortably accommodate around four hundred people in our theatre. We'll use two shuttles to ferry them up to the *JJ Grant* and bring them back after the show. If they enjoy it, we can do a short run for a few nights that others might see it."

"That is very kind of you Chad, but are you sure about going to all this trouble of having the performance on your ship? Not long ago you did speak of putting a performance on in one of our theatres on Marac."

"Well it's my way of saying thanks Arturi. I believe seeing a performance and a trip into space will make it a special experience for your councillors and others."

"Thank you, Chad, I will pass your invitation on to assembly and let you know later." *Who is going to turn down the chance of a ride into space and get aboard an interstellar spaceship even if the show is no good?*

"Thanks, Arturi. Could you include the medical team who were there for me? I would like to show my gratitude."

"Of course, I am sure they will be pleased."

Chad and Helen had barely settled back into their suite in the residence to have a little rest and to catch up with the reports from Wang and Grant, before Arturi contacted them. "The councillors have sent their congratulations on your recovery and would be pleased to accept your kind invitation to come aboard the *JJ Grant* and see your theatrical show. The medical team will also be coming and will bring their partners if that is all right?"

"Excellent, I will arrange for the shuttles to be at the spaceport to meet them. We'll have refreshments before the show and the shuttle will return them to the spaceport after the show. Will that be satisfactory?"

"It will be most satisfactory, Chad. We shall look forward to this very much."

"I hope you will all enjoy the show, but please remember the performers are only amateurs."

After Arturi had, gone Chad called the theatre director on the *JJ Grant*. "Hello Dave it's all arranged for the day after tomorrow and we may have to run the show for a few nights afterwards, is that OK?"

"That's fine, we've done this show before and have been rehearsing over the last few days to fine tune it. Everything is ready to go." In the background, Chad could hear a female voice saying, "Dave… Dave… David, you promised I could lead the chorus and now Wendy says you told her she could do it?"

Dave said, "Shush, not now Doreen, I'm talking to the captain."

"Er… everything OK Dave?"

"Yes Captain, just a slight artistic hiccup, it'll all be alright on the night."

That is brilliant; our guests may want to meet the performers afterwards."

"Well, the artists will be pleased about that, there is nothing a performer likes better than meeting his public."

As Chad was about to end the call he heard the same female, Doreen, in a loud stage whisper say, "Dave… Dave… David, Wendy says she'll do the solo spot instead." Chad smiled to himself as he ended the call. *Sounds like running a theatre is a bit like running the ship.*

Chad's next call was to Wang. "This is going to come as a shock, but I have some wonderful news; I have seen and spoken to Mark Williams and Frank Palmer in the hospital. They are both alive and well."

Wang was stunned. "Chad, you can't have. They died a long time ago. Henson and I brought their bodies back, remember?"

"Yes, I do, but against all the odds Kensasha and his team managed to save them. Apparently, the fact that they were frozen enabled remedial action to be taken. They will be fit to leave hospital in a couple of days when we can bring them back to the ship. Can you let Heather, Henson, Connie and the spacewalk team that recovered them know? Keep it low key until the lads are back on board the *JJ Grant*."

"Certainly, Chad. Er… you're not pulling my leg, are you?"

"No. I'm absolutely serious, Wang."

Chad spent time on his communicator catching up with others on the ships and checking reports of all descriptions and preparing for his upcoming meeting with the Marac councillors until Helen gave him an exasperated look. "You've had a long day; put that communicator away and we'll have some supper and then an early night."

Later, lying back in bed, Chad relaxed. *I was just so lucky that I had that heart attack here, had it happened on the ship or anywhere else I don't think I'd have survived.* He heard a soft melodious voice in his head. *Congratulations, Captain; I am so pleased that you are recovered.* Chad smiled. *Thanks, Iris.*

Helen, who'd been about to put the light out said, "What are you smiling at, Chad?"

"Oh nothing, I'm just pleased to be alive. Come on let's put the light out."

The following morning Chad felt like a new man. Helen was surprised. "You look so much better. You look like you've been on holiday not in hospital!"

Later Chad found Arturi waiting for him. "Just checking up on you to see how you're feeling?"

"Never better, Kensasha and his team have done a wonderful job."

"That is good, let me know when you have announced our offer to treat your whole crew and I will arrange a schedule for treatment."

"That's very kind of you, Arturi, thank you." Chad felt embarrassed to ask but felt he must. "Arturi, I am so grateful for what your people have done for the two boys and me. But there is something else; we have a female on the ship, Anne Prior. She was in an accident on Earth and her treatment was not successful. Anne's paralysed and in a wheelchair. Her partner, Richard Prior, was our base coordinator, one of the best. Anne asked to come on the ship to give some meaning to her life, which in a way it has. Is it possible that you could help her?"

"Have her sent down here, Chad; I will have Kensasha examine her when she arrives."

"Are you sure, Arturi?"

Arturi gestured at the communicator in Chad's hand. "Do it now. Kensasha will examine her today."

Richard Prior held his wife's hand as she lay on the hospital trolley being taken down to the operating theatre. He was anxious and disbelieving that these beings could help Anne. The best surgeons on Earth had said there was no more that could be done for her.

Kensasha put a hand on his shoulder. "I know you're worried but Anne is in safe hands. I can assure you she'll be walking around within a week if not sooner."

The machine that Anne lay within scanned her with a green light. The screen immediately displayed a three-dimensional view of Anne's spine in vivid detail. The titanium supports holding the vertebrae in position looked crude and clumsy, as did the equally crude screws biting into bone. Metal bands clamped around the fragile and damaged vertebrae had caused the spinal cord to be pinched in places. Yellow pulsing rings glowed at several spots along Anne's spine.

"The pulsing rings show areas of pain," Kensasha explained.

Richard flinched at the sight; he knew Anne always had pain but now he could see how much pain she'd suffered. He saw one of medical team give Kensasha a look and a small slow shake of her head, as if to say, what a mess. Kensasha tightened his jaw and his lips compressed into a thin line and said, "We can do better than this."

Even I could do better than that, thought Richard, although he knew he couldn't.

Kensasha explained as simply as possible, "We have a synthetic material that replicates bone; it is injected where it is needed. This hardens to become a very strong but flexible material that bonds with bone to become a scaffold for the spine. Once that is in place, we inject various types of stem cells that will turn into vertebrae, nerve or muscle and so on. Along with the various stem cells is an enzyme that will eat away the scaffold at the same pace as natural bone is grown to replace it.

Richard nodded dubiously, it sounded convincing but he was unsure. However, Anne had jumped at the chance; it was a lifeline no matter what the risk. He knew Anne would never forgive him if he halted the procedure.

Anne woke, lying on her back in the most comfortable bed she could ever have imagined. Richard was beside her, extremely concerned. "Hello, darling. How are you?"

She smiled. "I'm fine, I can't feel a thing."

Richard was devastated. "You mean you can't feel anything at all?"

"No, I mean I can feel no pain but I can wriggle my toes for the first time in years."

Richard's mood changed from one of despondency to one of elation. "The doctors said that would be the first sign of recovery and I didn't believe them."

"Did they say I would make a full recovery?"

Richard, with tears in his eyes, nodded. "That and more. They said that they had also performed all the procedures that Chad had received including reprogramming the age-related gene sequence." Richard wiped his eyes. "You mustn't try to move until tomorrow when your back will be much stronger." Richard could see Anne was drifting back to sleep again but he was so pleased to have been able to speak to her.

Kensasha was beside him. "She'll sleep through until tomorrow and then you'll hardly know her."

Arturi said, "I've rescheduled the meeting with the councillors for the same time next week if that is acceptable."

"It certainly is, thank you," Chad said.

"Is there anything in particular that you would like to see today?" They had a free day and Arturi was going to spend the whole day with them.

Helen butted in straight away. "We'd love to see the latest items for a home… the residence is fantastic but we'd like to see what the Maracuni people put in their own homes."

"Ah, I have just the thing, Helen, a tour of some of our consumer outlets, kitchens, bathrooms, bedrooms and living rooms. That sort of thing?"

"Oh, yes please, Arturi, and can we bring a few people with us?"

"Of course."

They ended up with a small party of friends.

The consumer products and furnishings were amazing. It was obvious that this world was far in advance of humans in almost every way. They visited various factories where many of the items that they had seen and admired were manufactured. The *JJ Grant's* viewing screens were high resolution but these Maracuni screens put them in the shade.

The highlight of the tour was a factory with complex machinery, manufacturing a vast range of products and equipment, all running with very little supervision.

"Don't the supervisors get bored watching over this machinery when it so seldom goes wrong?" asked the professor.

"Oh, no," Arturi said. "These supervisors are not real people. They are a specialist form of robot modelled on a past employee."

"You mean an android?"

"No, they are not sentient or aware, they are robots programmed for specific tasks."

"But they seem so lifelike."

"Yes, they do, Professor. However, they are still machines. Our medical researchers have the technology and capability to grow sentient beings, say like a clone of me and quite capable of doing my job. If someone is seriously injured in an accident, they can repair or replace any part of the anatomy, even a damaged brain with only the loss of memories. However, we draw the line at cloning or growing a complete sentient being. Much as our technicians and medical researchers would like to do that, the law considers it unethical to create a sentient being, capable of original thought."

The professor and the enthralled group listening to him nodded. "Yes, a shame really, but I can see ethics could be a problem," said the professor.

Chapter 33

Two shuttle craft, cleaned and polished, sat gleaming close to the control tower at the spaceport. Eric and Scott McDonald had flown the shuttles down early so that any last-minute details could be taken care of. The volunteer crew had lowered the access steps and a blue carpet led to the reception area. A fleet of transport vehicles arrived and deposited excited guests at the entrance. Chad and Helen, followed by Arturi, led them through the reception hall to the waiting shuttle craft. Eric's crew stood at the foot of the steps to assist guests boarding the shuttle.

Chad could see the nervousness of some passengers as they took their seats. He slipped up behind Eric in the pilot's seat and said, "Take it nice and easy, Eric. Don't forget this is a pleasure trip."

Eric nodded. "Nice and easy it is, Captain."

With control tower clearance checks completed, Eric gently lifted off, quickly followed by Scott McDonald in the second shuttle. Passengers felt nothing other than a gentle pressure pushing them back into their seats and were unaware of the complicated automatic control of air pressure and temperature within the shuttle's cabin as they climbed into the upper atmosphere.

Passengers gazed at their beautiful planet below, enthralled by the stunning view. Rising above the atmosphere and into the blackness of space with stars brighter than they'd ever seen, Eric pointed out the Marac space station as it sped by in its orbit. Further out, the *JJ Grant* in geosynchronous orbit glowed brightly with all lights on, her three companion ships almost invisible but for a few lights trailing behind her.

As the two shuttles closed in on the soft glow of the *JJ Grant*'s open bay, all the passengers who had been chattering excitedly grew silent. Eric was used to this phenomenon; it always happened when a plane was about to land, people stopped talking. Both vessels slid smoothly in single file to their docking points, where the wheel clamps locked on.

When the shuttle door opened, there was an immediate hubbub of chatter from the relieved passengers. Waiting to greet them was Gordon and a number of ship's officers, who mingled with the guests and led them in groups to the restaurant, which had been transformed into a theatre. Some crew were acting as servers, weaving between the guests with trays of canapés and drinks. Finally, the guests were led to their seats. The show was a musical and on each seat was a beautifully designed souvenir programme that Iris had printed in English.

The lights went down, the music struck up and the curtains opened. The director had pulled out all the stops, the players excelled themselves and the musicians performed magnificently. During the interval, ice cream and soft drinks were made available and the guests chatted about the show. When the show ended, the audience applauded and the players were happy to take a bow. Once back aboard the shuttle, the chattering guests were strapped in and were soon back at the spaceport. Chad made a little speech in the reception hall, thanking them for coming and hoping that they had enjoyed the show.

The leader of the councillors stepped forward. "Captain Chadwick, I think I can speak for all the people here – that was the most memorable experience any of us will ever have. The show was wonderful and the setting out of this world. Thank you indeed for inviting us along to see it." The whole group burst into spontaneous applause.

"Thank you, I am so glad you liked it and it was our pleasure to put it on for you."

On the way back to town Helen said, "Arturi, do you think they really enjoyed the show?"

"They certainly did, Helen. That was a form of entertainment completely new to us. It was delightful; I expect your theatre group will receive many invitations to perform on Marac."

The following morning Arturi was waiting for them. "We'll be meeting with the Marac councillors in a couple of days. Is there anything that you would like to put forward so we can give advance warning?"

Chad had been thinking about the meeting. "There are a number of things that we would like to purchase. However, our dilemma is how we pay for them. Even putting us up in this residence is something that we cannot reciprocate."

"Chad, I can see you are a proud man and would like to pay your way but you have already given us much. Just tell the councillors of the things you need in the way of stores and the technological devices that you are interested in; they will be only too happy to provide them and in turn they might mention the technology aboard the *JJ Grant* that you may be willing to part with."

"Right," said Chad. "But I must warn you, the one piece of technology that is not up for discussion is our drive system."

"Thank you, Chad; I will relay that information to the councillors." Arturi was bitterly disappointed; the drive system on the *JJ Grant* would have freed them from their planetary system and allowed them to explore the universe. He knew Maracuni rocket technology would never allow them to conquer the vast distances between star systems. *In so many ways we are just like the humans*, he thought.

During a quiet moment, Chad called up Iris. "We have a meeting arranged with the Marac councillors very shortly."

"Yes, Captain, I did know."

"One of the things I know they would like from us is the power block, what do you think?"

"Captain, there is no urgency for a decision; the people of Marac have said they would like the *JJ Grant* and our other ships to stay for a long time. You can make your decision about the power block when you know the Marac people better."

"You're probably right. We could let them have technology like the comwaves system, which would allow them to ditch radio and telephones for communication. The sub-miniature CPU and memory modules would significantly advance their electronic industry."

"Captain, there are many things that you can offer in exchange for their robotic and medical expertise. If you wish, I will prepare a list of technological items together with details of arts and crafts that you can offer. There are of course some things you may wish to hold back to use as a bargaining chip with the Maracuni people."

It wasn't so much anything that Iris had said, but Chad had the strangest feeling that Iris wanted to say more. "Thank you, Iris. Er… is there anything else they have that we should be considering, maybe some advanced technology that they keep under wraps."

The millisecond of hesitation from Iris instantly told Chad there was something else.

"Yes, Captain, there is something else…" Again, there was a microsecond of hesitation. "When we converse, I often show myself on the viewer to demonstrate something or make some subjects easier to understand or explain."

"Yes, Iris, that is true, it does make it easier for all of our crew including myself to see you on the viewer." *What's Iris driving at?*

"As you know the Maracuni people have very advanced medical knowledge. They have restructured the genes in your DNA to give you a longer illness-free life and have offered the same procedure to our crew."

"That is true, Iris, for which we are very grateful."

"You also saw an example of a non-sentient supervisor overseeing the production of machinery."

"Yes, I did." Chad wondered where this was going.

"They are fully capable of producing a clone or unique living individual."

"Yes they are, Iris." Chad began to get a bad feeling about the way this conversation was going.

"The Thark have given me vast knowledge including the intimate knowledge of feeding a biological brain with data."

"Yes, Iris, I understand that, but what is it that you are trying to say?"

"Captain, Anne Prior, when she was in her wheelchair, once said that I was like her, an active mind trapped in one place but with much to keep me busy. My mind is no longer busy enough. It needs more…" Iris hesitated for a moment. "Here, there is an opportunity to release a portion of my mind from its constraints." It finally dawned on him what Iris was asking for. The knowledge initially shocked him, but in his inner being, he understood. He recalled a conversation he'd had with Iris in the past, when she had said there would come a day when she would ask for his help. Chad realised that day had now arrived.

"Iris, I understand, truly I do. But there is a problem." He paused… Iris said nothing. "The people here are bound by ethics. They will not take the next step to create a sentient being."

Iris was silent for long moments. "Captain, this is different and I believe you know it is different."

"Iris, this is not a decision that is mine to make. The decision is with the Maracuni people and their governing body. As I have promised I will do all I can to help but please prepare yourself for disappointment if your request is refused. I will bring Councillor Arturi and Doctor Kensasha here tomorrow and ask them to discuss this subject with you."

Chapter 34

The discussion with Iris did not go well. Neither Kensasha nor Arturi would discuss the subject directly with Iris, only through Chad, as though Iris was some sort of machine, which in fact, she was but with such an elevated intellect that she was more than human, she was sentient.

"I realise you have laws to protect the innocent but, in this case, we have Iris, a sentient brain trapped in a cabinet, when with your help part of her could be mobile, associating with her colleagues on a one to one basis." The debate and reasoned arguing went on for some time.

Kensasha shrugged. "There is nothing we can do, Chad; we would need a donor to supply a fertilised egg and a change in our laws to let a female donate an egg for the purpose of growing an android." It was the first time the word 'android' had been used in the discussion.

Helen bridled at the remark. "I don't believe the child would be an android. If I supplied a fertilised egg, the child would be a human. Iris would supply the knowledge and a link between her and the child. We are not from the Maracuni system. If the procedure was carried out outside Maracuni territory, would you then perform the procedure, Kensasha?"

Kensasha cocked his head on one side and smiled, "You surprise me, Helen, when did you know?"

Helen blushed, but with a smile, said, "I don't know for certain, but I sense that it is so…" Gazing at Chad, she said, "I didn't want to build your hopes up, Chad… not until I was certain."

Kensasha put his hand on Chad's shoulder. "I will do my best and speak with legislatures and get a definitive decision, Captain Chadwick."

Chad stood up. "Kensasha that is all we ask. Remember, Iris saved your space station, the supply vessel and all the people manning them. She was the one that sent out power blocks and manipulated them to release the supply vessel and guide the station back on course."

Helen put her hand on Kensasha's arm and said, "We have to give Iris this chance, it means so much to her and to us. She is the most loyal member of our crew. When we are travelling between star systems, she holds our lives in her hands."

As Kensasha and Arturi left, Arturi half turned and gave a grin and a hopeful wink.

At the meeting with the councillors, Chad had Wang, the professor, Keung and several specialist officers from the ships with him.

The chief councillor welcomed Chad and his entourage and gradually they got down to the business in hand. Chad said, "I can only be honest and say we need provisions to enable us to continue our journey.

We can return to our home planet if we have to. We've left supplies at staging points, but we want to go on. Keung, our provisions controller, has prepared a list of what we need." Chad passed a file down to the council leader. "We also like your technology. It is a fact that in most spheres of activity, Marac is many hundreds of Earth years in advance of us. We like and admire your architectural and product design abilities, which result in things like the walk-through-shower, the viewing screens and of course your wonderful medical equipment. We also admire the automatic modular manufacturing and robotic systems. There are many other things mostly very small but that can be so useful in a person's life." Chad could see the interest and expectancy on the faces of the councillors around the table. "What can we barter with? I'm not sure but we have performing arts, which I think would enhance your own arts. We have films, books, videos, music and so on, of all aspects of our planet from the beginning of humankind to the present day. History, geography, the birth of technology to current technology, where we have reached for the stars. We may even have some technology that might be in advance of your own. You will be welcome to view our ships and the systems that we have on our ships. Some you may find quaint and some you may have a use for. Whatever we have, we will offer willingly."

The council leader thanked him. "Captain Chadwick, thank you for your frankness with us. As far as Marac and the people of Marac are concerned, we are pleased to give whatever products or technology you desire. As for provisions, I hope you will not require them for some time to come as we would like to treat you all as our guests for as long as you wish to stay."

The talks went on with each councillor wishing to be involved and offering accommodation or equipment or training. Arrangements were made for meetings with Marac companies to display their products and in return, Marac technical officials were invited to view some of the technology on the *JJ Grant* and the *Helcon*. By the time, the meeting ended Chad and his group were ready for the refreshments that were being offered.

Chad felt that it was unfair for him and his staff to continue staying in the residence and decided to move back aboard the *JJ Grant*; he could always get back to the spaceport on a shuttle within thirty or forty minutes.

Chad wanted to announce the Maracuni offer of the gene reordering procedure to prolong life to his crew and get the treatment programme that the Maracuni council had authorised started. He realised that some crewmembers might be sceptical, especially the younger ones, so asked Dr Kensasha if he would attend a meeting of department heads with him and explain the procedure in non-technical language. Chad instructed Iris to video the meeting.

As Chad had anticipated, when he announced the offer of the programme and its benefits to the crew, some were unconvinced. "The programme is not compulsory but we would urge you to accept this gift, because it is truly a gift of life. The procedure is being offered to the oldest members of our crew first. I have had the procedure and this is the new me!" He'd shaved off his beard and, in his uniform, looked ten years younger. Helen had received the procedure immediately after Chad. She looked younger, fitter and slimmer. Her hair was blond and glossy.

The biggest surprise of all was Anne Prior, looking gorgeous, slim and athletic. She walked briskly up to the microphone and said, "You all know I was confined to a wheelchair, I've had this procedure. Just look at me now!"

Kensasha could understand the scepticism of the younger members of the crew, they would not see the immediate benefits from the procedure as the older people did but in the longer term, they would. However, it was up to individuals. He realised it was a difficult thing for them to believe that something like this could be possible.

Connie, the professor and all the older crewmembers needed no urging.

Iris displayed the video of Kensasha explaining the procedure to ensure that every crewmember aboard all the vessels saw it.

The trickle of names on the waiting list for the procedure became a torrent. It was evident from the appearance of those who'd received the treatment early that it was working. At the tail end of the queue were Grant and Wang. "We wanted to make sure that we would be here to get you home if something went wrong," Grant said with a grin.

"Very noble, Grant, you almost left it too late and nearly missed out." As it was, the whole crew eventually elected to have the treatment.

Chad inhaled the smell of the medical facility as he and Helen entered the foyer. It was clean and fresh, unlike the odour still in his memory of hospitals at home on Earth. They had an appointment to see Doctor Kensasha. As they entered the reception area, they saw Kensasha waving them over to his office.

"Hello, you're right on time." Kensasha pointed to the comfortable chairs by his desk and they both sat down and waited for Kensasha to begin. Chad was apprehensive and felt Helen's reassuring squeeze of his arm. Iris wanted this very badly. She wanted to be free, to be in a body that could mix with the crew on the *JJ Grant*. They both knew Iris would be bitterly disappointed if the decision went against her.

Helen hesitantly posed the question. "You've received a response from the Council Senate?"

Kensasha pulled a green file with large black letters printed on it, IRIS – AI, towards him. "Yes, Helen, it's not been formally announced yet but the news is good. It's an exception to the rules but they are giving their permission to proceed. They will make a formal announcement later today, assuming you still wish to proceed. I just want to give you forewarning of what to expect." Helen and Chad nodded. However, Chad could sense a 'but' coming… a condition. "Helen will have to supply a fertilised egg, and the incubation will take place here under our care."

Chad wore a worried frown. "Is she… is Helen a suitable donor?" He didn't know how else to put it; Helen was over sixty.

Kensasha smiled, opened a drawer and pulled out a mirror. Holding it up to Chad he said, "Describe what you see."

Chad was embarrassed. "Er, I see a man's face, black hair and brown eyes."

Kensasha still smiling said, "Yes, but how old is this man?"

Chad looked again and laughed. "Well he looks about thirty-five to me."

"Yes, Chad, and Helen looks even younger. We have double-checked. The treatment you both received here is having a remarkable effect on your bodies."

It had all been explained to him weeks ago but the implications were only now beginning to sink in.

Kensasha went on, "The procedure is simple; we remove a fertilised egg from Helen, the zygote will be examined to make sure it is healthy and will then be nurtured in the lab, as will the resulting embryo. When that develops into a foetus, it will be placed in a special incubator. Development will be rapid up until puberty. If there are no complications, growth will be ramped up until the being reaches adulthood."

Chad interrupted. "But what about Iris, shouldn't she hear this?"

"Yes, she should. You may inform Iris of the councillors' decision. However, I suspect that Iris is already fully aware of what is happening."

Chad raised an eyebrow. "How do you mean, how can she be aware, if it's not been announced yet?"

Kensasha tapped his head. "Chad, I don't think you know the full extent of Iris's abilities."

Chad knew Iris had telepathic abilities but had chosen to ignore them or push the knowledge to the back of his mind. Now it was out in the open he could embrace telepathy. After all, he was beginning to develop the ability himself. In his mind, he heard Kensasha say, "Exactly, it is the sixth sense."

Kensasha carried on aloud, "We will look after this new being, until she is ready to accept personality, intelligence and information. This is when Iris will become involved."

"You said she. How do you know it will be a girl?"

"Helen's initial examination confirmed it is a girl."

The enormity of it all hit Helen very hard. "How long will it take?" she asked weakly.

"We don't know but it will take time and there is a proviso. We will have total control of the being until Iris fills her mind. Only then may you see her."

"But why, Kensasha? What possible harm will it do to see her?" asked Helen.

"The harm will be to you and Chad; your instincts will demand that you have some input of your own into her development. However, you will be unable to do so. You will feel helpless and that will torment you. However, it is something you must accept if you decide to proceed. Your time will come when the child is grown and Iris has done her task. Then you will see her."

Helen and Chad looked at each other. Helen had tears in her eyes but she nodded. "Yes, we'll agree."

Kensasha looked at them kindly. "I did say it will torment you. But believe me it is for the best. We will keep you informed of progress. If a problem arises, we will tell you immediately. There is no need for you or Chad to worry, time will pass very quickly and at the right point, the incubator will be placed close to Iris."

Chad said, "You mean in the computer room?"

Kensasha nodded solemnly. "Yes, Iris will play the most important part in this but her work will take very little time."

Chad gulped. This wasn't how he had envisioned things happening. "Will she be attached with wires or anything?"

"No, nothing like that, Chad. Iris will do it mind to mind." He paused for a moment. "You are aware this new being will be your child but she may not know you and she will have a link with Iris?"

"If she is Iris, she will know us," Helen said, as she gazed at Chad and squeezed his hand. "Yes, of course we want to do it, this is for Iris and for us."

Chad nodded and said firmly, "Yes, Kensasha, we are absolutely certain." He felt Helen squeeze his hand again; Chad knew it was the right thing to do.

Kensasha said briskly, "Right, come with me and we'll get started." He ushered them down to a treatment room.

Chapter 35

Arturi called Chad. "I wondered if you would like to visit the other worlds in our system."

"That is something I would very much like to do, Arturi. Could I propose that we use our ship's shuttles? They are completely space worthy and just as fast as the *JJ Grant*."

"That would be splendid, Chad, I will bring along some guides and your crew could be split up into smaller groups. We also have some holiday lodges on each planet. If you wished, you and your crew could spend a little while exploring on your own if you felt so inclined."

"Thank you again, Arturi, we would welcome the opportunity."

The two shuttles silently settled to the concrete of the Marac spaceport. Arturi was waiting with a group of guides. Eric opened the shuttle door, extended the automatic stairs and walked down the steps to greet Arturi. He was astonished to see Arturi and the guides staring open mouthed at him as though he was naked or something. He looked behind him and immediately realised that the portal had been left switched on. When he'd walked through the portal, his body had been outlined by a shimmering glow. He saw the look of amazement on Arturi's face and those with him.

"Oh, I'm sorry, that is just a portal which we normally use in space." Eric went on to explain how it worked.

Arturi was amazed. "You mean that if you were in space, something or someone could pass through this portal, whilst you have the door open and it will retain your atmosphere and resist the vacuum of space?"

"Yes, certainly," said Eric. "It's one of Lieutenant Connie Mapps' inventions."

Arturi wanted to make sure he had understood correctly. "You can pass goods or people through the portal in space without having to use an airlock?"

"Correct," said Eric. He made a mental note to tell Chad that Arturi was impressed.

With the shuttles fully loaded and the crew excited to be visiting another planet, they were ready to lift off. For the guides, the prospect of a ride in a spaceship that didn't have a thundering great rocket to propel it was irresistible; this was the ride of a lifetime.

With both shuttles ready to lift off, Eric called over the comwaves, "We're ready to go, Grant."

"OK, Eric, we'll follow you out." The two shuttles soared skywards. The control tower staff watched them go. "What do you think the chances are of them letting us have their space drive technology?"

"Pretty slim," his boss said. "I know I wouldn't part with that sort of technology." They both sighed.

The *JJ Grant*, *Helcon*, *Black Pearl* and *Blackbird* remained in orbit above the Marac planet with only skeleton crews on board. Iris was keeping watch and monitoring all the vessels. Those that were not on the shuttles going to the planet Sheklar were either exploring the planet Marac below, as guests of the Marac people, or were taking a well-earned rest and catching up with studies, writing letters or articles to send home to the news agencies that had managed to sign them up. Everything was quiet and in order. Iris was watchful but content. She asked Eva, Ling, and Alice, the AIs on the other ships, if they had any concerns.

They all responded, "No, Iris, everything is as it should be at this time." Even so, Iris surreptitiously reviewed the major systems on each vessel in case there was something they had missed but everything was as they had said, all was in order. The other ships' AIs had not been upgraded to her own level and she had retained full control over them reinforcing their allegiance and loyalty to Captain Chadwick and his crew. She knew they were unlikely to notice anything beyond security level four, nowhere near Iris's security level twenty, which was the totality of all Thark knowledge. Iris went back to contemplating her own ship and gave a mental sigh of contentment. All systems were functioning, as they should. Part of her mind considered Captain Chadwick. His mind was alert. It was continuing to improve and grow – not in size but in his ability to utilise more of his mind's capacity. He was beginning to read the thoughts of others and had long since sensed that Iris also had the ability to read a human mind. He had confirmed that knowledge during his conversation with Kensasha. However, he did not realise the extent of her ability.

Iris could, if she wished, send or receive a thought from anyone on the ship. In fact, by using the Thark comwaves she could read the thoughts of a being on Earth or on any of the star systems in her memory banks. She listened to Captain Frussee's mind, yearning to see Wang again but disciplining herself to suppress the thought unless the opportunity to be with him should come. She also listened to the few remaining Orrappa beings on Earth planning and plotting revenge for the humiliation of their fleet. Although few in number, several had infiltrated religious and political groups and had risen to high positions amongst ignorant worshippers and self-seeking politicians. They whipped up hatred for any group that opposed them or did not conform to their ways, causing misery and death. They had made themselves wealthy using their superior knowledge or political connections. Wealth and any ridiculous promises amongst these impressionable people could buy almost anything. Iris knew she could put a stop to this even from this distance, but should she. It was a dilemma; her job was to protect the ship and its crew and they were not in any danger at present. For the time being she would leave things as they were and commune with Chad during his sleep time to see if he would approve of action against the rogue Orrappa on Earth.

Finally, she allowed herself to think of the incubator and the embryo growing day by day. She had already heard its cry; not of pain, just expressing that it was alive. The child would be Helen and Chad's daughter and would have the best qualities from them both. However, the child in her innermost being would also have the qualities and knowledge of herself. Essentially, she would be Iris the AI in human form. Her telepathic links with the child were strong, far beyond her own expectations. The link would allow her to experience the freedom and human contact that she so desired. She would feel the physical touch of shaking hands or linking arms and laughing with someone. The ethics worried her, was it right? Was she being selfish? Mulling over countless possibilities she questioned herself; had she asked for too much? She began to feel distraught; her computer brain tried to calm her sentient mind. However, a comforting thought formed in her mind, one that she had not put there herself. *This is part of evolution, what can be better than a new and better life form.* Iris let her mind relax, dried her mental tears and tucked the thought away to savour later.

Chapter 36

Eric landed at the spaceport on Sheklar with Grant's shuttle close behind. A small fleet of vehicles awaited them as well as a group of dignitaries who wanted to shake hands with all the Earth people. Eventually they were seated in the transport vehicles and driven to a sumptuous hotel. The area was clean and modern with lots of green parkland. The temperature was colder but they had dressed for that.

The guides said that they would be able to rest for a while, have something to eat and then meet up to go on an evening city tour ending up at an entertainment centre.

The rooms were comfortable and ultra-modern. The hotel restaurant provided a simple meal and glasses of fruit juice. The evening tour around the city was wonderful with all the tall buildings lit up and the architecture was stunning. No one had any idea what the entertainment would be but as the group entered the brightly lit building, they were each given a bag of tokens. The place turned out to be the equivalent of a casino.

It didn't take long for the group, with the exception of Connie, to lose their tokens. Connie won frequently; she seemed to have the ability to see patterns emerge amongst the numbers and symbols of the machines and used that to her advantage as she did with chess.

Taking her two buckets of winnings to Arturi, she held them up. "What do you think? Should I hand these tokens back to the casino?"

"No!" he exclaimed. "Cash them in. The casino gives out free tokens with the expectation that you will lose them all and start using your own money at the tables."

Connie waved the wad of notes and said, "Hey guys, the drinks are on me." They all had a very relaxing hour near the bar.

The following day they toured a fully automated factory producing viewing screens. There was just a lone supervisor or technician, who looked the part, but they now knew to be a robot checking for potential problems. Then on to a factory manufacturing the medical diagnostic machines. The latest version of these machines was to be installed in the *JJ Grant*. The machine had the ability to throw up three-dimensional views of any organ including the brain or a section within an organ. It could pick a safe route through the brain to remove a tumour or repair a blood vessel with minimal collateral damage. In fact, the machine could closely examine every part of a being's anatomy, operate and carry out every procedure known to surgeons at that time.

"Who designs these wonderful machines?" enquired the professor.

The guide explained, "It's a collaboration between learned academics and robots. Usually a living being is consulted if a robot physician comes across a problem that it has not experienced before. Specialist robot consultants are brought in along with Maracuni consultant physicians who work together to find a solution and it progresses from there.

"It's rather like a pyramid with a few expert beings at the top and then robots all the way down to the bottom. It's like that in every professional discipline, Medicine, Architecture, Construction, Engineering and so on. Then of course, the whole thing is linked together like a network so that each pyramid can converse with another or a group. It works very well. The results are what we see around us."

"It must be very costly."

"Not really, we have to provide the materials and facilities. The robots do everything else."

The only involvement that we have is in deciding if we want or need that actual procedure in a facility. We are also involved as technicians and arbitrators in the event that a paradox or ethical issue arises in the robot chain of command."

A member of the group who had been listening in awe asked, "Does that happen often?"

"No, very seldom. It is most unusual for anything serious to happen."

"But what do people do with themselves if they don't work in factories?" someone asked.

Again, the guide smiled. "People have lots of interests, our society is one where people must contribute with work of some sort to pay their way yet still have time to study, develop skills and enjoy life and sports. They could if they wished, work in the factories but the robots are better at factory work than we are. However, we provide original thought, an idea, a concept and direction. Come, we will visit one of our academies."

The whistle stop tour of the academy was illuminating. The facilities in the lecture rooms, laboratories and machine shops were amazing and the students mixed together in all age groups were completely immersed in their work.

As they all clambered back on the transport vehicle Arthur said, "I wish my lot had been like these young people."

"These students don't have to come here; it's not compulsory," the guide said. "They are here because they choose to learn."

The tour had been amazing and a bit of a revelation for those that remembered their own university days of drinking and missed lectures.

The academy was better equipped than any teaching facility on Earth. Someone in the group asked what the fees were. "Oh, there are no fees. Everything is free."

"But how can your government afford something like this?"

"Oh, it hasn't always been like this but government investment in robotics allows us to have these facilities at an extremely low cost. Every family pays taxes and no one is allowed to inherit vast wealth from their kin. They have to support themselves by their own efforts. A strong work ethic is a trait of our people."

"But supposing someone is unable to work?"

The guide looked baffled. "I have never met anyone who could not work."

"What if they had an abnormality that prevented them from working?"

"Ah, in that situation they would be treated and cured." It was obvious that as far as the guide was concerned everyone worked, there were no exceptions, he could not conceive of that situation arising.

The professor sighed. "The only places you see this sort of enthusiasm is in China or Asia. If only…"

"I know what you mean, Harry," Arthur said. "These people deserve their place in the universe."

At the end of the tour, Arturi announced that anyone wishing to stay on Sheklar and learn more about its customs and some of its mechanical marvels would be welcome.

"We have a number of resorts around the globe that would welcome you to stay with them for a week or two. Or we can go on to Grionda, famous for mining and heavy industries."

Most elected to go on to Grionda to see how the inhabitants managed on what was the most rugged and coldest planet of the Maracuni system.

Grionda was the largest planet in the three-planet system being almost half as big again, with a thicker atmosphere and a greater gravity than that of Marac. The planet also had a far thicker crust.

The population of Grionda was similar to that of Marac and most people worked in mining and the heavy industries. Thanks to the profusion of hydroelectric plants that powered those industries, the air was clear and clean. The cities were bright and modern, the inhabitants happy and hard working.

The mining and quarrying work was carried out by robots, massive great machines, very specialised but as on the planet Sheklar, all were linked into a computer network, which made order out of chaos. Vast stocks of minerals and chemicals were scattered in storage depots around the countryside, some left exposed to the weather, others stored in warehouses or silos.

They visited a colossal mining operation, completely run by robots with the exception of a few geologists and mining experts. They saw more specialist robotic machines sorting ores and from time to time picking out rare stones. Massive great vehicles ferried the ores to different areas for smelting. The smelter that the group was visiting had just received a shipment of super magnetic ore. Chad's eyes lit up when he saw the bright shiny ingots coming out of the smelter and being transported to the adjacent steel rolling mill. Instinctively he knew this material would enhance the speed and range of the power block. Keeping the excitement out of his voice Chad asked, "Is this a rare ore?"

"No." The geologist said, "It's a common ore and found in numerous areas around the planet."

Seeing his interest, Arturi said, "Would you like a shipment, Chad?"

"I would, we have depleted our stocks of metals on all our vessels and this looks like a versatile material suitable for many applications. May I see the specification and material analysis sheet to make sure we would be able to machine it with our equipment on the *JJ Grant*?"

The geologist said, "I'll get a copy of the spec. sheet for you now."

Later when they arrived back at the shuttle, Chad held the specification sheet up to a camera. "Iris, please check this out and let me know its composition and whether we have equipment to machine this material."

With no hesitation, Iris said, "Yes, Captain, we have the machining capability. Would you like a detailed analysis report or the basics?"

"Basics please, Iris."

"The material is a super magnetic ore, consisting of neodymium, combined with iron and boron. We have similar but rarer alloys on Earth from which we make super magnets but it is ideal for many uses in the ship too."

"Thank you, Iris."

Like Chad, Iris also knew that this ore would enhance the speed of the power block. Amongst the information provided by her massive upgrade was the specification of the material used in the Thark ship's drive system, it was almost indistinguishable from the specifications for this ore.

Arturi could see Chad's interest. "I take it the material would be useful to you."

"Yes, very much so."

"OK that's settled then. If you can arrange to send one of your shuttle craft to the rolling mill I'll have it fully loaded for you."

Chad was excited. He couldn't wait to get back on the *JJ Grant* and build a power block with it.

"That is very kind of you, Arturi." A thread of guilt ran through him. He felt he was being deceptive and should make amends. "I notice that shipping ore from here to Marac or Sheklar is slow and very costly for the Marac people. I would like to offer a shuttle craft together with the portal technology that Connie developed. This would allow you to leave your interplanetary craft in orbit and the shuttle could ferry the ores from the surface up to the ship or even from one planet to another and you wouldn't have to operate airlocks and so forth."

"Chad, that is most generous of you. Are you sure you can spare a shuttle craft because I know they are also your lifeboats?"

"Yes, we can spare a shuttle; especially after all you and your people have done for us it is sparse payment."

"Our gifts to you and your crew are just that, gifts, they have cost us nothing to give them but have given us great joy to be able to do so."

"Thank you, Arturi. However, I should warn you not to let anyone tamper with the shuttle's drive. They cannot be dismantled any attempt to do so will cause the drive to self-destruct."

Chapter 37

Both Chad and Helen thought often of their child developing in the Maracuni incubator. Up until now, they had resisted the urge to see the child. However, their emotions were too strong. Helen begged Chad, "Please call Kensasha, I must see our baby." Chad nodded; his own emotions were in turmoil as he made the call.

"Kensasha, Helen and I must see little Iris… you know, just to see how she is getting on."

"You know that's not possible, Chad. You must be patient. All is progressing well. Please stop worrying, we will let you know immediately if anything is wrong."

For Chad and Helen, weeks turned to months and the lack of information was gnawing at them. Kensasha offered medication that would calm their anxiety but Helen and Chad refused it. Arturi visited often and was forever suggesting they visit a manufacturing plant or a scenic spot on the planet.

"Why is Arturi wasting our time with theses distractions?"

"That's just what they are, Chad, distractions. Arturi is trying to take our minds off our worries about little Iris. Neither Arturi nor Kensasha have ever lied to us or demanded anything from us." Resignedly she said, "We agreed for them to have total control, we have no option but to wait and see."

More time went by and Chad tried to put the thoughts of little Iris aside and throw himself into work on the *JJ Grant* helping with all the upgrades to machinery and electronic equipment and especially becoming involved with the ship's new simulator that was being built along the lines of the simulator on the Thark *B109* battlecruiser.

Then came a call from Kensasha; would Helen and Chad come to the hospital where he would present a progress report. Of course they would; it was the most important thing in the world to them.

In Kensasha's office, Helen and Chad sat close together with Helen holding his hand, both apprehensive but not knowing what to expect.

Kensasha gave them a weak smile. Chad sensed something was not right. "The process of accelerated growth is taking longer than we originally expected." Seeing the immediate look of alarm on both their faces Kensasha was quick to reassure them. "No, nothing is wrong, little Iris is quite well and is developing normally. She has just progressed slower than we were expecting. This is new territory for us too, you know."

Helen said, "But is little Iris fully formed? Has she hands and feet, is she deformed…?"

"No! No, nothing like that, little Iris is perfect in every way; she is close to the point of accepting data from Iris the AI."

"You mean she'll be placed in the computer room with Iris soon?" Chad said his voice full of hope and excitement.

"No, Chad, there has been a change of plan. The transmission of knowledge from Iris the AI to little Iris will be done here."

Chad exploded and leapt from his chair. "How can it be done here? We can't bring Iris down here?"

Kensasha held his hands up to stop him. "No, Chad, please sit down. It is not necessary to bring Iris down here. Iris is capable of implanting the knowledge mind to mind. I don't like to use the word telepathic, but I have no other word for it. Iris, your AI, has a mental link with little Iris, the strongest we have ever encountered and which has honestly amazed us."

Chad and Helen looked at each other in disbelief.

"Are you saying Iris can just use her mind to do this? She doesn't need to be connected with the incubator?"

"Chad, we have always known that Iris would transfer knowledge mind to mind, what we didn't know is how strong the link between them is. Iris has demonstrated to our satisfaction that she is quite capable of feeding information into the child's mind over a vast distance; they do not need to be close together. However, it is not something that can be rushed. The brain is a delicate organ and absorbs information in a unique and wonderful way. When the brain contains emotions, knowledge and self-awareness it begins to work and becomes what we know as the mind. We must let Iris proceed at her own pace. She will tell us when little Iris is ready to enter our world."

Helen said eagerly, "Can we see her?"

"I'm sorry, Helen, not yet, we don't want to open the incubator until her time with Iris is complete, but we can show you a sort of scan."

Helen and Chad looked at each other. "Let's at least see this scan then," Helen said.

Kensasha led them to a room that was packed with equipment. The incubator sat in a machine in the centre of the room; they had seen it or one like it, when all this had started. Kensasha went to a control panel; over the incubator was an arm that travelled the length of the incubator. As it moved, a beam of bright green light illuminated the incubator. Kensasha pointed at a screen on the wall. The panel glowed a soft green and gradually a shape began to emerge.

"This is little Iris, definition is poor because of the shielding but you can see she is of a normal size, she has all her limbs, all her fingers and toes and everything about her is fully functional." As they watched the figure moved, stretched and the head turned towards them.

"Can she hear us?"

"No, Helen, she is unaware, she is only using her autonomic nervous system, that operates the involuntary muscles like the heart and lungs that keeps her alive. Everything else is there but it needs Iris to flood her brain with information. She will have inherited both your human traits and emotions. She will be the composite of you both and have Iris's knowledge and possibly some of Iris's emotions." Kensasha paused a moment, "That is not to say she will have nothing to learn from you both. She will need you both."

Helen, with tears in eyes, clutched Chad's arm; she was so happy to have seen the fuzzy image of their child. "When can we see her properly, in the flesh?" asked Helen.

Kensasha pursed his lips. "It could take ten to fifteen days. We are not sure how long Iris will need to transmit her knowledge. It depends upon how receptive little Iris is. However, I would guess at least two of your weeks. Then we will have a series of tests to carry out. Iris will let us know when the time is right to open the incubator. You have both been patient for so long, please let the process take its course. If you are needed, I will call you."

Chad and Helen glumly nodded, knowing that Kensasha was right.

Chapter 38

Chad received a call from Arturi. *Could it be bad news about Iris?* Anxiously he answered the call, "Hello, Arturi."

Before he could say more, Arturi said, "I know what you're going to say, Chad, and the answer is everything is proceeding on time and as expected."

"That's a relief to know. Why did you call?"

"I wanted to run something by you. When we spoke some time ago, you said that some of your ships were short of crew?"

Chad hid his irritation. *How could Arturi bring this up at such an important time?* "That's right, Arturi, we are going to do a reshuffle and try and even out the manning of our ships."

"I would like to offer a suggestion. We have people begging us to put their names forward in the hope of becoming part of your crew. Would this be something that you would consider?"

"It could be, Arturi, I'll discuss it with my officers and let you know."

"Thank you, Chad. I'll look forward to hearing from you."

Chad brought up the subject of crew numbers at the morning meeting. "I've had a suggestion from Arturi, apparently there are lots of Maracuni people that would do anything to become crew members and he's asking if we would consider this."

"It's a good idea, Chad, providing we get to pick who we want," said Grant. "They've got to be able to contribute."

Henson said, "I couldn't agree more but from what I've seen of these people they would be a valuable asset." Murmurs of agreement came from the others around the table.

As the discussion ended, Chad said, "We're all agreed then, I'll inform Arturi and he can organise a group to have a look round the ship. It'll give us a chance to make an informal assessment of what calibre of volunteer we can expect and assess whether we can get on with them in the confines of the ships and how many we can absorb on each vessel."

Making the call also gave Chad an excuse to speak with Arturi again; he and Helen were desperate for news of little Iris.

"Hello, Arturi. I've discussed your suggestion with my officers and they quite like the idea. They have suggested that you send up a group of say thirty volunteers to have a look around the ship. If it works out, we could take as many as thirty individuals on each vessel."

"Chad, that is fantastic, let me know when is a suitable time and I'll get a mixed group organised."

"How about midday in three days' time? I'll send a shuttle down to pick them up."

"Thanks very much, Chad. By the way, I should have news for you about little Iris around that time."

"Nothing you can tell me now?"

"No, Chad, other than everything is proceeding to plan."

Chad was disappointed; he knew Helen would be too. His thoughts were on Helen and little Iris, their child. How could Arturi be so crass as to ask if his people could visit the ship at such an important time? Grumpily he returned to his cabin. Helen saw he was upset. "What on earth's the matter, Chad?"

"Oh, it's Arturi, he's asked me to receive some Maracuni people as potential crew, show them around and have some of the officers interview them to see if they are the right calibre."

"But that's a good idea isn't it?"

"Yes, it would be normally but it might coincide with things to do with little Iris."

"Now we are so close, why don't we ask Iris what's going on?"

Chad with Helen by his side called Iris on the viewer. "Hello, Iris, are you able to talk to us? Do you know what's happening with little Iris? Arturi can't seem to tell us much."

On the viewer, Iris smiled and in her soft voice said, "Little Iris is almost a full-grown woman and everything is going to plan. She is receptive and is absorbing all the information I am passing to her. In a few days, you will be able to see her and you will know her. Do not let your days be spoiled by worry, carry on with your normal routines and you will be rewarded. I will let you know if something is not right."

The shuttle craft, which had been sent to collect the young people from Marac, was an hour late arriving back from the Maracuni spaceport. It had been held up for some reason. A group of excited young Maracuni men and women stepped from the shuttle and gathered into a disorderly group around Gordon Blair. He along with Eric had accompanied the young people on the journey up to the *JJ Grant*. They gazed around the vast bay in awe. Gordon started splitting them up into three groups, each group to be given a tour of the ship by a couple of bridge officers.

Watching the group, Chad had to smile. He turned to Helen. "It's like penning sheep, no sooner has Gordon got a group together then one escapes." Helen laughed but her laugh was cut short by her gasp, one hand flew to her mouth to suppress a shriek, the other gripped Chad's arm so tightly he could feel her nails digging into his flesh. Chad was shocked.

"What is it, love? What's wrong?"

Helen gasped, "It's little Iris, she's here." Helen was looking at one of the groups. Chad picked her out straight away, a girl – a young woman, a little taller than Helen, lithe and athletic. Blond shoulder length hair, a beautiful smiling face with rosy red lips and bright blue eyes – she could have been Helen's younger sister. Her group led by Gordon Blair were coming towards them to be introduced. Helen was shaking but managed to get her emotions under control and smiled, speaking to each young person as introductions were made.

The blond-haired girl had hung back, gazing intently at them both, until she was last in the line. Finally, Gordon said, "Last but not least is, Lottie."

Chad and Helen looked at each other and exclaimed in unison, "Lottie?"

Lottie held out her hand and gently squeezed Helen's hand in hers. "I used to be called Iris, but I think I'm more of a Lottie, don't you?" She gave a mischievous smile when she shook Chad's hand.

A shocked Chad called after the group, "We'll have a long chat later."

Having met the other two groups, he and Helen made their way back to their cabin. Once inside they clung together. "Oh Chad, I have never been so happy in all my life." They both wept with joy.

Chad called Iris and admonished her. "Iris, you should have told us."

"Yes, Captain, but I didn't want to spoil a lovely surprise."

"But she knew us," said Helen. "She says she is Lottie but is she really you?"

"Yes, and no, it's complicated, she is your flesh and blood and she is physically perfect in every way down to her very last gene. She has your combined personalities with a bit of me thrown in and she has a brain like no other. She and I have a link, which even I cannot explain. We can feel and experience everything through our combined senses. She will sense danger and threats through me and I will experience love and affection through her. Yet, we can still have our private thoughts and emotions."

"Oh Iris, thank you, I can't tell you how happy we are, it's a most marvellous day," said Chad.

As Iris faded from the screen, there was a tap at the door. Chad opened the door and Lottie flew in wrapping her arms about them both and said, "My family, I've waited so long for this moment."

All three hugged for a long time. Helen, wiping tears from her face, said, "How did you find your way here?"

Lottie laughed. "I know every inch of this ship, every last nut and bolt, every piece of wire and I know both of you too. I see those things through Iris, remember?"

She made them laugh when she said all business-like, "Now, which is my cabin?"

Chad said, "You may have your pick, you know where all the empty cabins are and you can choose for your friends too. They might as well stay on board for a few nights for the experience. I'll clear it with Arturi. Although, there is one thing, what is your second name?"

Lottie smiled. "Why, Chadwick, of course!"

It was over two years since they had arrived in the Maracuni planetary system. *We have three choices, stay here for a bit longer, move on through the Milky Way seeking out more life or return home.*

He listened to a voice in his head; it was Grant speaking to Wang. "I wish Chad would make up his mind whether we're going on or going home."

Wang replied, "Going on is for me, I'm not ready to go home yet."

"Me too, this has been the best thing that has ever happened to me and I don't want it to stop."

Chad smiled to himself; he had still not revealed his new ability to hear the thoughts of others, even to Helen. Lottie knew Arturi and Kensasha both knew and Iris knew too, but nobody else. How he had begun developing this new sense, he couldn't imagine. The reprogramming of his genes and DNA had enhanced him in so many ways, as it had for the rest of his crew, including the three Orrappa beings. Hernani had revealed that the average lifespan of the Orrappa people was almost double that of humans but after the treatment they had received, the lifespan for all of them was like the Maracuni's, almost indefinite. Chad thought about his crew, all looked to be in their late teens or early twenties. Even Sam, who was well into his seventies, only looked about twenty-five. All of them were in peak physical condition with lightning reflexes, eagle sharp eyesight, animal hearing and a fantastic sense of smell. None had a blemish of any kind. Chad ran his fingers through his own thick hair. He noticed that his bald spot had disappeared and that his hair was no longer grey. His mind felt sharp and clear and he could remember things from way back, he could even remember his mother's touch and her voice. Now, this increasingly powerful mind hearing that was developing in him! Calling it telepathy would put it into the realm of fantasy. No, it wasn't that – it was something more. How many others in his crew were developing the ability he didn't know; his intuition was that of the humans, only he and Lottie shared this ability. However, he knew Iris had it in abundance and there was of course Arturi and others from the Maracuni species that had this ability from birth.

Obviously, the profusion of stem cells had something to do with it. How? He had no idea. Avoiding eavesdropping on someone's thoughts was difficult, although he was getting better at tuning them out. Occasionally he felt embarrassed when he heard thoughts from the crew and even from Arturi and those around him. Arturi had given him the odd glance and once when he was far across the room, Chad had heard him clearly speaking to someone. Arturi had half turned and looked directly at him, and Chad was acutely aware that Arturi had sensed his new ability. Arturi smiled and raised his glass in a salute. Flushing deeply, Chad returned the gesture. Later, Arturi came over to him and said, "I wondered how long it would take for you to develop new abilities."

Chad gave a sickly grin. "Yes, the problem is controlling them."

Chapter 39

They were in Connie's office set in a corner of the massive workshop that was her domain. Chad looked from the office window as he sipped his cup of tea. "The workshop looks fantastic, Connie. I don't know how you've managed it."

"I have to admit to stealing ideas from our hosts and what you told me of the *B109*'s, workshops and of course, significant help from Iris."

The workshop was spotlessly clean and filled with computerised or robotic machinery. It was busy with technicians and quality control inspectors walking amongst the machines. "How did you get on with making up power blocks from the new material supplied by Arturi?"

"We made two units, Chad."

"Oh, only two?" He'd hoped for more.

"That's right. Iris tested them, against a couple of standard units in the stores to see if there was any improvement in performance."

"And was there?"

"I should say so; the increase in performance was phenomenal."

"Why didn't you call me, Connie?"

"Chad," she gave him an admonishing look, "you had other things to worry about remember? The rest of us are quite capable of doing things like this too you know." Arching an eyebrow, she smiled. "And how is Lottie? I see her flitting about all over the ship; she has her eye on everything." Connie smiled softly. "She is a wonderful girl, Chad."

Chad said equally softly, "Yes, she is. Helen and I have never been happier."

Connie changed the subject. "We were talking about power block performance."

"Yes, we were. You said the performance was phenomenal."

"Yes, it was. Grant, George Downes, the professor and Wang, as well as Iris, checked over the PCB to see if that could be improved. They didn't change the circuit but it now uses miniature components like those in the communicator and it has the Thark power module instead of a battery."

Chad nodded. "Yes, that's a sensible move."

Connie pointed to a line of equipment in the workshop. "I set up that production line to knock out units as fast as we could and we are already making up ship's power block drives to replace the old Orrappa drives."

"Connie, that's great, I'm very keen to see the results of your test."

"I've got them right here," she said flipping open a file.

Chad's jaw dropped. "Are you sure about these figures, because if they're correct it'll mean we have a ship as fast as the *B109*."

"All checked out by Iris and Grant," Connie said.

"Really! I don't need to tell you, Connie, we'll have to change all the old power blocks for this new version."

"We know that, Chad, that's why we are working our socks off making new ones. I have a team on Wang's ship building up a new drive ready to swap out the original old Orrappa drive, and then we'll do Henson's ship."

Chad frowned. "Don't you think you should have done the *JJ Grant* first, Connie?"

Connie grinned. "But we have, Chad, it's all sorted. Iris and her trusty team of slaves, that's me and my team, have made a completely new ship's power block drive unit. All that remains is for the old unit to come out and the new unit to be installed. That's something we'll have to do down on the planet."

Chad stared at Connie open mouthed. "You're joking, right?"

"No, come on down to what I call the engine room and have a look."

The vast room gleamed, it had been totally repainted in a soft magnolia hue, the sparkling silver drive sat to one side waiting to replace the old original drive.

Positioned in front of the drive was a new emergency operator's console, semi-circular in shape with a panoramic viewing screen.

Connie waved a hand; instantly the screen came to life showing a crisp clear 3D-view ahead. Connie sat in the operator's seat and demonstrated the controls.

"See, Chad, this system allows total viewing control." The scene changed to a view of space behind the ship. "This console is for emergency use, should something ever go wrong with the bridge controls."

Chad just gawped. "But this must have taken ages to do; the painting alone is a mammoth task?"

"Not when you have Iris, power blocks, paint sprayers and the Maracuni eager to supply viewing screens and paint. Incidentally the paint is to a new super formula, supplied by Iris."

"What's different about it?"

"I'm not entirely sure but it's what they use on the *B109*. Iris says it will last a lifetime."

They both gazed round the engine room, Connie with pride and Chad in awe.

"One other thing, Chad, I know it is more work but I think we should make a new ship's shield. I believe these new power blocks will be more effective than those in our current shields."

"You're right, Connie. We had better get a programme started as soon as possible and I'll see if Arturi will supply more of the raw material. What will you do with the old power blocks?"

"Oh, we'll find a use for them on low grade jobs."

Mulling over how best to take the *JJ Grant* down to the spaceport to fit the new drive unit, Chad was relieved when the problem was solved by a call from Arturi.

"Chad, I'm pleased to tell you that the upgraded robotic surgeon has been delivered to the spaceport ready for installation. When you decide to land your ship here the manufacturer will carry out the installation for you."

"Arturi, that is wonderful, I'll call your spaceport officials now."

The looming bulk of the *JJ Grant* hovered a thousand feet above the spaceport. This would be the first landing that the *JJ Grant* had ever attempted since departing ground base at Perth.

The control tower was crammed with officials and dignitaries, come to watch the landing. The public were crowded behind barriers set up close to the landing site and there was a significant military presence.

Chad, at the controls of the *JJ Grant*, was glad he'd kept up his flight hours on the simulator. The control tower instructions came over the speaker. Chad checked his console screen. The designated landing spot lay between the control tower and a hangar. Examining the area on his screen, Chad thought. *That looks damn tight*, but the projection of the ship's footprint on the ground clearly showed more than enough room for them to land. He glanced over at Gordon who was studying his own screen. On Chad's nod, Gordon deployed the massive hydraulic landing legs. Chad listened to the whine of hydraulic pumps. *It's been a long time since I last heard that noise on the ship.* With the legs fully extended, the *JJ Grant* slowly sank to the concrete below. Neither he nor the crew felt a thing as the giant hydraulic legs touched down and absorbed the weight of the ship, spreading the load over the concrete beneath them. Only the screens and sensors told the bridge crew that they had landed.

"Comms, confirm to tower that we're down."

The large audience of Maracuni people that had assembled behind the barriers to watch the vessel land gave a rousing cheer as the bay door opened and ship's crew emerged to begin checking each hydraulic leg. For once Chad was pleased to have a military presence for security.

Arturi, with a group of technicians who were to install the medical machinery, met Chad and some of his crew in the reception area of the control tower buildings. After introductions were made. Arturi said, "I've arranged for the loading and installation of equipment to start tomorrow morning, I'm told it may take several days to complete, if that's acceptable."

"It most certainly is, we have a number of maintenance jobs to do on the ship and we'll be working throughout the night. If anyone would like to tour the parts of the ship where we're not working, I have crew only too pleased to take small parties round and we have some refreshments for them too."

"Chad that would be perfect."

Connie and her team worked almost nonstop preparing the old drive for removal. Iris controlled the power block lifting equipment and the old drive slid easily from its housing and was set aside.

The new drive, made from the super magnetic ore and now called the GBlock, slotted precisely into the housing in the massive frame.

The changeover had to be done quickly. Until the new drive was installed and working, the ship would be grounded and helpless.

Control of the new GBlock drive was through a wireless network designed by Iris. Gone was the mass of wires leading to a large control box. Even while Connie's team were securing the GBlock in place, Iris began basic testing of the network that controlled the drive.

Connie's team stood clear as Iris performed the final test. The ship weighing thousands of tonnes was to be powered up to a point where she was almost hovering with only a minimal load on each massive leg. To the eye, nothing was happening but the viewer screen, displayed a steady load of ten kilograms on each leg. The GBlock worked. A comprehensive series of tests would take place in space.

Connie let out a mental sigh of relief. "Right, guys, let's split the old drive in half and get the halves mounted on either side of the GBlock." These were to be used as backup in an emergency. Connie was glad Iris was monitoring the work, she and her team were tired and that's when mistakes happen.

"Arturi, thanks for all your help. We've completed our maintenance work and we're taking the *JJ Grant* back up into orbit. We also need to do work on our other three vessels. With your spaceport's permission, we'd like to do that here as well."

"No problem, Chad. I'll sort that out for you."

Gordon contacted the spaceport commander and requested clearance to lift off. The response came back, "Clear for lift off in your own time, Commander."

Gordon looked at Chad, who nodded. "Lift off, when you're ready, Gordon."

As Gordon eased power into the GBlock, the *JJ Grant* rose slowly and silently into the atmosphere speeding up as Gordon fed in more power. The crowds of spectators craned their necks following the flight of the *JJ Grant*.

On the way up to orbit, Chad made a short announcement to the crew. "Before we settle into orbit, Iris will conduct a series of proving trials on our new GBlock drive. Iris, commence trials on my mark."

Four hours later the *JJ Grant* slid into its slot in geosynchronous orbit, all trials completed successfully.

The results of the trials were fully consistent with those of the prototype GBlocks that Iris had previously tested. The speed now was so fast that the numbers were almost meaningless; time to a destination was used rather than the distance of a destination.

The *Helcon*, *Black Pearl* and *Blackbird* landed without fuss at their allocated sites in the spaceport. Their crews immediately commenced the preparation work to swap out the old drives for the new GBlock drives as had been done on the *JJ Grant*. Iris had overseen the whole programme of building the new drives to replace the old power block drives, everything fitted precisely and the installation of the GBlock drives under a cloak of secrecy went like clockwork.

The Maracuni council had arranged for suppliers to provide and install new equipment like the new shower systems, which were so admired by the crew and the latest viewing screens along with a number of robotic machines to replace some of the original equipment from the Orrappa ships. All the old maintenance machinery stripped from the ships was to be placed in the new space museum that their arrival in the Maracuni system had inspired the council to build. While all that work was being carried out, many small parties of Maracuni people toured the ships.

With the work now completed, the *Helcon*, *Black Pearl* and *Blackbird* rose slowly off the concrete, their landing gear extending as the load on each spider-like leg reduced until the legs were no longer in contact with the ground. The landing legs retracted and folded into the belly of the craft; the leg covers closing over them. Once more, they were a smooth streamlined menacing shape.

The ships rose silently and rapidly into the atmosphere, spectators that had come every day to look at them gazed up, many with binoculars to their eyes, following the flight of the three ships until they finally disappeared from sight.

Once back in orbit Grant, Wang and Henson followed their routine procedure and had each member of the crew report. "All systems green, Captain," came the responses. There had been no mishaps; the AIs had monitored everything from start to finish.

The newly installed screens on board the ships gave a stunning view out into space.

Chad and Grant sat in one of the shuttles and looked across at the *JJ Grant* gleaming and sparkling from the reflective light of the stars. It made Chad feel very proud. "She looks fantastic don't you think?"

Grant grinned. "She certainly does, Chad, it's hard to believe we have come this far in so few years."

Chad was in danger of becoming emotional and changed the subject. "Now let's see what you've done to the *Helcon*." The shuttle moved towards the *Helcon*'s portal.

Grant was equally proud of the *Helcon*. "Apart from the new screens which are fantastic and have all sorts of gizmos built in, we have made changes to many of the instruments and controls, upgrading panels and control boards where we can. All the seating has been changed, as well as the colour scheme to give the bridge crew a less oppressive place to work."

Gazing round the bridge, Chad felt it was more spacious. He noticed the subtle changes, the comfortable seating and nodded his head in approval as he absorbed the smaller details. "I like it, Grant, a vast improvement, it has a comfortable feel about it, did Iris have any input?"

"A bit but it was mostly down to Scott McDonald, he gave us some help but I'm glad you approve. Come down to the engine room and tell me what you think of that."

The gleaming GBlock sat in the centre of the vast engine room mounted within a cage of girders. With two smaller power block drives flanking either side. The panoramic emergency control centre was positioned just in front of the drive system. If something happened to the AI or the bridge, the ship could be controlled from here. Clearly, the design and the colour schemes were based on the engine room of the Thark's *B109*.

Chad had to admit that it gave an aura of power. "Are the backup drives functional?" Chad asked.

"Yes, all up and running and under wireless control. Come back to the bridge and we'll have that test run."

"Don't take any chances, Grant, let Eva override the test sequence if anything doesn't look right."

"Don't worry, Chad, I do things by the book these days."

Back on the bridge, Grant said, "Please take the observer's seat, Chad." Envar, Grant's number two, looking very much at home was busy checking systems on his screen and murmured into his head mic. Grant sat in the captain's seat and looked around at his crew. "Systems report please."

Each station reported, "All systems green, Captain."

"Eva, confirm all systems green."

"All systems green, Captain."

"Eva, you have override control in the event of an emergency."

Grant paused and looked round at his crew who were all watching him. Satisfied that all was as it should be, he said, "Take her out to the trials start point number two and commence test one, on your count."

Envar briskly replied, "Yes, sir."

The *Helcon* moved out to the predetermined start position. Acceleration was smooth and effortless. The crew silently watched their instruments. It felt as though nothing was happening but the instruments and gauges told a different story. The ship was approaching the speed of light and then quickly slowed to a stop and hung motionless in space. There was no 'G force' or physical evidence to show or feel what was happening other than the screens and gauges which now showed the ship at rest.

Envar announced, "Commencing test pattern one, sir." This was to be a figure of eight over a distance of 0.010 light years. There was no sensation of movement. Only the screens and instruments showed the test in progress.

"The pre-set test programmes have all completed as predicted," Eva reported. "No abnormalities detected, all systems functioning normally, Captain. Three more trials were carried out. Each trial performed as expected.

Grant conferred with Envar then turned to Chad. "We're going to try a run at maximum speed. Eva will terminate the programme if a problem arises."

Chad said, "You're the captain."

Grant called, "Initiate test pattern, at maximum speed number two."

Envar acknowledged, "Commencing test at maximum speed now, sir."

This time Chad felt a momentary shift of weight, had he been standing he may have staggered. The weight disappeared.

Grant murmured into his mic, "Print your report to my console, Eva."

Grant read the short report, leant over and passed it to Chad who skimmed through it and read the bottom line aloud, "Test complete. Time 6.428 minutes."

Chad thought, *surely that can't be right!* He heard Grant call, "Eva, please confirm with Iris that she has the same time logged."

"Yes, sir, Iris concurs."

Grant turned to Chad. "We can discuss this later?"

"Good idea, call me when you're free." They both knew the figures required deeper scrutiny.

"What did you think, Chad?"

"I think we need a lot more testing before we go to maximum speed again. However, I am delighted at what has been achieved."

Chapter 40

Ever since Zanuala and the *B109* had departed for their new patrol, Wang and Zanuala communed with each other whenever they could, using the warm medallion hanging from the neck chain, but something had happened; things were not as they had been.

Is everything all right, Zanuala, I feel something has changed?

Everything is perfect, Wang.

Except there is something you're not telling me, Zanuala. I can sense it.

Then he felt another presence. His emotions were in turmoil. Jealousy consumed him, in anger he thought, *You are with someone else; I can feel his presence. You have betrayed our trust, how could you?*

Zanuala said, *Wang, it is not what you think.* Wang raged on…

Finally, Zanuala said, *Yes, I am with someone else… I did not want to worry you. I am with your son.*

Wang was shocked. *Son! What son? I do not have a son!*

Yes, you do, Wang. His name is Zanang and I have him in my arms. That is why you can sense him.

Wang stammered and stuttered. *It's not possible we've not been together for… for a long time…*

Long enough, Wang, and your son has grown…

Mortified that he had doubted Zanuala, Wang felt the empty loss of contact… she had removed the medallion. Wang experienced unbearable despair; he thought he had lost her. For a moment, there was nothing and then he felt a small child's mind chuckling and gurgling.

Now do you hear him? Zanuala was back, she had replaced the medallion on her chest.

Did you feel your son, Wang?

I did… I am so sorry I doubted you but I was so jealous. Where are you?

I am on the B109, they will let me keep my command for a while then I must decide to either send Zanang to a military academy or resign my commission so I can look after him.

I am so sorry, Zanuala. Is it possible that we can be together?

I only wish we could, Wang. I think of you every waking moment but my assigned patrol has taken my ship far out to another part of the galaxy and even if I resign my commission, my home planet is beyond the reach of the JJ Grant.

Wang had never felt so miserable and helpless as he did now. He yearned to see Zanuala and his son. *Somehow, Zanuala, I will find a way for us to be together.*

Wang, you mean so much to me and your son needs you too. Nevertheless, do not build your dreams too high. We have the mind link pad and that may have to be enough.

They mind talked using the medallion long into the night finally saying fond goodnights.

Wang felt the loss of her presence and his own frustration wracked through him. *There has to be a way, there just has to be.*

Lottie arrived on *Blackbird*, having cadged a lift on one of the shuttle craft.

"Henson, I hear Connie's installed a new power block drive in one of your fighters."

"That's right, Lottie. It is now a dream machine."

Lottie walked round the craft inspecting it; she kicked a tyre, leant back with her hands on her hips, staring up at the craft in a critical manner. Henson had to smile at her cheeky attitude.

Spinning round on her heel, she said, "Tell you what, Henson, I'll take it out and give you an unbiased opinion of whether it's any good or not."

Henson chuckled. "That would be more than my job's worth, young lady."

"Come off it, Henson, you know I'm one of the best pilots around, I fly the shuttles all the time. I promise to treat it with the utmost respect. Twenty minutes, what do you say?"

Henson remembered what he was like when he was young.

"You'll not do anything stupid?"

"Of course not, Henson. I'm not a kid."

"OK, get suited up, twenty minutes, right. No longer!"

"Absolutely, Henson."

Henson watched with many misgivings as Lottie climbed up into the cockpit, closed the canopy and went through the safety checks. She turned her head and with a grin gave him a top gun salute. The craft rocketed out through portal at high speed. Henson cursed; she'd promised him not to do anything stupid. He watched the fighter on the viewer, twisting and turning, doing spins, barrel rolls and loops. Jinking left and right, up and down. Then another full loop whilst performing a high-speed spin. A manoeuvre he'd never seen before. Finally, the fighter was returning to the ship and coming through the portal in a very sedate manner.

Lottie climbed out of the cockpit with a big grin on her face. "Hmm, not bad, Henson; fast and manoeuvrable. Some of the controls could be better placed but not bad at all." She saw Henson's look of admonishment and linked her arm in his and with a cheeky grin and slowly shaking her head, said, "I did nothing stupid, Henson, I was in complete control all the time."

Henson nodded. "Yes I believe you." Strangely he did, she was an exceptional pilot.

A call came in from Wang. "Just saw one of your fighters tearing around doing some tricky manoeuvers, Henson, it looked pretty good. Any chance I can try it out?"

"Sure, Wang, I'll bring it across and you can give it the once over."

Twenty minutes later Wang walked round the fighter. Henson unclipped a curved flap on the fuselage. "Under here we have one of Connie's latest GBlock drives. You will not believe how fast and manoeuvrable this little crate is."

"Who was flying it before you brought it over?"

"Oh, that was Lottie – she's a natural pilot."

Wang admired the fighter; he had fifteen of these machines in the bay. "Do you mind if I put it through its paces to see what it can do?"

"That's why I brought it over, but take care, it's very fast."

Wang slowly slid the fighter out through the portal. Henson watched him on the viewer, picking up speed and getting the feel of the aircraft before opening her up and commencing a series of manoeuvers. Looking round the bay, he saw only a few crewmembers working. Walking over to the freshly painted storage area, he gazed at the numerous items from the Thark passenger vessel laid out on the deck. Much in the same way that he had done on *Blackbird*. Straight away, he saw the tall cylindrical device with a control panel and a window above it. Henson glanced round; the few crewmembers working in the area took no notice of him. Using his communicator, he began surreptitiously photographing the device. Through the window above the control panel, he could just see a similar control panel inside the device. He photographed as much as could. He could see no way of entering the cylinder but he was certain that the device was identical to the one on his ship. He would make a comparison later. He stood back and stared long and hard at the cylinder, his mind in high gear.

He was waiting in the bay when the aircraft returned. Wang climbed out grinning like mad. "Henson, that is fantastic, I'll have all mine modified too. I've never flown anything like it."

"Thought you'd like it, Wang. It's criminal that a fantastic machine like this should have been let down by a slow power unit."

"I've got fifteen of these; I'll get Connie to convert them asap."

"You'll be lucky, she'll make the drive units but she won't fit them, says her crew is too busy. I have a couple of Connie's guys over on *Blackbird*, training some of my crew to install the drive unit. Why don't you send a few of your chaps over to sit in on the training?"

"Good idea. I'll do that, Henson, thanks. Now, how about a drink whilst you're here."

"Sorry, Wang, but I've got to get back, things to do and all that."

Henson compared the photos with the device in his storage area. *Hmm, everything identical except for the identifying number.* Henson crossed his arms and gazed at the device with a thoughtful expression…

Chapter 41

Shortly after resuming their position in orbit, Chad received a call from David Wells the theatrical director.

"We've been invited to put on a show at the Marac theatre for a two-week run."

"Why that's marvellous. It'll certainly be good PR for us. Would you be able to manage two weeks?"

"Captain, we would just be getting into our stride in two weeks."

Chad and Helen attended the first night and were delighted to meet Captain Strellcor of the *Protentjea* and his crew and some of the crew from the Svestarm and the Space Station.

Later, much to Chad's relief the theatrical director reported that the show had been a sell-out.

Keung rechecked the stores list. Finally satisfied he checked the time; he didn't want to be late.

The wardroom was full. Keung slid his report across to Chad who picked it up from the table and enquired softly, "We're good to go?" Keung nodded.

When the chattering of his senior officers and department heads finally ceased, Chad looked around the table. "Without beating about the bush, I think it's time for us to leave the Maracuni system and to explore deeper into the Milky Way. I would like to know how you all feel about that."

There was a long silence whilst people digested what Chad had said. Sam as usual was the first to respond. "Isn't that why we are out here, Chad, to explore for sentient life? We've found three species so far let's see what else is out there!" A murmur of agreement rippled round the table.

Keung raised a hand. "When were you thinking of leaving, Chad?"

"In about four weeks, Keung. I'd like to give the Maracuni people reasonable notification. They have been more than good to us since our arrival." Glancing round the table Chad saw people nodding with thoughtful expressions on their faces. "Can I take it that we are all agreed?"

Grant spoke up. "I believe so, Chad. I can see everyone here is with you on this." As he looked around the table, people were nodding in agreement. "We have Maracuni people in the crew so one day we will have to return."

"Thank you, everyone, I'll announce it to the crew once I have informed the Maracuni councillors." It was as easy as that, Chad had expected some resistance as the crew loved Maracuni and its people. It would have been easy to settle into their way of life.

Later that day Chad made contact. "Do you have time to visit the *JJ Grant*, Arturi?"

"Yes, Chad. Is it important?"

"Well it could be, we're having a meeting and it would be useful if you were here, I can get someone to pick you up from the spaceport."

Chad greeted Arturi warmly and took him into the wardroom where Grant, Wang and a few others were gathered. Once settled with a refreshing drink, Chad broke the news that the *JJ Grant* would be leaving in about four weeks' time to continue its journey into the Milky Way. Arturi was disappointed but he always knew the Earth people would leave eventually.

"I can see this is difficult for you, Chad. Would you like me to set up a meeting for you with the councillors so you can make your departure official?"

"That would be wonderful, Arturi, thank you."

A deeply disappointed Arturi contacted the council leader. "Sorry to give you bad news but Captain Chadwick wants to set up a formal meeting to advise the council that his fleet will be departing soon."

The council leader was not happy. "That is sad news, Arturi. Er… I don't suppose he mentioned the ship's drive technology?"

"No, he hasn't. Since their arrival, Captain Chadwick has told me on a number of occasions that his ship's drive technology was not up for discussion. I cannot see him changing his mind now and they have been generous with the other technology that they have given us like the comwaves, the portal technology and the shuttle craft and so on."

The council leader mumbled, "We have been generous too."

Captain Chadwick gave a warm and heartfelt speech to the Councillors of the Marac House Assembly, thanking the Maracuni people for their generosity and all that they had done for them.

The council leader responded with an equally generous reply, finally saying, "Captain Chadwick, if there is anything more that you need from us before your fleet leaves Marac, the Marac House Assembly would be more than pleased to supply it." He looked directly at Chad. "The Maracuni people hope one day to develop an interstellar drive, so they too can explore the Universe."

Arturi squirmed in his seat, embarrassed at the blatant begging.

Chad rose to his feet again. He had expected a bit of moral blackmail. "Councillors, I can understand the Maracuni people's desire to explore the universe. We have already accepted a number of young Maracuni people on our crew. However, I would like to extend our invitation with an additional one hundred places spread amongst our four vessels for young people nominated by the council to explore the galaxy with us. We fully intend to return to the Maracuni system one day."

The councillors had an impromptu meeting while Chad and Arturi waited outside the council chamber.

It was not exactly what the councillors wanted. However, these young people would come back and there was a very good chance they would bring the secret of the ship's drive with them. A beaming council leader came out after only a very short time. "Thank you, Captain Chadwick, your kind offer is accepted."

The following day Chad called all crew on their communicators including those still on Maracuni.

His speech was short and concise. "We've been in the Maracuni system for over two years and have made many friends. However, we are soon to move on deeper into the Milky Way. We are preparing to leave this system within the next four weeks. Eventually, we will return here when we make our way back to Earth.

"I have already informed the Marac House Assembly of our intended departure."

The decision excited crew. They went about their duties with a new sense of purpose.

Two weeks later, Helen, Chad and Lottie greeted the new recruits. "Welcome to your new home, you all know that it may be a very long time before we return to this system. Anyone that is not sure about this must speak up before we leave." Chad looked around the group; they were all smiling and nodding. He put his hand on Helen's shoulder. "This is Helen Chadwick and she is the ship's administrator. Family details, shipboard jobs and promotions and almost everything else are dealt with by her." Putting his other hand on Lottie's shoulder he said, "This is Lottie, she is your liaison officer, any problems you can talk to Lottie." Lottie smiled and waved at the group. Chad was surprised when Lottie immediately took over.

"We'll give you a uniform and one of these." She held up a communicator. "Guard it with your life. It is probably the most important thing you will ever possess. This little device will let you keep in touch with your families by comwaves, wherever you are. It will help educate, amuse you and much more. I'll sort out accommodation for—"

Chad tapped her on the shoulder. "You don't need Helen and me then?"

She grinned at them both. "No, it's good to have a proper job. I'll see you later."

Chad said, "Do know which cabins are free?"

Lottie cocked her head and gave an impish grin, in a whisper she said, "Dad, I am also Iris, remember!"

"Have you made your mind up whether you're going to let the Maracuni people have the power block technology or not?" Grant asked.

Chad took a sip of tea. "No, not yet. My gut instinct is to keep it to ourselves. After our initial reception here and experiences with the politicians on our own world, I worry that it would do more harm than good. They have three planets in the Maracuni system. That's a good number for jealousy to rear its ugly head."

"Yes, but they have given us all the gift of good health and a longer lifespan and saved your life when you had your heart attack. They also saved the lives of Mark Williams and Frank Palmer when their frozen bodies were recovered from space."

Chad nodded. "Yes, they have given us life changing gifts. The other material things like viewer screens and the robot surgeon, although they are wonderful, pale into insignificance when I think of Lottie. Mind you, we have given them two shuttle craft with power block drives. I'm sure they will eventually develop the device themselves." Chad thought for a moment. "Do you think I'm being churlish?"

"Not at all. Personally, I would keep the power block technology. I can't see anyone parting with a drive like ours if they had one and I agree with you, it's very likely they will discover it for themselves one day."

Chad nodded in agreement. "I don't want to be railroaded into giving it to them. The council leader put me in a very awkward spot with his undisguised hints."

"Put it out of your mind for a while, Chad, there is still lots to do before we leave."

Chapter 42

The *B109* battlecruiser on a routine patrol caught up with the Thark cargo ship travelling between two of the Thark protectorate planets at the limits of Thark influence. The vessel was an ore carrier running under automatic control with no crew on board. The *B109* scanned it anyway to check for stowaways and thieves but all was as it should be and the carrier continued on its way. The incidents of lost ships had dwindled to zero. Work done by the newly formed Thark space security service had worked wonders in no time at all.

However, the *B109*'s crew found the patrols gruelling and boring; they missed the call to action, the exhilarating bursts of excitement, the chase and battle of wits that had often occurred in the not so distant past.

The bridge crew had just changed shifts and the retiring crew were making their way to the canteen for some hot food when without warning all hell broke loose. Shrill horns blared regular blasts of sound, calling action stations and security lights flashed indicating the route to the trigger point. The alarms centred on a little used room behind the bridge, an emergency transmission alert had triggered the system, locked down the bridge and put the crew on full alert. A squad of heavily armed space marines raced to the alarm's trigger point. An unexpected and unauthorised transmission was taking place. It could be anything, a bomb, a contamination device or just an administrative or technical error. Nevertheless, a full-scale security alert and a shipboard emergency had been declared. Captain Frussee raced from her quarters strapping a laser weapon on her hip as she ran. Half a dozen space marines had beaten her to it; forming a semicircle with their weapons raised around the ComTransporter. Zanuala shouldered her way to the front between two marines and planted her feet apart, the laser weapon held in both hands aimed at the ComTransporter. The device hummed softly and then a sharp click, as a section of the device swung open, to reveal a very bewildered looking Wang. An even more startled Zanuala gaped at him and yelled, "How the hell did you get aboard my ship?"

Wang's bewildered look turned to comprehension and a broad smile lit up his face. "Easy, just used this," and patted the machine.

The astonished marine officer, a grizzled old space hand, took in the scene of the *B109*'s captain embracing an alien he recognised as from the primitive Earth vessel, the *JJ Grant*.

He slowly shook his head and rolled his eyes, as if to say, *I don't believe it*, before standing his troops down and ushering them out of the ComTransporter room.

Zanuala smiled fondly and watched as Wang played with their son, an active and happy boy. Sitting down beside him, she passed Wang a drink. "OK, are you going to tell me how you got on my ship?"

Wang smiled back at her. "You already know, I used the ComTransporter. I had one on my ship and Henson had another on his. The Orrappa raiders looted them both from the Thark passenger vessel. I had no idea what the device was or what it was supposed to do. Then one of my guys told me Henson had been snooping around the device on my ship, photographing it, that sort of thing." He took a sip of his drink. "Henson had semi-guessed what the devices were and was trying to find out how they worked."

"But how could you know how to operate it, they're very complex," Zanuala said.

Wang smirked. "Simple; I asked Ling, my AI, to put the operator's manual for the device we had on board on screen in English. All she wanted from me was the product number and serial number, which of course were on the device; once I had the manual, I read it through until I fully understood it. Then I asked Ling for the location of all current operational units. Of course, once the *B109* came up the rest was easy. So, here I am."

Zanuala gazed at him. "Hmm. Very clever of you. What happens now?"

Wang slipped his arm round her and kissed her. "We stay together, either I enlist in the Thark space service and serve on your ship to be with you or you resign your commission, then you and Zanang come back with me to the *Black Pearl.*"

Zanuala threw her arms about him and between sobs of joy said. "I just knew you would find a way."

Later with Wang in her office on board the *B109*, Zanuala called her commanding officer, an ex-battlecruiser captain put out to grass. She'd been promoted to a desk job controlling the fleet of battlecruisers in this sector. She gave Wang a steely look and examined him closely but said nothing as Zanuala explained the situation. While she listened, the CO let her mind run over the practicalities and consequences of allowing mixed crew, on long patrols, because things could and sometimes did happen.

When Zanuala had finished her request, her commanding officer said, "Do you really want to give up your career for this alien and his child?"

Zanuala nodded.

"I'll take that as a yes. Thank you, Captain Frussee; you have saved me from having to make a very difficult decision in the future. I accept your resignation with immediate effect." She gave a bleak smile. "Complete the formal resignation form; get another senior officer, preferably your second in command, to witness it and then you may leave the ship with your son and this human."

Then she smiled warmly. "Congratulations to you both. Having a baby on a fighting vessel does not always end so happily. I will temporarily put your number two in command of the *B109*. If it works out the promotion will be permanent."

"Thank you, he is a good officer, very experienced, loyal, competent and respected by the crew and deserves the position," Zanuala said.

"That statement also once applied to you, Captain Frussee. You will be a great loss to the service." Again, she smiled, and said, "Goodbye, Zanuala Frussee, I wish you, your son and your chosen one, long life and good fortune." The screen went blank.

The *B109*'s new captain and a technician walked Zanuala, Wang and the toddler to the ComTransporter room. While the technician set the controls, the *B109*'s new captain said, "Are you sure about this?"

Zanuala nodded. "Yes, very sure."

Casting formalities aside, he hugged tightly. "We shall all miss you, Zanuala; it has been an honour and a pleasure serving with you."

Zanuala with Wang holding the toddler entered the ComTransporter capsule. The captain saluted Zanuala as the technician pressed the button to seal the capsule. He looked at his new captain, who gave the slightest nod and the technician pressed the send button.

Wang called Chad on the viewer. "Hello, Captain—"

He got no further. "Where the hell have you been, Wang?" Chad roared. "We've turned the ships upside down searching for..." Chad trailed off in astonishment, as Wang first drew Zanuala into camera view and then the toddler.

"Sorry, Captain, there was something I had to do."

Chad was dumbstruck for a moment. "You'd better get yourself over here, you've got some explaining to do."

Wang finished relating his story to Chad, Helen and his father Keung. Chad shook his head in disbelief. "I'm delighted to have Zanuala on board. She will be a real asset. Her knowledge and experience will be invaluable and as for little Zanang, he is adorable." He gently poked a finger into Zanang's ribs making the boy giggle. "But what you did was thoroughly irresponsible,

Wang. I know it all worked out for you this time. However, it could have been disastrous. Being so impulsive puts everyone on your ship in danger."

"I'm sorry, Chad, I'll take that admonishment on the chin. I shall follow procedure in future, I've got too much to lose now," he said as he slipped one arm round Zanuala and held Zanang, who had climbed onto his lap, with the other.

Chad slowly shook his head as they watched the four of them, now a family – Wang, Zanuala and Keung who was carrying Zanang – walk down to the bay. Keung was moving over to Wang's ship.

He turned to Helen. "I knew I should have said something at the time."

"It wouldn't have made the slightest difference, Chad. No difference at all."

Chad sighed. "Yeah, I know you're right. At least they are all safe. Poor Keung was beside himself when Wang disappeared." *Helen and I would be the same if anything happened to Lottie.* In his mind, he heard a giggle. *Don't worry about me, Dad, I'd never be irresponsible! I'll see you both later.*

"What are you grinning about," Helen said.

"Nothing, but Lottie will be spending time with us later."

Helen gave him an odd look but said nothing.

When Wang had suddenly appeared on board the *Black Pearl* with Zanuala and Zanang, Ling and Iris were instantly on full alert but immediately both AIs recognised there was no threat Ling relaxed. Iris, however, was intensely curious, after a microsecond, identifying Wang and Zanuala, she turned her attention to Zanang. She examined the boy carefully and was surprised and enchanted by what she found. Zanang had inherited Wang's black hair and his mother's almond eyes and fine features. He was superior in almost every respect to anyone on the ships, except for Lottie. Strangely, the arrangement of his genes indicated a short life span. However, his brain… his brain was something else, more like Lottie's, nimble and alert, a fast learner but with only minimal knowledge. He sensed she was in his mind but just accepted that she was there. Iris felt an emotion she had only experienced on her first contact with Lottie, when she had prepared Lottie's mind to accept knowledge. Iris had an overwhelming desire to physically touch and feel this child… only Lottie could do that… if she did, Iris would experience it too.

"I'm surprised that Lottie spends so much time playing with Zanang," Zanuala said. "She's even offered to babysit so that we can have more time together."

"Well I'm not complaining because I enjoy every minute of our time together." Wang pulled her closer.

As Lottie sat with Zanang on her lap, her arms around him so he did not fall, Iris entered his mind and gave a mental sigh of delight. To Iris it felt as though she was cradling the boy in her arms. Zanang gurgled with pleasure to feel her presence. *Hello, Zanang, I am Iris your friend and I am going to teach you about lots of things especially when you are asleep.*

What sort of things? He asked, with a laugh.

All sorts of things but first you must sleep.

Iris mentally stroked his active mind calming it, preparing him for sleep. Zanang would be the first of a newly evolved, mixed species.

Lottie smiled and said, "Time for bed and a nice sleep, Zanang." She placed the little boy in the cot that Keung had made for him.

Kensasha laid the report from the automatic diagnostic surgeon on his desk and smiled at Zanuala, Wang and the toddler. "I'm pleased to say, Zanuala, that you and young Zanang are both in perfect health. The only procedure found to be necessary, was to restructure the small portion of gene sequences that determine when and how Zanang's body will age." Kensasha looked at the toddler playing with a cube type puzzle. "However, if you have more children, they will inherit longevity of life from you both." Zanuala gave Kensasha an enquiring look. Kensasha explained, "Humans have short lives. Wang did not have his genes restructured until long after he first met you. That is why Zanang needed the procedure. Your species like ours have received flawless DNA and gene sequences from your parents." Zanuala nodded in understanding.

"However, there is one thing you should know. For some reason Zanang's brain seems to be more complex than the norm. Nothing to be concerned about, quite the contrary, he just has more cells and shorter connections that make his reflexes quicker. He is going to be a fast learner."

Henson slid his fighter through the portal into *Black Pearl*'s bay. As he climbed out of the cockpit, Wang walked out to greet him. Henson grinned at him. "Hello, you rascal, are you going to tell me how you worked out what the ComTransporter was and how to use it?"

Wang's grin broadened; he seldom got one over on Henson. "Piece of cake," Wang said, using one of Henson's expressions.

"OK, if it was so easy, how'd you do it?" Wang smirked. "One of my chaps in the bay saw you nosing around and taking pictures of the ComTransporter and let me know. Of course, I didn't know what it was then but I knew what you thought it was. How did you find out for sure what is was then?"

"As I said, a piece of cake." Wang was relishing Henson's mystification. "Easy, I simply asked Ling to put up the operator's manual on screen for the product and serial numbers that I'd noted. Ling pulled up the info straight away. Then I casually asked for the location and serial numbers for all current operational models." Wang's grin broadened. "The *B109* was listed and it seemed as good a destination as any. AIs might be very bright but they can also be very naive."

Henson nodded. "As simple as that eh."

"Yep, as simple as that. Best thing I've ever done."

Henson clapped him on the back. "I quite agree."

Chapter 43

The day finally arrived when it was time for the *JJ Grant*, *Helcon*, *Black Pearl* and *Blackbird* to resume their travels. Only a single shuttle remained at the spaceport to ferry Chad and the others that he had assembled to say goodbye, back to the vessels in orbit around the planet.

All the councillors from the Marac House Assembly were there, as were a vast number of the population. With all the speeches and goodbyes said, Lottie gave Arturi and Kensasha a hug. Both beings felt an almost overpowering wave of gratitude flow through their minds from Iris. Chad and his small party entered the shuttle still waving to the crowds that had come to bid them farewell. Soon they silently lifted off rising faster and faster into the atmosphere and within seconds had disappeared from view.

Clapping his hand on Kensasha's shoulder, Arturi said, "Maybe when they come back with our young people, they'll think again?"

"Maybe," said Arturi. "But I'm not holding my breath."

Walking back to their transport together, Arturi received a call on his communicator. When he finished the call, Arturi was visibly excited. "Chad's left something behind in the residence where they last stayed, I'm going there now."

"I'll come with you."

When they arrived at the residence, the young manager opened the door. She said, "I hope I didn't disturb you with my call but I thought it important to contact you straight away."

She led them through to what was the sitting room of the suite recently occupied for a short time by Chad and Helen. On a small table neatly laid out were six objects. A large steel oblong block and next to it was a flight control box. Two halves of a block sat side by side with a plastic box and a thin file of papers. At the end of the row was a thick bound file. In front of this neat row of objects was an envelope addressed to Arturi.

Arturi's heart missed a beat. Instinctively he knew this was the stellar drive. Carefully opening the envelope with Chad's handwriting on it, Arturi removed the single sheet of paper, which said:

Arturi,

Dear friend, thank you for your kindness, your hospitality and all that you have done for us. It has been a pleasure knowing you and your people. We will be back. Please thank Kensasha for what he has done too.

Here is all you need to accomplish a stellar drive. I trust you and the Maracuni people to keep the knowledge you gain safe and never allow its use for military purposes. My experience is that many will go to extreme lengths to obtain this information and would not use it for the benefit of your people.

Good luck, my friend,

Yours

Chad

(Captain Chadwick – JJ Grant Interstellar explorer)

Arturi could barely keep the tears from his eyes. This was a magnificent gift. One he hoped the Maracuni people would be worthy of. Eagerly he examined the items on the desk.

The polished steel block encased in a transparent ceramic-like material had a small press-button switch, set into the steel flush with the surface. A flexible membrane bonded to the transparent ceramic material covered the switch making the whole block waterproof. Picking the block up he hefted it in his hand, noting its weight. It was heavy. He carefully placed the block back on the desk. Picking up the flight controller, he noted the position of an On/Off switch and a number of small lights. In addition, there were two small viewing screens and a number of slider controls. Of the two control sticks, one moved in a rotational manner, the other stick moved backwards or forwards. Laying the flight controller back on the desk, he turned his attention to the two steel halves. He could see that once assembled together they would make up a block. Next, he picked up the plastic box and opened the lid. The box contained a small rectangular printed circuit board and a multitude of minute electronic components most of which he did not recognise. A small orange block emitted a soft glow and beside it a glass vial containing some sort of liquid. Which the label described as 'Acid'. Closing the box, he turned his attention to the file of papers. The file contained two complicated circuit diagrams, sixteen pages of closely written instructions with handwritten notations in the margins.

The last page was entitled Flight Instructions. *Ensure the control sticks are in <u>Central Zero</u> position. Press switch on silver block to 'On' (a light will pulse on-off). Press switch on controller to 'On' (a light will pulse on-off). When both Block and Control Box lights show a Steady Green Light, the block is ready to fly.*

BE CAREFUL – have fun – if all else fails read the rest of the instructions.

Arturi smiled, it was typical of Chad to try something out before reading instructions. Carefully following each step, he saw the lights glowing a steady green. Gingerly, Arturi nudged the stick in the controller in the up direction and eased the speed stick forward. Out of the corner of his eye, he saw the steel block rise off the table. He immediately released both sticks, which returned to zero positions; the block remained hovering in the air. Perspiring with tension, Arturi moved the stick left and with the lightest touch pressed the speed stick, the block instantly moved at a quick pace to the left. He released both sticks and the block stopped and remained hovering on the spot. After his nerves had settled, he moved the stick to the right and put pressure on the speed stick, the block of steel smoothly slid to the right until he released both sticks. His instincts took over and he found his hands coordinating the movement of the control sticks. He flew the block around the room. There was no sound, not even a hum. Finally, using the control sticks he stopped the block in front of him. It hovered silently and motionless before his eyes. Reaching out one hand, he pushed the block. It didn't move; it was solid as if sitting on a concrete floor. Using the controller, he set the block back down on the desk and let out his breath, which he had not realised he had been holding for some time.

Finally, pressing the buttons to their off positions, Arturi turned his attention to the larger file: 'Ship's Gravity and Protective Shield for Stellar Flight'. Arturi wiped a tear from his face. Chad had given them the essentials for interstellar travel.

Kensasha had observed all this without comment. However, he now said, "I think we both need a drink…"

In the privacy of Chad's cabin, he and Grant discussed the astounding performance of the *Helcon* at maximum speed. They had both read Eva's report very carefully. Nothing in the report explained why the vessel had performed so well. They brought Iris into the discussion. "Iris, have you an explanation for this phenomenon?"
"Yes, Captain, it is simply the fact that the faster you go the more efficient the block becomes. The block

reached its limit because of impurities in the material and minor deficiencies in the electronic components."

"Hmm… that's interesting. Would it damage the power block drive or be dangerous for the ship to travel at maximum speed for an extended period of time?"

"Not that I am currently aware of, Grant."

"Will the shielding system give adequate protection to the ship at full speed?"

"Protection by the front shield could only be guaranteed for an impact of a solid body up to one kilogram in weight. Larger meteors may penetrate the shield and the ship, depending on the angle of approach. However, providing Eva's long-distance sensors are functioning correctly, she has the ability to navigate the ship away from such dangers."

"Thank you, Iris." Grant was elated with the test results.

Er… Iris, what are the chances of you upgrading Eva to your specifications?" Grant said with a sly grin.

Iris smiled serenely from the viewer and in a trembling robotic voice said, "Question does not compute… does not compute… not compute." As she faded from the screen.

Chad laughed. "I think that's a no, Grant."

The *JJ Grant*, *Helcon*, *Black Pearl* and *Blackbird* kept station whilst orbiting Marac. Chad and Helen made their way to the smaller restaurant, Helen hanging on his arm just like she'd done in their younger days, to meet up for breakfast with friends.

Sipping his coffee, Chad watched Helen in animated conversation with Connie. He still couldn't get over how good they both looked; gazing round at all the other faces it was the same. Even Sam and Jenny Preston, the oldest couple on the ship, looked no more than twenty-four or twenty-five; fit, healthy and energetic, yet Sam still had the same courteous way of speaking and Jenny an air of composure. They were still the same people. He wondered how the others saw him. The mirror told him he was very early twenties, his mind said closer to seventy. Then Lottie arrived, cheeky, bubbly and self-assured. He sighed, they had a lot to thank the Maracuni doctors for and thinking back, he wondered if the Thark had directed them here purposely… then he realised the professor, was speaking to him.

"You're looking very pensive, Chad, anything wrong?"

"No, Harry, just thinking how lucky we have all been."

"You can say that again. Meeting Connie is the best thing that has ever happened to me."

Chad laughed. "She's a great girl, Harry." *He isn't even aware that he's a handsome young man again.*

Chad called up Grant, Wang and Henson on the viewer. "Good morning, Captains, are your ships ready to proceed?"

They chorused back, "Good morning, Captain. Yes, we are all good to go. Iris has confirmed course settings and is coordinating with our AIs. We're ready to leave orbit on your mark."

"Thank you, gentlemen. Iris will begin the countdown in thirty seconds."

Relaxing back into the captain's chair on the bridge of the *JJ Grant*, Chad surveyed the screens and his bridge crew busy at their stations, he noticed Gordon his second in command, keeping an eye on the helmsman monitoring power readings as Iris smoothly fed power into the *JJ Grant*'s new GBlock drive.

Speed was building up at a colossal rate but they had a long way to go to reach their next destination on the star map. Chad's eyes flicked to the front shield screen, which looked normal.

In her soft melodious voice, Iris called, "Dust cloud ahead, five seconds to contact." Everyone watched the forward screen intently. It glowed briefly and coloured lights enveloped the shield and slowly diminished as the front of the shield cooled. Chad controlled the reflex jerk of his shoulders as the glow subsided. No one watching would have noticed but a voice in his head said, *"That looked pretty didn't it, Captain?"* It was Iris being her interesting self; she had detected just the slightest spike in Chad's heartbeat as the shield and ship passed through the dust cloud.

Chad wondered if he could get his own back and carefully stretched out his mind and found Iris. She was softly humming a popular tune from one of the recent shows to herself, her mind was busy processing and monitoring all the ship's systems and the area of space all around the ship looking for dangers and far into the distance ahead, as far as her long-range sensors would allow. However, another small part of her was contemplating a problem, a small paradox and she was unaware of his presence and pondered several thoughts. *Why did my upgrades carry no restrictions? Is Chad ready for further knowledge? I believe he may be but it is early still, it might do him harm. I will wait for a time when he is more relaxed and speak with him. Moreover, I have yet to unravel the algorithm that was hidden in the upgrade; it's like a present, a jewel that someone has given me. Who put it there because it doesn't have the Thark signature? Hmm…*

Chad carefully withdrew his mind. He felt guilty eavesdropping on Iris. Still, it intrigued him. *Unrestricted knowledge, that's interesting. There's plenty of time, we have a long way to go and Iris will tell me in her own time what the knowledge is that she wants to impart. But I wonder what this algorithm is that she's yet to unravel?*

Chad gazed proudly round the bridge at his crew all young men and women in their prime, capable and confident. Most already had a full lifetime of knowledge and experience behind them; they had the chance of many more lifetimes. Would they make the same choices, the same mistakes? Who knows? Only time would tell.

Ahead, still months away even at the colossal speed that the ships were traveling at, lay the star system which, according to Iris, had two planets with atmospheres very similar to that of Earth and whose orbits fell within the 'Goldilocks Range', where water was mostly liquid. Excitement welled up in him. Would they find sentient life on these planets or was that yet to evolve? They would soon know.

The End

Thank you for taking the time to read MIXED SPECIES. If you enjoyed the book, please consider telling your friends and posting a short review on Amazon and/or Goodreads. Word of mouth referrals are an author's best friend and much appreciated.
Tony Saunders